OZZY

CONTENTS

Book Cover by Y'all. That Graphic

Edited by Victoria Ellis, Cruel Ink Editing

Proofread by Rosa Sharon, Fairy Proofmother Proofreading

CHECK YOUR TRIGGERS

Your mental health and emotional well-being matters to me. You can find a list of possible triggers on the book's page on my website or by scanning the QR code below.
Xoxo

PROLOGUE
Ozzy

The downtown bar in Boston is stuffy as hell. Everyone here has a pint of Guinness or Amstel with a shot of whiskey sitting next to them. Gramps and my dad managed to drag me and Knox to this little bar they visit every time they come out this way. Not that either of them do often. When Gramps retired from his presidency of the Black Roses, my old man took over. But most of his time is spent in his office doing a bunch of mind-numbing paperwork. Add in the daily pain in his hands and it seems the presidency is going to go to me sooner rather than later. Arthritis is a bitch for my dad, and he doesn't think he'll be riding much longer.

In any other club, they would probably vote in a new president, but in ours, it's handed down—unless the guy next in line for the president patch is a complete and utter failure and can't handle putting the lives of his brothers and the good of his club before his own. Thankfully, I'm not that man. I learned what loyalty and family mean at a young age, and I'll be damned if I ever let my brothers down.

Knox, my best friend since high school, sits on one side of me, and my pops is on the other with Gramps next to him. The bar isn't what you would call packed, but the woman behind it is running her fine ass off, seeing as she's the only one here at the moment.

I have to hand it to her; she's doing a damn good job of making everyone at her bar feel welcome. Running the show yourself can be a pain in the ass, I've had to do it plenty of times at the club's bar back home. And I'm not nearly as pretty to look at.

"Another pint?" she asks, pointing to my almost empty glass.

"Sure, sweetheart." I tip the corner of my mouth up and shoot her a wink. The slight blush on her cheeks and the extra sway she puts in her hips as she walks to the tap tells me she might consider giving me more than a refill later tonight.

"Dad, when do you expect your friend?" my dad asks Gramps.

"Walter said eight o'clock. He and his grandson are taking a little East Coast tour on their bikes. The boy just retired from the service and decided to come to the States," Gramps replies. "I think you'll like him, Trick."

My dad looks at Gramps and raises a brow. "Are we meeting with an old friend to shoot the shit, or do you want this kid to prospect for the club?"

Gramps shrugs. "Walter said the boy doesn't want to stay in London, but he also doesn't want to work for his brother. Figured you could meet him, and if you and

Ozzy like him, they could come back to Shine for a few days."

Not sure how appealing the small town of Shine, Massachusetts is going to be for a guy who's used to the hustle of the London streets. My dad and I both know Gramps well enough to pick up on the fact that this plan has most likely already been solidified with Gramps and his friend. Hate to see all their secret planning be for nothing.

My dad chuckles. "Okay, old man, I'll keep an open mind."

"That's all I can expect from you, son." Gramps shoots my dad a victorious smile.

Gramps's gaze shoots to the door, and a wide smile overtakes his face.

"Walter," he calls out, raising a hand.

The three of us turn toward the door and see a man about Gramps's age walking toward us with a younger guy trailing behind him. They both have the kind of tan you can only get from riding a bike for days on end. I miss the days when I had that same tan. Being vice president of the Black Roses has severely cut into my riding time. It's been far too long since I've had the opportunity to take my bike on a cross-country trip with no cares except where I'd lay my head for the night or if there would be a warm body next to me. I don't regret my decision to go all in with the club for one second, though. My dad gave me a choice when I was a senior in high school. After everything... happened.

The only thing he cared about was my happiness. There hasn't been a day I've had second thoughts about my decision, but there are some days when I think about the what-ifs.

"Arthur," the older man says when he reaches Gramps. They give each other backslapping hugs, both with beaming smiles on their faces. "You got old, mate," Gramps says with a chuckle.

"I see the years haven't been kind to you either, Art."

Both men laugh, and Walter turns to his grandson.

"Art, this is Jude. Jude, Art." Gramps shakes hands with Jude, who looks to be a couple years younger than me.

Gramps turns to the three of us sitting at the bar. "Gentlemen, this is my son, Trick, and my grandson, Ozzy. And the boy at the end is Knox."

I chuckle at the introduction. Only Gramps would refer to Knox as a boy.

We all shake hands and decide to move to a table off to the side of the bar top.

I raise my hand to get the bartender's attention before going to sit with the rest of the guys. When she stands in front of me, her arms spread across the bar top, and she leans over so I don't have to yell. Or maybe so I could look down her tight, low-cut T-shirt. Naturally, my eyes wander to the cleavage she has on display, and when my gaze meets hers again, a half smile tilts the corner of her lips.

"Can we get six pints and six whiskeys, sweetheart?"

"Sure thing. I'll bring them over."

I shoot her a wink before she turns to pour the beers, then I head over to the table.

Gramps and Walter are telling stories about their time in London as I take a seat at the table. Walter looks over to me and smiles.

"You look so much like your grandmother, Ozzy. God rest her soul," he says as the bartender delivers our beers and shots. "I met her a few times when she was studying in London."

Gramps has a soft smile on his face, the same one he always has when anyone mentions my grandmother, Janine. She passed when I was fourteen, but everyone loved her, and she made every stray in town feel like they had a family, including my best friend sitting next to me.

Walter turns to my dad. "Did Art ever tell you we met her the same night? I noticed her first and took a shot when your dad was in the loo. I nearly had her, too, until Art came back and bumped into me, spilling my pint down her dress."

"Bullocks," Gramps says, rolling his eyes. "You never stood a chance. One look at me and Janine was smitten."

"Aye," Walter replies. "That she was, mate." Walter raises the pint in front of him. "To Janine. God rest her beautiful soul."

The rest of us raise our beer glasses and toast to my grandmother.

I look through the plate-glass window of the bar, surveying the busy Boston street. I hate big cities. Too many people are in a rush to get somewhere without paying attention to the meaningful things in life—like family and celebrating memories with old friends. Honestly, I feel bad for the people out there who don't have what I have with my family and my club. They'll never understand what it means to live for something bigger than you, to know what true family and loyalty are.

On the other side of the window, a long mane of dark-blonde hair catches my attention. The girl turns slightly, laughing at whatever the man next to her says. My breath catches in my throat when I recognize her profile. I haven't seen her face or heard her laugh in five years, but the memory of that sweet sound rings through my ears as though she were standing right next to me.

Freya Campbell.

My first love, shit, my first everything. The only girl I've ever seen myself with for more than a few nights and a bit of fun is standing five feet from me, but it may as well be five thousand miles.

The man next to her leans down and places a sweet kiss on her lips. I remember when those lips were mine to kiss. She looks into his eyes like he's the only person she sees on the busy sidewalk. Memories of her looking at me the same way wash over me, followed by the red-hot rage that only comes with remembering the night five years ago when she was almost taken from this world. It was the same night I knew I'd lost her, that staying with me could cost her everything she wanted for herself. I close my eyes and remember when I told her she needed to leave Shine.

"Freya, I wish I could tell you what you want to hear. I wish being with me didn't put your life in danger, but that's not our reality. You have so much to do in life, pretty girl. But I'm not the guy who's going to be by your side."

When I open my eyes again, the happy couple is gone, leaving nothing but strangers and memories in their place.

"Jesus Christ, what the hell do I have to do to get a drink in this shithole?" I hear some asshole at the bar shout to the bartender. The woman rolls her eyes as she tends to another customer, which further pisses off the loudmouth who forgot his manners at home.

"Did you just roll your eyes at me? Maybe instead of trying to suck that guy's dick, you should pay attention to your other customers."

There are few things in this world that piss me off more than a man disrespecting a woman. Especially one that's trying to do her job. Add in the fact that I just got slapped in the face with memories I've worked damn hard to keep buried these last few years, and I'm a fucking ticking time bomb ready to go off on a dumb motherfucker.

"Bitch," he says loudly to his friends, and they have a nice little chuckle at the scene this idiot is causing.

I look toward Knox, who's waiting patiently for me to make a move, then my eyes dart to Jude, who looks as ready as I am to put this asshole in his place. I tilt my head to the guys at the bar and Jude lets a sinister smile spread across his face. Standing from my seat, Knox and Jude do the same and we walk up behind the four knuckleheads who have no idea what kind of hell they just unleashed.

Tapping the shoulder of the loudmouth, he turns to face me with a disgusted look on his face. The man is obviously drunk as hell and judging by his pinprick pupils and preppy rich-boy clothes, probably high on coke.

"Apologize," I tell him.

"Fuck you. I don't have to say shit to some slut behind a bar."

Turning my head to the side for a moment, a dark chuckle escapes me before I look him dead in the eye. "I gave you a chance."

Without giving him a second to open his mouth again, my fist slams into his jaw.

His other three friends yell and try to come to his aid, but Knox gets there first and grabs two by the collar, throwing them backward as Jude gut punches the other one. Dumbass Number One tries to swing, but it goes wide, leaving an opening for me to take advantage of, and I throw two punches to the fucker's kidneys. That should have him pissing blood for the next week. Jude has one pinned on the ground as he rains down blow after blow to the guy's face. I grab my guy by his neck and drag him outside. Knox and Jude follow with the other three, and we watch for a moment as the four assholes groan on the ground.

"Use your manners next time, you fucking twats," Jude says before kicking one of them in the stomach.

The three of us head back into the bar, and everyone inside gives us a wide berth. Looking at the other two, I realize we must be quite a gruesome sight. Jude has blood dripping from his knuckles, and Knox is a sweaty mess. Gramps and my dad are still sitting at the table, sipping the whiskeys in front of them while Walter laughs.

"Jesus, boys. You sure know how to make a point," Walter says.

I walk over to the bar and meet the bartender's gaze.

"Sorry about that," I tell the woman. "But there's no way I was going to allow that shit in my presence."

She nods and looks at my swollen knuckles. "You want some ice?"

I shoot her a wide smile. "Yeah, sweetheart, that would be great."

She grabs a towel and scoops ice into it before handing the makeshift cold pack to me.

"You got a name?" I ask, purposely running a finger over her wrist before I take the pack from her hand.

"Darcy," she says with a smile.

"Those assholes ever been here before?"

She shakes her head. "I've never seen them."

"Good. Hopefully they won't be back."

She chuckles and leans forward, resting her elbows on the bar top. "Doubt it. What about you? I've never seen you here before either."

I quirk my lip in a half smile. "Just in town for the night. Meeting up with some old friends."

"Hmm. Well, if your friends can spare you, I get off in an hour." Darcy bites her bottom lip and looks at me shyly from under her long lashes. "I could show you the sights," she suggests.

In an hour, it's going to be almost ten o'clock. I have a pretty good idea there's only one *sight* she plans to show me, and that sounds just fine to me.

"Yeah, Darcy. I think we'll be all caught up by then."

This is exactly what I need. A good fight and a good fuck to end my night. Not thoughts of the blonde from my past who left town with my heart five years ago.

CHAPTER ONE
FREYA
TEN YEARS LATER

"Good night. See you bright and early," I say in an overly sweet singsong voice to my paralegal. Clara shoots me a sly smile and waves.

We've been burning the candle at both ends while getting this case ready to take to trial. Working in the US Attorney's Office in Boston is never dull, and to be honest, every assistant US attorney works ridiculously long hours. I thought Harvard Law was rough but soon realized it was a cakewalk compared to here, especially with this case. We're going after the Cataldis, one of the oldest Italian Mafia families on the East Coast. My dad assisted on a case against them when I was in high school. I almost lost my life when some young capos decided to try to make a name for themselves. Wrong place, wrong time. You could say all the grueling hours I'm putting in to see the head of the Cataldi family behind bars for the rest of his life is some sort of vendetta. You would also be one hundred percent correct. I lost a lot more than blood the day those men came into the Black Roses clubhouse and shot the place up. I don't give a shit if the old man says he didn't sign off on the attack. I've done enough research on his organization through the years to know nothing happens without his say-so or, at the very least, his knowledge.

I followed in my father's footsteps for the most part. There were a few years of teenage rebellion, but I never veered from my plan of becoming a lawyer. The stress and long hours of fighting for justice took a toll on my dad. He ended up having to retire a few years ago after a heart attack—not that my mom gave him much of a choice. He never went soft on the Mob, and neither will I.

"Good night, Phil." I wave to the old security guard in the building I work in, making my way through the doors and onto the busy Boston street. It's not often I get out of work before nine at night, but I promised Kasey I'd have drinks with her while she and her husband are in Boston for some fundraiser. The senator's wife and I have been friends since college. It's not often we're in the same city at the same time and actually have the chance to get together.

Instead of taking the train, I decide on a cab. It won't necessarily save me time, but I can work more comfortably in the back of a cab. Kill two birds with one stone, as the saying goes.

When we pull up to my little brownstone apartment building, I pack my laptop away and check my phone. I still have time to get changed and freshen up my makeup before meeting Kasey. I bought a little two-bedroom, one-bathroom apartment with some money my grandmother left me when she passed. That's the only way I could have afforded the place on my salary. My parents thought it was a waste of money, complaining I could get more for my money outside the city limits. Real estate in Boston is outrageously expensive, but I wanted to live closer to the city, not in a suburb. I'm not ready for the white-picket fence life quite yet. Plus, there's no one in my life to share the fence with. And that's perfectly fine with me. I've worked hard for the career I have, and so what if my dating life took a back seat? I live my life on my terms, not anyone else's.

I open the door to the smaller building and my downstairs neighbor, Mrs. Flemming, pokes her head out.

"Freya, you're home early."

"For once," I joke, making my way up the stairs.

"You shouldn't work so much, dear. You're never going to find a husband with the hours you keep."

"Oh, Mrs. Flemming. If any man has a problem with my work schedule, then he definitely isn't the right one for me."

Unless I decide to go into private practice, my hours won't be changing anytime soon.

"I just want you to be happy like my Ernest made me. Fifty-seven amazing years together."

I smile fondly at my neighbor. She means well, but the two of us have very different ideas when it comes to the importance of marriage.

"I wish I would've had a chance to meet him." Experience has proven there's no use in trying to convince her that being single isn't a death sentence. "I have to cut this short though, Mrs. Flemming. I have plans in about a half hour and need to change." I smile and begin walking up the stairs.

"A date?" my nosy neighbor asks with hope ringing in her voice.

"No. Just drinks with a friend from college."

Mrs. Flemming lets out a long-suffering sigh. "Okay, then. Have fun and be safe out there. This neighborhood isn't what it used to be. Especially if you don't have an escort after dark."

"Good night, Mrs. Flemming."

Instead of waiting for her to extrapolate on all the other reasons having a man is the most important thing in the world, I hurry up the stairs.

Before I unlock my door, my phone pings with a text.

Clara: *Xander just sent over another file for the Cataldi case. I'm sending a courier to you so you have it over the weekend.*

Me: *Great. Thanks Clara.*

Of fucking course. He was supposed to have everything to me before I left. Xander is a paralegal for one of the other attorneys working on the case, but the kid never has his shit together. Looks like I'll be a little late for drinks.

Me: *Hey girl. I'm going to be running a little later than I thought. Thirty minutes tops. Maybe. Hopefully.*

Kasey: *No worries, friend. I'm still at the hotel.*

I throw my phone on the sofa in my small living room and head to my bedroom to change from an overworked lawyer to a thirty-three-year-old single woman who has their shit together. Well, that last part is stretching it a bit.

While I'm fixing my hair in my tiny bathroom, the buzzer sounds.

Walking over to the intercom, I press the button to speak to whoever is trying to get buzzed in, hoping it's the courier with the file.

"Yes?"

"Delivery for Ms. Campbell."

"Thank you." I press the buzzer to allow them in and wait.

The knock sounds at my door a moment later. That's one hell of a courier service to get here so fast. I'll have to ask Clara to keep them on speed dial.

"Freya Campbell?" the one in front asks.

"Yes," I reply with hesitation in my voice. These men aren't dressed like typical couriers.

Before he says another word, Guy Number One punches me in the jaw. Blinding pain, along with fear and utter confusion, causes me to freeze for a moment too long, giving them the opportunity they were looking for. Before I can let out a scream, they've both entered. Guy Number One has me by the throat. The unconcerned emptiness in his gaze sends terror rushing through my body. I claw at his leather-clad arm, desperate to get his hands off me, while Guy Number Two slams the door.

"Toss the place. Make it look like a robbery."

My air supply is being cut off by the asshole with his hand around my neck. I kick and try to fight, horrified by the realization that if I can't get away, I'm as good as dead, but the man has at least a hundred pounds on me. I manage to land a kick to his thigh, even though I'm aiming for his balls. The kick pisses him off, making him tighten his grip around my neck.

"Bitch," he spits out, slapping me hard across the face. He sweeps my feet from under me and lands on top of me. The air whooshes from my lungs before he straddles my waist so I can't move.

Leaning down, he whispers in my ear, "You're going to lose some evidence for us, Ms. Campbell. Or next time we come, it's going to be more than a few bruises to your face and ribs."

As soon as I think about the fact that he hasn't touched my ribs, his partner walks over to me and kicks me in the side. The debilitating blow to my ribs from the man's wing-tipped loafers sends a wave of nausea through me, and I try to choke back the bile threatening to erupt.

"Do I make myself clear?" the man pinning me asks.

Tremors of panic and pain rack my body, making it difficult to nod as tears and snot dribble over the side of my face.

"Good." The sadistic smile on his face makes the tears flow harder. "One more thing..." He punches me hard in my temple and consciousness leaves me.

"Oh my God. Call an ambulance," I hear Mrs. Flemming call to someone. "It's okay, dear. You're going to be just fine."

Why is she telling me that?

The terror and searing pain come flooding back the same moment I feel her thin hand caress the side of my face.

I blink my eyes open, and a painful groan escapes me as I attempt to sit up.

"No, no. Stay right there," she says, patting my shoulder. "You don't want to make anything worse."

"I'm okay," I croak out, not wanting to stay on the hard floor.

"Honey, by the looks of your face, you're anything but."

A weak smile forms on my lips, but the movement causes my cheek to ache even more.

"Shit." I tentatively touch the side of my face and immediately feel the swelling and tenderness. "That asshole got me good."

I look to my doorway and see a shaking young man who can't be more than twenty. He's on the phone with whom I assume are the police, and a manilla envelope is clutched in his tight fist.

"You must be the courier," I say, trying to stand. A jolt of pain slices through my side, nearly knocking the wind from my lungs.

"This is why I told you not to move," Mrs. Flemming admonishes.

Ignoring her warnings, I hobble over to my couch and slowly sit down, trying not to jostle my ribs, which are most likely broken.

"Can you bring me the file, please?" I ask the obviously terrified courier. It's not every day you show up to deliver a package and find the recipient beaten and unconscious on the floor of her apartment.

"The ambulance is on the way, ma'am," he replies, handing me the Cataldi file.

"How long was I out for?"

"No way to know for sure. The boy kept trying to ring your apartment, and when you didn't answer, he rang mine. Who did this to you, Freya?"

Poor Mrs. Flemming. Her daughter has been trying to get her to move south with her, saying the city isn't safe for a woman living alone. This incident probably tipped the scales of that decision in her daughter's favor.

"I'm not exactly sure, but I know what they were after." Something I'll never give them. Instead of being afraid like any sane person would be, I'm fucking pissed. Those assholes broke into my apartment and attacked me, threatened me. If I wasn't determined to put Cataldi away before, I sure as hell am now.

"I really don't think you have anything to be worried about." The reassurance sounds hollow even to me.

"Of course I'm worried," she exclaims. "You could have been killed, and I was just sitting in the apartment right below yours. I feel awful. Did you get a good look for the police?"

Yes, I did. But I'm not entirely sure this should be reported. The Cataldis have dirty cops in their pockets. I'm going to put these fuckers away no matter what, but I'd like to keep my life at the same time.

"I'll talk to them at the hospital," I assure her as the EMTs make their way into my apartment.

After checking me over, they suggest a trip to the ER. Since I'm sure my ribs are at least bruised to high hell, if not broken, I'm inclined to agree.

The gravity of the situation hasn't completely sunk in yet as I waver between numbness and fiery anger. Right now, getting from point A to point B is all I can manage.

"Call me when you're on your way home, sweetheart," Mrs. Flemming tells me while the EMTs carry me on the stretcher down the stairs.

I shoot her a weak smile. My face is throbbing more and more by the second, and exhaustion is beginning to take over. I read somewhere you shouldn't fall asleep if you suspect a concussion, but the thought of a nap is more than a little appealing to me, at least until they can give me something for the pain. I'd much rather sleep through this bumpy-as-hell ambulance ride.

Oh, shit. I just remembered drinks with Kasey.

Instead of texting her and attempting to read my screen with this raging headache, I hit the call button.

"Hey girl. Where are you?" she asks when she answers. She must have been waiting for at least an hour by this point.

"There was an accident at my place. I'm on the way to the ER."

"What kind of accident did you have that warrants a trip to the hospital?" I hear the concern in her voice over the sounds of the busy bar she's waiting at.

"The breaking and entering kind with a side of assault."

"Oh my God, Freya. What hospital?" The volume of Kasey's voice is not helping my headache situation.

"Mass Gen." I look toward the EMT who is sitting next to me for confirmation, and she nods.

"Donovan and I will meet you there."

"Kasey, you don't have—"

"Shut it, Freya Campbell. I'm calling him now, and we'll meet you there."

You do not argue with Kasey Hayes when her mind is set.

"Okay, see you in a little bit," I relent as another wave of nausea somersaults through my stomach.

We hang up right before pulling into the ambulance bay. The bright lights and loud noises of the hospital have me squeezing my eyes shut, which only causes the swelling on my face to ache more. When I get to a bed, the doctor comes in and asks me about my injuries. The same lie I plan to tell the cops spills easily from my lips. I have no idea who the guys were or what they wanted. I am the victim of a home invasion and that's that. They were wearing masks, so I didn't get a look at their faces. The doctor orders a CT for my head, and now all that's left to do is wait.

"Knock, knock." A familiar auburn head peeks inside the curtain.

"Wow, they'll let anyone back here," I quip.

She shoots me a wry smile. "Being a senator's wife has its perks." Kasey's eyes soften as she looks me over. "How are you feeling?"

"Like I got punched in the face and kicked in the ribs," I reply dryly.

"Stupid question," she says with an apology in her tone. "Have they given you anything for the pain yet?"

"Any minute." Which is a minute too long.

"What happened, Freya?" she asks, taking the seat next to my bed. "Did this have to do with the case you're working on?"

My head nods stiffly in affirmation, the reality of the situation sinking in. The enormity of it hit me when the nurse asked if I needed a rape kit. Those men could have done anything to me, and I wouldn't have been able to stop them. And if Mrs. Flemming had heard something and decided to come check on me...God, I can't even think about it.

"Freya, you need to take this seriously. You have to file a report. You need protection."

A caustic laugh escapes me. "Kasey, the Cataldis have people in the department. If I make a report, chances that it gets back to them are pretty fucking high."

A tear escapes as my mind plays the coulda, shoulda, woulda game. Maybe if I had fought harder or closed the door as soon as I opened it and knew in my bones something was off. Now, there's no doubt they know where I live and, most likely, where my parents live. Going to them is out of the question.

"Have I ever mentioned the guys that helped us find Lindsey when she was kidnapped? The owner of the security firm is friends with Aiden, Donovan's security specialist."

I wipe the tear from my cheek and nod. When Kasey's sister was kidnapped, Donovan's security specialist called in a favor to an old friend from the Royal Marines to help with the search.

"He still talks to him. In fact, Aiden helped him out not too long ago. I could put you in touch. He has contacts all over the place. You need to get out of town for a while. Work remotely until this case goes to trial. He could find somewhere safe for you."

Blowing out a shaky breath, I look one of my oldest friends in the eye. "That would be a good idea."

I have no intention of reporting this to my office. I'll be damned if I'm taken off the case for my "protection." This case is why I became an attorney, and no one is going to take away my satisfaction of putting Francesco Cataldi in prison.

Kasey offers me a sad smile. "It won't be forever, honey. Just a little while. As soon as they take you for tests, I'll get his number from Donovan."

"Where is your husband, by the way?"

"In the private waiting room."

"I don't want to keep you from your plans. You don't have to stay." Kasey and I both have an uncomfortable past with being in hospitals.

"Well, my plans were to have drinks with you tonight. Instead of wine, I'm sure someone could scrounge up some delicious apple juice."

I scrunch my nose and chuckle, immediately regretting it. Kasey notices my wince.

"Headache?"

"Like a motherfucker."

"Wow, being in the hospital brings out your sailor speak."

"I'm not the biggest fan of them." Not since my hospital stay fifteen years ago when my life changed forever.

"I'm sorry. I know you have a history with them."

The orderly comes in before we can talk about why exactly I hate them, not something I care to discuss at the moment, and wheels me to the imaging department. The scan takes less than thirty minutes, and I'm wheeled right back to the curtained-off area I was in before.

"The doctor will be in shortly," the orderly says, and I offer him a gracious smile.

Kasey is by my side again moments later, and she hands me a piece of paper.

"This is the guy's number. His name's Liam Ashcroft. Kind of a pompous asshole, but he's great at his job. These are the only guys Donovan would trust with something like this."

I take the piece of paper from her hand and stare at it. This is what it boils down to. Years of hard work are now being compromised so I can go into hiding because I was attacked. I'm not saying it's not the best option, but goddammit, it pisses me the hell off.

"Do you want Donovan to make the call for you?" Kasey asks, mistaking my reluctance for something other than being angry with the fact I have to make this call in the first place.

"No, I got it."

Picking up my phone, I dial the number Kasey gave me.

"Hello?" the man on the other end answers.

"Hi. Liam Ashcroft?"

"Freya Campbell, I presume," he replies.

"How do you know my name?"

"I could say I have the number of every federal prosecutor in my phone, but that would be a lie. Senator Hayes texted and said you would be calling."

OZZY: THE BLACK ROSES MC, BOOK THREE 25

This fucking guy.

"Did Donovan tell you about my situation?"

Liam hums. "He briefly ran me through it. It just so happens I have a friend who owes me a couple favors. I think we could have you set up somewhere out of the city in no time."

Relief washes through me. "That's exactly what I need. Where am I going?"

"Have you ever heard of a little town called Shine, Massachusetts?"

CHAPTER TWO
OZZY

This paperwork in front of me wouldn't be so bad if I wasn't hungover as fuck from last night. Ah, the illustrious life of an MC president. It's rare I indulge to the point of a hangover this bad, but it's that time of year for the memories of a night I wish to God never happened to play on a constant loop.

The words and numbers are jumping around on the paper at this point, making my headache a million times worse. Or it could be the asshole that keeps calling me. Liam Ashcroft has been ringing my phone since last night, and frankly, I have nothing to say to the arrogant prick. Who the hell did he think he was sending me a fucking invoice for jet fuel for the planes we used to rescue Jude's woman and all the others from that cult compound a few months ago? It was for his brother, for chrissake. If it weren't for the fact he helped us out with the compound cleanup, I would have made a special trip to Philly to punch the bastard in the face. That option still isn't off the table, but I have too much fucking work to get through here to make it a top priority.

Rubbing my tired eyes again, I think about fucking off and getting into the bottle of whiskey in my desk drawer to alleviate this damn hangover. I've been busy as hell the last couple months with paperwork, building out the women's shelter to house the influx of residents from that damn compound, and more paperwork. I haven't had time to take my bike out when shit gets to be too much, hence the binge I went on. Alcohol isn't something I want to use to drown my pain, but the day my life changed fifteen years ago is right around the corner.

I don't often let myself think about Freya, not since seeing her a decade ago in Boston, but a couple of my brothers are pretty close to being wifed up, and I don't know, it's bringing up memories from the past. Freya and I were only kids, but at the time, I saw myself with her for the long term. Maybe even getting married after she was done with college and law school. Stupid, childish dreams I had when I considered what life would look like after graduation, but the thought was there, nonetheless. Then the Italians came in and shot the place up, and her dad decided to move her the hell away from here. Can't say I blame the man, but fuck if it didn't hurt.

Blowing out a breath, I look at the stack of papers, then to my desk drawer. Nope. I have too much shit to get done. I gave myself last night to ponder the what-ifs, and today, it's back to reality. The club needs me present. I still have invoices from the bar and strip club we own to go through, and I need to work on payroll for the bike shop. Cash would help with this shit if I asked, but my dad always impressed upon me the importance of crossing every t and dotting every i myself. It's not because I don't trust the other brothers to handle it or even Tanya, my dad's girlfriend and bike shop manager, to help out. It's so there's never a question of that trust. Cash is the treasurer and he's damn good at what he does, but this system worked for Gramps and my dad, so who am I to argue?

The last few months have certainly proven once again how much trust we have to have in each other. When Linc and Jude's women came to the club, they brought a boatload of trouble with them. Our club banded together with some help from the Irish and handled shit like I knew we would, but we weren't without losses. We lost Cooper—and he would've made one hell of a brother. Which reminds me, I need to call his sister again and try to convince her to cash the damn check I sent her. Even though Cooper was still a prospect, I didn't have it in me to leave the girl with nothing. I know he was sending her money every couple weeks, but he never said what it was for, and I wasn't going to pry into his personal business without a reason. The first time I called Nova, she told me to fuck off. I figured it was the grief talking. From what Cooper said about his family, it was just him and his little sister. He never mentioned how damn stubborn Nova was, though. Months later, the money is still sitting in the club's account.

Cooper died protecting Lucy. While his death hit us all hard, Lucy's had a hard time moving on from it. There's been a few times I've caught her staring at his picture hanging above the bar next to his prospect patch with tears in her eyes. She was there and watched him take his last breath. I've tried to talk to her, but she clams up and busies herself with something for her sister or the shelter where many of the women we saved from that horrid compound took up residence. Jude says he has it under control, and it's his woman, so I'm not about to argue. Some of us need more time to deal with loss than others. Living this life prepares you for the possibility that the brother standing next to you today may not be there tomorrow. Though Lucy's seen a lot of shit in her life and is one of the toughest women I know, she wasn't prepared to watch her friend die. Shit, there's no way to prepare for something like that.

The knock on my door thirty minutes later is a welcome reprieve from the paperwork and maudlin thoughts jumbled in my head. Jude pops his head in with a slightly apprehensive look on his face.

"Got a minute, Oz?"

"Yeah." I rub my tired eyes and lean back in my chair. "I'm just about seeing double at this point."

I wave him in and open my desk drawer. May as well take a much-needed break.

"Want one? We have a shit ton." The Monaghans sent us two dozen cases after helping them out with getting rid of one of the brother's old lady's ex and keeping some important information out of the Italian's hands.

I pour some whiskey for each of us and hand him a glass. Taking a sip relieves some of the pressure behind my eyes. Not as good as being on my bike, but it will do for now.

"What's up, Jude?" The need to get out of this office and go on a long ride to clear my head is strong. Especially considering more paperwork tends to find its way to my desk the longer I sit here.

Jude rubs the back of his neck. It's still strange to see him with shorter hair. He chopped it before we went to rescue his woman from her crazy-as-fuck family in the Nevada desert. It sort of reminds me of the old days before I was the club president.

"My brother called. He needs some help."

I blow out a long breath. I knew this day was going to come sooner rather than later. Liam made it clear when he helped out with the trouble that followed Linc's old lady that he would be calling in a couple favors.

"What is it?" There's no doubt in my mind this is going to be a big ask. Even though the man pisses me off, there is no way in hell I can say no to him. I made a deal with the devil, and now he wants his due.

"There's a girl—" Jude begins.

"There always is." I shake my head as a sardonic chuckle escapes me. It's always about a girl these days.

"She's pissed off some dangerous people. People we've had dealings with."

The feeling of a rock dropping in my stomach hits me when he says those words. I have a good idea of who he's speaking of, and there's no doubt it's going to cause a whole mess of problems I didn't want to deal with right now.

"Don't tell me," I groan out.

"The Cataldis."

He had to tell me.

I haven't wanted to go anywhere near those Italian bastards. It doesn't mean I didn't know I would have to at some point. There's been too many instances where they've seemed to have a spoon in the pot of shit that's been stirred around here. I just thought I had more time. Looks like times up, though.

"Fuck," I say, clenching my jaw. "Okay, what does he need?" I have no idea what we can offer this girl that Liam can't, considering he's the one she reached out to.

"He said he's stretched thin at the moment, and this girl needs a safe place to lie low for a while until some shit gets sorted. That's all he told me."

"Did he say anything about who the girl is or what the 'shit' is?" Leave it to Liam to only give the bare minimum of information.

"She's some lawyer in Boston who's been working on putting the high-ranking capos behind bars. She has some pretty hard evidence, and they want it back and want her gone. They've already tried to get to her once. Seems she has some friends in Philly who hooked her up with my brother."

"Fucking great. Are we turning into protection for hire or some shit?" I tip back the rest of my whiskey and remember why we have an endless supply. The Irish were more than grateful all those months ago when I turned over the notebook Charlie's ex wanted to give to the Italians that had a whole lot of sensitive information about the Irish. We gave her a place to stay when she was on the run, same with Lucy, Jude's old lady. Shit, maybe we should start charging. Wouldn't be the worst business decision.

"Liam said she grew up here and you, Linc, and Knox went to school together."

That piques my interest. Not a lot of the girls I remember from high school stuck around our little town, which never bothered me in the least. Most of those girls were stuck-up bitches, and I was more than happy when they moved on.

"Yeah? What's her name?"

"Freya Campbell."

The tiny amount of ease the whiskey has given me vanishes in an instant. Jude may as well have reached into my chest and wrapped a fucking fist around my heart when he said her name. I stare at him, not quite believing I heard him right, but at the same time, sure that I did. That's a name I haven't uttered to another person in almost fifteen years. I'm sure I've never told Jude her name, either.

"Who did you say?" I croak out.

Jude's brows lower, a concerned look in his eyes. "Freya Campbell." He tilts his head, still staring at me. "You okay, mate? You look like you've seen a ghost."

A humorless chuckle rumbles through my chest, which causes Jude to look even more uneasy than he did moments ago.

"Oz, I'm getting a little worried here. Who the hell is this Freya Campbell girl?"

I blow out a long breath and stare at the ceiling for a few moments. There are so many different ways to answer the question. My first love, my first heartbreak, the girl I almost gave everything up for when we were only eighteen because I couldn't imagine loving another woman the way I loved her. I can take my pick.

"You've heard the story about the Italians coming here fifteen years ago and shooting up the clubhouse." It's not a question. Even though it happened five years before Jude got here, it's a well-known story among the brothers. We all remember the bloody aftermath. My dad and Gramps, who was retired from club life for a lot of years by that point, made sure to handle those responsible. "She was my girlfriend at the time, and she was shot."

Jude looks at me with wide eyes and slumps back in his seat. "Shit, Oz. I've heard the stories and knew a girl was shot, but I don't remember anyone calling her by name."

"Because no one would. I don't talk about it."

Jude looks like he wants to ask more questions but wisely decides against it. Good thing because I have no intention of going down memory lane with him.

Of all the dumb fucking luck, Liam *would* need me and the club to help her. Why did I ever think when Liam called in his favor, it would be a simple favor that wouldn't involve something that could potentially break my fucking heart all over again?

"I need to call your brother. Go let Knox know what's going on." Oh, he's going to love this. He was none too happy with me after she left, and I became a raging asshole.

Jude stands but doesn't look too keen on leaving me alone. "Okay, Oz." He heads toward the door. Before opening it, he turns back to me. "Listen, if this is going to be too much, I'll call him myself and tell him to fuck off and find someone else."

"Really, Jude? You think I need you to hold my hand or fight my battles for me? I think I can handle seeing my ex-girlfriend." I roll my eyes and wave him off.

"I know you can. I just wanted an excuse to tell my asshole brother off. I'm sure I'll come up with something else in no time."

"Get the hell out of here," I say on a laugh.

Jude smiles and shoots me a two-finger salute before shutting the door behind him.

What I wouldn't give to rewind time to fifteen minutes earlier when all I had to worry about was the mountain of work on my desk.

I pick up my phone and stare at it for several minutes. There's no way for me to tell Liam no. And if I'm honest with myself, I don't want to. In fact, I want Freya here now. What the hell happened to her? Yes, when Jude said her name, I was thrown for a fucking loop, to put it mildly. But that doesn't mean I would ever turn my back on her if she needed help. Considering she reached out to Liam, she must have found herself in a world of trouble. Now that the shock has worn off, the only thing I can think of is I will destroy the motherfucker who had the audacity to touch her. She may not be mine any longer, but she was at one point. I couldn't do anything all those years ago, but I'll be damned if I can't protect her now.

I hit Liam's contact and listen to it ring.

"Ozzy, so nice of you to finally call me back," he answers with a snarky bite to his tone.

"Well, when you send me a bill for over a hundred grand for jet fuel used to save your brother's girl, did you really expect me to jump when you called?"

"Jesus fucking Christ, Oz. It was a joke. You're familiar with the concept, yes?"

"First of all, it's Ozzy, as I'm sure I've reminded you before. And second, your jokes are funny to exactly one person on this planet, and I'm talking to him now."

Liam has always derived some sick pleasure from getting under my skin, but I suppose I'm the dumbass who lets him.

"Jude said you needed to speak to me about a protection job."

"Ah, yes. Freya Campbell. I wasn't aware of her history with the club when I suggested going to Shine. She was a bit apprehensive at first."

A scoff escapes my throat. "I'm sure."

"Be that as it may, I'm handling a heavy caseload at the moment and can't spare anyone. You owe me a favor, and this seemed like a good time to call it in. Win-win."

"Did Freya see it as a win?"

It occurs to me that this is the first time I've said her name out loud in years, maybe more than a decade.

"She's scared and desperate to stay alive and wants these people behind bars. Any situation that makes that possible is a win for her, I'm sure."

"So, what you're saying is she's desperate enough and doesn't feel she has any other choice."

I've become well versed in Liam speak, which usually entails hearing the things he doesn't say.

"Precisely," he replies.

"What happened to her?"

"A couple of Cataldi's goons broke into her place and roughed her up. Didn't break anything but threatened to come back if she didn't lose some evidence."

"All this for a few capos? Why would they put their organization at risk for that?"

Capos are a dime a dozen to the Cataldis, proven by the fact that the old man didn't do jack shit when my dad and Gramps put a few to ground fifteen years ago.

"She's not going after capos. Or not just the capos. She's going after the old man."

"Francesco?"

"One and the same."

"Shit." I lean forward and rest my head in my palm, massaging my forehead with my fingers. What the fuck is this woman getting herself into? "Why hasn't the US Attorney's Office given her any sort of protection?"

"I haven't the foggiest. Budget cuts would be my guess."

He's lying through his teeth.

"She didn't tell them, did she?" The Freya I knew in high school was as stubborn as they come. If she thought, even for a second, this would affect her case, she'd keep quiet.

Liam's answering chuckle is the only confirmation I need to know she hasn't changed that much in the last fifteen years.

I inhale a deep breath and sit up straight. There's a quick knock on my door and Knox pops his head in with an irritated scowl on his face. Jude must have found him. I wave him in and point to the phone in my hand, mouthing Liam's name. Knox shakes his head as he has a seat in the chair across from my desk.

"Okay, Liam. When do you expect her to be here?"

"I plan on escorting her there myself tomorrow afternoon. She's still pretty banged up, though, so be prepared."

"Are you warning me out of the goodness of your heart?"

"I do have one, you know," he grumbles.

"Yeah, I'll remember that the next time you decide to play one of your 'jokes.'"

"I'm simply letting you know, Ozzy, that she looks like hell. And if there's one thing I know about you lot, you'll run headfirst into any situation when you see women in this condition. Don't do that here. She needs to be kept away from these assholes, and that means they can't know she's there."

"I got it, Liam. This isn't my first rodeo."

He seems to be inferring I won't be up to the task, further grating on my fucking nerves.

"Alright. See you tomorrow, then."

I hang up without saying anything else and meet Knox's weighted gaze.

"Freya's coming here?"

"Seems so."

"Well...fuck."

Yeah, my sentiments exactly.

CHAPTER THREE
FREYA

"Don't look so nervous," Liam says to me as we drive out of Boston. "Ozzy was more than happy for you to come to the clubhouse."

I can't contain the laugh that escapes when Liam attempts to reassure me. "Do you honestly expect me to believe when you talked to him, he had nothing to say about me coming?"

If this guy thinks I haven't gotten to where I am by *not* reading between the lines, he's a lot dumber than I give him credit for.

"Well, he had his concerns, naturally, but he didn't say he didn't want you there."

I wish I'd been a fly on the wall during that conversation. Never in a million years did I think Ozzy would turn me away. Even though it's been fifteen years, there has to be more to the story than Liam is letting on. Ozzy may not have expressed his reservations about having me in the clubhouse to Liam, but there's not a single doubt in my mind he doesn't have any. Hell, I have several. Namely, the anger I've never quite been able to let go of from all those years ago.

When I was eighteen and lying in a hospital bed, recovering from a gunshot wound, he came in and told me it was over. After everything we shared just a few days prior, he was so easily able to discard me. That kind of rejection sticks with a girl, no matter how honorable the intentions behind it were.

"It doesn't sound as though you believe me, Ms. Campbell," Liam says in a mock offended tone.

"Well, Mr. Ashcroft, this isn't my first trip around the sun, so it's safe to say you're correct in your assumption."

Liam chuckles and nods his head. "You're what many would consider a ballbuster."

"You're also correct in that assumption."

I give the man a small smile and look out the window as the car travels down the small two-lane highway that will take us to Shine, Massachusetts. It's been years, fifteen to be exact, since I've traveled this road. Last time, I was headed in the opposite direction, being whisked away from everything I grew up with.

Before the incident at the clubhouse—and my subsequent heartbreak—I couldn't wait to get out of this town, although it didn't occur to me at the time that I'd have stayed away for so long. It's not like there was much to bring me back, though. There's only one person I'd have truly missed. When he ended it, there was really no reason for me to come back. I couldn't stand most of the girls who went to my high school. The only people I felt comfortable being myself around were Ozzy and, for a short time, Linc and Knox. Well, maybe not Knox. He's always been the scary, silent type. Wonder if that's changed?

Not wanting to talk to Liam about how I'm feeling in regard to going back to Shine or being in the clubhouse again, I pull out my laptop and start going through the motions that have yet to be filed with the court. Work. Work has always been my safe go-to when emotions try to take over. I don't have time to worry about the danger I'm in or what seeing Ozzy again is going to do to my heart if I keep busy. It's how I made it through prelaw, after all.

We've done so much preliminary work on this case, making sure everything is set and we have an argument prepared for every possible objection that could be brought up by the defense. There's no telling what will actually happen once the case goes in front of the judge, though. The fact that we got an indictment against Cataldi is a fucking miracle in and of itself. Many have tried, but so far only me and my team have succeeded. Sure, a few other high-ranking capos haven't had the best luck when it comes to trial, but this is the first time anyone has been able to get charges to stick to Francesco Cataldi. The way he laughed at me when I offered him a plea deal was probably the highlight of my year. I didn't want to offer it, but my boss insisted. When he laughed in my face and told me he'd see me in court, the utter glee I felt was written all over my face.

Let the man's ego be his downfall. It usually is for men like him.

What seems like only a few minutes but is probably closer to two hours later, we're driving through downtown Shine. There's a certain sense of nostalgia over being in my hometown, but there's also a bittersweet sort of feeling with seeing how much has changed and how much has stayed the same. A couple shops on Main Street are still here from when I was a kid, and a few have closed and are now replaced with new businesses. A smile spreads across my face when I see Cool Beans is still open. Betsy always made the best pastries and coffee. Nearing the end of the street, I see the bike shop Ozzy's dad and grandpa used to own. The Black Roses insignia is still painted on the sign, so I assume they still do. Trying not to look too obvious, I attempt to peek inside the open bays to see if I recognize anyone inside. Of course, I don't. It's not like I'm going to look over and see a teenage version of Ozzy working in there. I mean, I suppose it's not impossible to think he could've had a kid after I left town. The kid would probably be working in the shop just like Ozzy used to from the time he could hold a wrench.

Jesus, Freya. Get it together. Now you're making up imaginary children your ex may have fathered.

Okay, so I may be a tad bit nervous and overthinking what's transpired in Ozzy's life since I left. I'm a lawyer, for fuck's sake. Overthinking is in my job description. It's not as though I'd heard what happened to Ozzy after graduation. The only reason I know he's alive and still in Shine is because Liam is taking me to him. He never called after I left. No letters or text messages. Not even a smoke signal. There was zero communication after he broke my heart in that hospital room all those years ago.

I've rarely let myself imagine what it would be like to run into him on some street in Boston or something of the sort. Would I smile? Would we have a cup of coffee and chat? Would it be possible for me to be that mature, or would I break down crying because of all the unresolved feelings toward the sudden and entirely unexpected demise of our relationship? Of course, those musings haven't crossed my mind in ages, but driving through downtown is transporting me back to that time in my head. So much was left unsaid. Would I have the courage to say it now? Or would it be better to let sleeping dogs lie until I can get back to Boston? This anticipation bullshit is quite the mind-bender.

The long stretch of highway out of town and toward the clubhouse reminds me of the only time I came out here as a teenager. It was the day before Thanksgiving and the day I was shot.

Before leaving Boston, I refused to consider the old feelings and memories being back here would bring to the surface, only caring about getting out of town and ignoring everything else. That was definitely an oversight on my part because I feel wholly unprepared now as we pull up to the gate of the clubhouse. Liam waves to a man wearing a vest that says *Prospect* across the back, and he lets us through.

"Come here often?" I ask him.

"My brother lives here, well, he used to. He's a member."

When Liam and I discussed sending me here to hide out, he never mentioned a brother.

"I didn't realize you had such a close relationship with the club."

"I don't necessarily, but they've needed my help from time to time, and it never hurts for the president of an MC to owe you a few favors."

I recall Kasey telling me there are two things Liam takes as payment: money and favors.

"I'd think your brother being in the MC would make them exempt from owing you favors."

"The last time I helped them was personal. But there were a few times before that. No matter how much I like the lumbersnack president, no one gets something from me without me getting something in return."

A sharp laugh escapes me. "You refer to Ozzy as a lumbersnack?"

"Well, not to his face." Liam shoots me a conspiratorial wink.

He parks, and I stare at the building in front of me for several long moments before either of us gets out of the car.

"You okay?" he asks.

"Yup. It's just a little strange being back here. It never occurred to me I'd end up in the place my dad took me away from for my safety, then come back to be protected by the club he swore up and down was dangerous."

Truth be told, when my dad moved me and my mom out of Shine, I never expected to come back for any reason. My parents have no idea I'm even here. The last thing they need to worry about is the Cataldis coming after me. Telling them I basically ran back to the MC they hated, for protection nonetheless, wouldn't make them feel any better about the situation, either.

I step out of the car and grab my bag from the trunk. Before hitting the road, we stopped by my place to grab some clothes and let Mrs. Flemming know I was going to be gone for a while. Thankfully, after the attack, Mrs. Flemming decided it would be a good idea to stay with her daughter for a bit and was leaving the same day. The assholes who attacked me did a damn good job of trashing my apartment. Kasey, Donovan, and Liam were with me, and it didn't take us too long to clean up my tiny apartment, considering the state it was in. Of course, Liam grumbled the entire time about needing to get out of town ASAP, but there was no way I would have been able to put it off. Knowing the mess would be there when I finally made it back home would have wreaked havoc on my slightly type A personality. Who am I trying to kid? I'm one hundred percent type A.

The nerves are battling it out in my stomach as Liam and I make our way to the door. A younger version of the man next to me steps out with a wide smile on his face.

"Liam, you fucking twat. Only you would be able to get under Ozzy's skin by calling in a favor steeped in unpleasant history." The man stops and looks at me. "No offense."

"Sorry for my brother. While I was raised to have manners, it seems he was raised by bloody wolves."

"For fuck's sake, Jude. Don't be a dick," a short woman with long black hair calls, walking up to him and smacking him in the arm.

He grabs the woman around the waist and lays a smacking kiss on her mouth.

"I apologized, Lucifer."

"That was hardly an apology." The woman turns toward Liam. "Liam, good to see you." She gives him a small smile.

"How's Little Bit these days?" Liam asks.

"Better. Thanks for the set of throwing stars you sent her." The woman shoots Liam a rueful grin.

"I figured it would do her some good to master a few different weapons," Liam replies with a shrug.

"So, you thought sharp projectiles were the way to go?" Jude asks.

Liam turns to Jude. "It didn't do you any harm."

The woman next to Jude shakes her head and turns to me, holding out her hand. "I'm Lucy, this asshole's old lady," she says, nodding toward Jude.

"Freya Campbell. Nice to meet you," I reply, shaking her hand.

"Come in and meet Charlie. We were just about to head out, but she's excited to have another woman here who isn't a bunny."

"Bunny?" *Do they have some sort of animal rescue here?*

"You don't know much about MCs, I take it."

"Not really. The only time I was here was back in high school during a big family dinner Linc and Knox's mom cooked for."

Lucy chuckles. "Yeah, they definitely would've made themselves scarce around Tanya." Lucy begins to walk toward the clubhouse, motioning for me to follow. "A bunny is a woman that lives here and 'services' the brothers, among other things."

My brows shoot up my forehead. "Not what I thought you were going to say."

Am I one to judge a woman for what she does with her body or how she chooses to spend her time? No. Am I looking forward to meeting a bunch of women who live here with my ex and probably have slept with him? Also, no.

"They're not too terrible since Ozzy kicked out the queen bitch, but they'll probably steer clear. Don't be shocked if you get a few dirty looks, though. They're pretty territorial, even though they have zero chance at being one of the brothers' old ladies." Lucy shrugs and opens the door.

It doesn't surprise me in the least that Ozzy wouldn't put up with any drama around here from whoever this "queen bitch" was. He was never the type to deal with it when I knew him. Nice to know that hasn't changed.

The clubhouse is just how I remember it. The main room is large, with a bar along the back wall, an area set up with a few sectionals and a large flat screen hanging on the wall, pool tables and a couple dart boards off to the left. Last time I was here, there were a bunch of tables set up with food spread all over and kids running around. This time there're no tables or large spreads. Only a few brothers milling about, shooting curious glances in my direction.

A woman bounds over to Lucy and me with a wide smile stretched across her face. "Hi. I'm Charlie," she says, coming in for a hug.

I'm not a particularly touchy-feely kind of person myself, but I return the embrace.

"Freya," I reply as Charlie pulls away.

"Don't mind her," Lucy starts. "She's excited to have another member of our girl gang."

Lucy and Charlie both wrinkle their noses.

"I thought we agreed that sounded stupid," Charlie says.

"I thought I'd try it out again. But no, it's still dumb."

I chuckle because, one, it is stupid to refer to a group of female friends as a girl gang, and two, I find both of these women charming.

Charlie looks at the injuries on my face with a small frown. "How are you feeling?" she asks.

"Sore as hell, but nothing was broken."

"I've been there. I think I have some arnica cream in my old room. It helps with the bruising and soreness."

"Thanks. I'd rather not be hopped up on pain meds." I offer her a smile.

"I'll introduce you to my old man...oh wait, I forgot you guys knew each other in high school."

A tall man with broad shoulders and short dark hair walks over and slides his arm around Charlie.

"Hey, Freya."

"Holy shit. Linc?"

Linc laughs and leans in for a brief hug. "One and the same. It's been a minute."

"It has. It's so great to see you again."

Gone is the young kid who was a bit of a flirtatious goofball in high school. In his place stands a man who I can tell is a bit more reserved and a bit, I don't know...edgier. And nearly twice the size he was the last time I saw him.

"Sorry it's under these circumstances," he says. "We've had some dealings with the Cataldis in the last few months. Fucking assholes."

"Well, they certainly aren't on my Christmas card list," I retort.

Linc laughs, and I feel a bit more at ease seeing a familiar face.

"How are your mom and brother?"

"Good. I'm sure once Oz tells her you're here, she'll be over and cooking up a storm. Knox is around here somewhere," he finishes, looking around for his older brother.

I see the man in question come from where I know the kitchen to be. The one I'd lain bleeding in fifteen years ago. Fuck, this is harder than I thought. I rarely think about that night, and now scenes from it keep playing in my mind over and over.

Knox walks over and gives me a stiff nod. "Freya."

"Hi Knox. Good to see you."

The only reply I get is a grunt before he turns to his brother. "I have some shit to take care of." He turns and leaves the clubhouse without another word.

"Still chatty as ever," I mumble under my breath.

Linc gives me an apologetic look.

"So Knox has always been like this, then?" Charlie asks.

"Pretty much. That's why I always told you not to take it personally, Charlie Pie." Linc leans in and kisses the top of his girlfriend's hair.

"Mate," Jude says, walking up to us. "Are you ever going to give up on the nicknames?"

"She's warming up to it," Linc replies.

"No, I'm not," Charlie says, rolling her eyes. "They're still ridiculous."

Seeing the way Linc looks at Charlie makes me happy for him. Granted, I know it's been years since being back in Shine, so of course, people have grown and changed, but in my mind, he was always the sixteen-year-old jock with an easy smile who enjoyed the attention of all the girls. This version of Linc only has eyes for the woman sitting next to him.

"Hey Ozzy," Jude calls, looking over my shoulder.

It's as though the air has been sucked from the room as I turn to face Ozzy again after fifteen years. The gray Henley stretched across his wide frame reminds me of the day I went to his house, and he was waiting on his front porch. His eyes burn into me from across the room as I take in how much he's changed in the last decade and a half. His eyes hold the same vibrant gleam, but now there are lines around them that weren't there before. Instead of the care-free, clean-shaven football star I remember from high school, he stands before me as the bearded MC president he's become.

One look at him and I can sense something in him that wasn't there when we were together. It's obvious, at least to me, that the weight of the world is visibly resting on his shoulders. His gaze doesn't hold the warmth and humor I remember. Instead, there's a dangerous intensity in it as he stares straight at me.

I often wondered how I would feel seeing Ozzy again. Now I have my answer—pure, unadulterated anger.

CHAPTER FOUR
Ozzy

It's as though I'm eighteen again as I look at the most beautiful girl with the brightest blue eyes I've ever seen. Never in a million years did I expect Freya Campbell would be standing in this clubhouse again. The next emotion that hits me square in the chest is raging anger. I knew she had been roughed up by those goons the Cataldis sent to scare her, but I was in no way, shape, or form prepared to see the bruises on her face and neck.

I'm going to kill the motherfucker that put his hands on her.

We stare at each other for what seems like hours but couldn't be more than a few moments. The clubhouse comes back into focus, and I notice the eyes of all the brothers in the room darting between Freya and me. I don't trust myself to speak yet, but I know I need to. Taking a step toward Freya, I notice her spine straighten and her chin rise. I'd observed her for a moment before Jude noticed me. She was relaxed, saying hello to Linc and meeting the old ladies who had recently come to Shine. That ease has been replaced with rigid shoulders and a tense jaw. Her gaze has now turned cold, nothing like the girl I knew before who always had an easy smile for me. There's a storm brewing in those blue eyes, and it's directed straight toward me.

"Hi Freya," I say, forcing myself out of the shocked stupor I spent an awkward amount of time in.

The lines around her eyes deepen, her entire demeanor screaming indignation when I greet her.

"Hello, Ozzy. Thank you for letting me stay here."

There is no warmth or gratitude in her voice. As far as reunions are concerned, this one could be going a hell of a lot better. I'm confused about where the anger is coming from. She's here because she needs me, not the other way around.

My brothers and their women stand around uncomfortably while Freya and I continue to stare at each other. She's as stunning as ever, even under her bruises. Her hair is shorter than I remember from the time we were in love, and I would run my fingers through her waist-length, dark-blonde strands. She had the softest hair I'd ever felt. Her blue eyes are the same, though now they possess a shade of resentment I've never seen from her before. My chest aches with sadness for a brief moment seeing what's changed and what stayed the same over the last fifteen years. And I wasn't there for any of it. The urge to wrap her in my arms and promise her that she's safe and nothing will ever touch her again is so strong that I feel my brain fighting with my natural instincts to take away her pain and fear. I can't, though. I lost that right years ago.

Liam clears his throat, taking a step toward me. "Right, then. Now that that's out of the way, Ozzy, how about you and I go to your office? Lucy, would you mind showing Freya where she'll be staying and then show her to Ozzy's office after she's put her things away?"

Normally, I would have nothing nice to say about the egotistical Englishman with a terrible sense of humor, but I'm grateful for him stepping in when I'm still trying to figure out how to keep my muscles locked so I don't wrap Freya in my arms and never let go again.

Lucy looks at me for confirmation, and I nod. She turns to Freya with a wide smile. "Okay, new friend, let's get you settled." She grabs Freya's bag from her and links their arms together.

When they walk past me to get to the bedrooms down the hall, my hands curl into fists at my side. It's all I can do to keep myself from reaching out and tracing the soft skin of her neck like I used to do when we were eighteen and thought love was enough to get us through anything.

"I have to tell you the story of when Charlie and I got here," Lucy begins. "There was this absolute bitch, Stacia..." Her voice trails off when they go around the corner to where the guest rooms are.

We have several empty rooms. My club is on the smaller side, and I like it that way. Not that I'm opposed to beefing up our numbers, but they have to be the right fit. Not every man who hangs around or prospects makes it into the club. I'm not going to ask my guys to put their trust and sometimes their lives in the hands of any asshole who walks through the door.

"Come on, Ozzy. I could use a whiskey. My brother says you stash the good stuff in the office," Liam says.

Speaking of assholes...

My head jerks in response, though my mind is still trying to process the events of the last three minutes as I lead Liam to my office.

"Have a seat," I offer, waving to one of the black leather chairs in front of my desk. The face of the tough-as-hell MC president slips back into place. It's time to get down to business.

Liam takes a moment to observe the space. He's never been in my office, not that he spends a lot of time in Shine. The walls are covered with family pictures of my grandparents and my dad when he was a kid and Gramps was president.

"You and your dad could be twins," Liam says, looking between the pictures of when I was patched in and when my dad was.

We were about the same age when we became full members, around nineteen or twenty. You'd think being the son of the prez would have afforded me or my dad special consideration. You would also be wrong. I wasn't treated any better than the other prospects, shit, probably worse. My dad was determined to make sure I had what it took to be a brother and the future president of the Black Roses. Years later, he said Gramps did the same to him, and if I had a son who decided to prospect, I'd need to do the same to him. I think it was also his way of getting back at me for my punk-ass teenage years. He smirked when I told him that but didn't deny it.

"Have you ever thought of updating the space? I could hook you up with a designer I know in Philly. Maybe add some color," Liam says, looking around. "Maybe even some accents other than skulls."

"You're not here to talk about my decor choices, Liam. Are there any leads on the assholes that did that to her face?" I ask, pointing at the door. "Because I'm much more interested in crushing the skulls of those pieces of shit."

Liam's eyes widen as he leans back in his chair. "Wow, mate. I've never seen you so intense. What exactly is the history between you two?"

I could tell him she was the first girl I loved, the first girl I slept with, or the only girl I ever saw myself having a future with. After Freya left that part of myself shut down hard. Witnessing how easily someone you love could be taken from you scared the shit out of me. Plus, at the time, I was convinced no one would ever mean to me what she did. Obviously, I know you can fall in love more than once in your life, but I've been perfectly content having no-strings hookups. Less drama and more time to focus on what matters, like my club and my family. High emotions can get you killed in this life. I never want to feel like I did when I was eighteen and watched my girlfriend bleeding in my arms. Now, the same girl is back with bruises all over her.

"Excuse the fuck out of me, Liam, but I don't need to sit here and have a heart-to-heart with you. The only thing I need right now is answers."

Liam studies me for a moment, then nods. "Fine, fine. No, there haven't been any leads on who exactly it was that broke into her place. We have footage of two men walking into the building, but Sawyer hasn't found any criminal records for them, so he'll be going through different avenues to try to identify them."

"Meaning what?" I ask.

"Meaning he's still working his magic, but so far, he hasn't found anything."

Liam isn't going to give me any hints about how his hacker finds information no one else would be privy to.

"They weren't ghosts, for chrissake."

"No, but from what Sawyer can tell, someone has gone to some lengths to make sure no one can identify the two guys."

"Why do you think that is?"

"Well, I have a couple theories on that. One is I don't think the old man is running the show as much as law enforcement is led to believe."

"That's an interesting theory, but what does that have to do with not finding these two assholes?"

"There's been a lot of talk in certain organizations about the Cataldis being involved in human trafficking."

Some of us suspected this, but until Charlie was kidnapped and almost sold into one of their rings, it was only the Irish throwing the idea around.

"Okay..." I trail off, confused about where this is connecting.

"The old man didn't really have a foothold in selling girls. They had their prostitutes and gambling enterprises bringing in plenty of money. Cataldi has always seemed content with his territory in Boston. They've made good money and, for the most part, have stayed out of the uglier side of the underworld."

"Are you going to get to the point anytime soon, Liam?" Jesus, this man loves to hear the sound of his own voice.

He rolls his eyes and continues. "My sources say things are heating up with his son. He's made it known to a few people that they shouldn't have to share any part of Boston, or anywhere else for that matter, with the Irish or other families. It would make sense for him to put a crew together behind the old man's back that can't be traced to him or any other organization. And he would go to great lengths to make sure this new crew is untraceable, especially if they're involved with human trafficking."

"How the hell do you know all this?"

Liam doesn't deal with the criminal underworld, as far as I know.

"I have ears everywhere. You never know what kind of information you'll need in my line of work."

"Didn't realize being a security expert has so many different facets." I've always suspected Liam has other interests that don't lend themselves to legality.

Instead of answering, Liam looks at me with an amused smile. He isn't going to give me anything else on his business, and he knows I'm fishing. That's fine. Having his brother in our club means it's highly unlikely we'll ever have to worry about his other pursuits, whatever they may be, touching us. If there's one thing about the Ashcroft brothers that I've always admired, it's no matter how much they irritate the hell out of each other, they are loyal to the death. Liam proved that when he showed up a few months ago with his entire team to rescue Lucy from that hellhole in Nevada. Liam knew we were going with or without any more firepower, and he wasn't willing for his brother to go there without all the backup he could possibly have. Liam and his team even handled the cleanup for us, making it look like a mass suicide if the authorities ever decided to come snooping around. If it wasn't for the invoice he'd decided to send me, I might have actually liked the guy at some point. Maybe. Well, probably not, but there was a fleeting thought.

"Is Freya aware of your theories?"

Liam shakes his head. "No, I haven't discussed this with her. Her office thinks putting Cataldi behind bars is going to be some huge boon. Our theories are hardly fleshed out at this point. It's more of a gut feeling right now."

"Do you have plans of sharing this information with her or anyone else in law enforcement if it proves to be credible?"

Liam's answering grin tells me all I need to know. "I'm exploring all avenues."

Meaning, probably not. When Lucy was taken, the pilot of the plane spoke Italian. It doesn't take a genius to figure out it was most likely the Cataldis who funded that little kidnapping mission. They fucked up when they helped those fucks come after one of my brother's women. Add in the fact it was Jude's woman, and they've created an enemy in Liam that I don't think the Italians are prepared for. And it seems Liam intends to keep it that way.

A light knock sounds at my door before Lucy pokes her head in. "Can we come in?" she asks.

I nod, and Lucy opens the door to reveal a slightly less angry-looking Freya.

No one says anything for a few moments, and the tension is stifling. Freya looks around my office. When her gaze lands on a picture of me in my football uniform with my dad and Gramps, a small smile ghosts her lips. Both of us had just turned eighteen, and no one knew we were dating yet. Keeping our relationship a secret was never really our intention; it's just how it evolved. Back in high school, being the son of the Black Roses president meant there was a stigma attached to me, no matter how many state championships Knox and I dominated. We were still biker trash. Freya never cared, but that didn't mean we were making out in the halls. Freya hated gossip and liked her privacy, same as me. A few short months later, she was shot, and her parents took her from Shine and away from me. There was plenty of gossip floating around after that. I'm glad she wasn't there for it, to be honest. I had a hard enough time dealing with it myself.

"Liam," Lucy starts. "Do you have time to come for dinner before you leave? I'm sure Cece would like to see you."

Liam has taken a big brother role with Lucy's younger sister, Cece, though I'm not entirely sure he's the best influence for a young girl who was raised on a cult compound and never knew any freedom until a few months ago.

"That would be great. She can show me the progress she's made with the throwing stars."

Liam stands from his chair and holds his arm toward the door. "Shall we?"

Lucy looks toward me, silently asking if I'll be okay with Freya. If Lucy is worried about me being alone with her, I can't help but wonder if Freya said something. I'll have to ask Lucy later. Any insight into what has her seemingly so incensed with me will make the time she'll be spending here a little easier.

"Freya, you have my number if you need anything. Same goes for you, Ozzy. Sawyer and I will be looking into everything we talked about," Liam says.

"Keep me updated." There is no question in my request.

Liam smiles but doesn't agree. He'll do whatever the hell he wants with whatever he finds out, regardless of anything I say.

"It was so nice meeting you, Freya," Lucy says, leaning in for a hug.

I watch Freya's reaction to Lucy. Back in high school, she had girlfriends, but she wasn't close with any of them. Not like she was with me. Shine High was filled with bratty teenage girls who cared more about image and social standing than anything else. There were two distinct groups. There were the ones whose daddies were rich and either owned their own businesses or worked some swanky white-collar job. Then, there were the blue-collar kids whose parents worked in the factories or auto shops. The kids who didn't have a lot of money and couldn't give two shits about social standing. Freya and I were from opposite ends, but we existed somewhere in the middle together, at least for a short period of time.

Freya returns the hug that Lucy offers with a warm smile. "I hope I'll see you soon."

"Oh, don't worry. Now that there's another woman here who doesn't hate us on sight, you won't be able to keep Charlie away." Lucy laughs and pulls away. "We'll be back in a couple days, I'm sure. How do you feel about guns?"

The tension in Freya's jaw is back. "Not great, to be honest."

Lucy closes her eyes and blows out a breath. "I'm an idiot. Jude told me what happened." She shakes her head. "That's okay. Charlie and I took a shit ton of self-defense classes when we lived in New Orleans. I help Jude teach a class at the women's shelter, too. If you're interested, Charlie and I could come by and teach you a few things."

"That would be great," Freya tells her. "Maybe you can bring those throwing stars Liam was talking about."

Lucy's face lights up with murderous glee. I don't know how Jude sleeps at night knowing his old lady is such a fan of sharp objects.

"It's a date. I'll get your number from Liam." She turns to the Englishman. "Let's go. Cece is baking bread and I'll be damned if Jude sneaks off and eats it all before we get there like he did last time." Lucy waves and heads out the door with Liam on her heels, leaving Freya and me alone for the first time in fifteen years.

"She's nice," Freya comments, turning toward me.

I nod in agreement and tilt my head toward the chair in front of my desk. "Have a seat."

Freya sits, and my eyes wander to the bruises on her neck. She's obviously self-conscious about the marks, pulling her hair forward to cover them.

"Tell me what happened."

"I'm sure you heard it from Liam," she replies, defiance in her tone.

"Okay, then tell me why you're so angry with me."

She stares at me for a beat. "I was getting ready to have drinks and my assistant was sending over some paperwork via messenger. I let the guys who attacked me into the building because I thought they were the courier at first. When I opened the door, one of them punched me and then they ransacked my place."

Though the short recount of what those bastards did to her sends a hot burst of anger through my body, a smirk ghosts my lips. So, she doesn't want to tell me about what's bothering her about being here. Fine, not like she's going anywhere anytime soon.

"What exactly did they want?"

"For me to lose some evidence or remove myself from the case. This is the first time in history we've been so close to putting Cataldi away."

"You've earned yourself quite the reputation of being a bulldog." I may have done a little digging of my own when I knew she was coming here. Her proud smile tells me she's aware.

"Checking up on me, Ozzy?"

"Looking into the trouble you're bringing to my doorstep."

Freya's eyes narrow and her spine snaps ramrod straight. "I could leave if it's too much trouble."

Fuck, why the hell am I making this so much worse?

CHAPTER FIVE
FREYA

This fucking guy. Like it's my fault I was attacked and threatened. Now I'm the one bringing trouble to his club?

"I could leave if it's too much trouble."

Ozzy's deep-brown eyes instantly shine with regret when the words leave my mouth.

"Shit, Freya. I'm sorry."

"For what? For my bringing 'trouble to your club'? Which, let's be honest, isn't exactly some innocent little group of guys who like to ride motorcycles. Or for making me feel worse about the situation I'm in after being attacked for trying to put the head of a dangerous organization behind bars?"

"I'm sorry for being an idiot and not thinking before I spoke. I'm sorry this world is touching you again." He mutters the last part quietly, almost to himself.

It's been fifteen years since I've laid eyes on the first boy I ever loved. The first one to break my heart. Really, Ozzy is the only one to ever have that honor.

Being back in the clubhouse where I nearly died has brought up a lot of emotions for me and presumably for the uncomfortable-looking biker in front of me as well. There's this irrational anger flowing just beneath the surface, looking for any excuse to erupt. It's like I'm eighteen all over again and can barely keep my feelings in check. But I'm not. I'm a thirty-three-year-old woman with a successful career and what I would consider a healthy state of mind for the most part. Granted, I was attacked and had to uproot my life for the foreseeable future, but this anger, this desire to lash out, is so beyond anything I've dealt with since...the last time I saw Ozzy.

Shit.

"I think coming here was a mistake," I say.

A panicked look runs through Ozzy's gaze, but he quickly schools it. "Where would you go?"

I shrug and look at the wall behind Ozzy's head, unexplainably sad he would let me leave. "I don't know. Maybe to my parents? I can always ask Liam to find me somewhere else to go. I'm sure he has other places he can stash me."

"No," Ozzy starts. "That's the last thing I want. If Liam thinks this is the best place for you, then you should stay here. Trust me, if he had another idea, I'm sure he would have sent you somewhere else."

I'm not sure that's true. "Listen, this came up last minute. I'll ask him to figure something else out. In the meantime, I'll stay here and out of your way."

I stand to leave the office, but Ozzy starts speaking again.

"If you want to leave because you're uncomfortable, I'll accept that. But know I want you to stay here." He looks at my bruised face and shuts his eyes for a beat. "I want to protect you from whatever those fuckers were going to do to you. If you go to your parents, you know you can't guarantee their safety. Or yours. At least if you're here, there's a clubhouse full of people who are armed and have a bone to pick with any Cataldi fucker who tries to walk through our doors."

He has a point about not going to my parents. The last thing I want is more people in danger because of me.

"Alright." I nod and turn toward the door. "I'll stay, but I am going to talk to Liam about other arrangements."

Ozzy doesn't look thrilled with the idea of me talking to Liam, but there really isn't anything he can do about it. This isn't his decision, and the short time I've been here hasn't exactly been some happy homecoming.

"I'm going to go back to my room." I'm fucking exhausted and need my pain medication. The stuff they gave me at the hospital made me too loopy, so I opted for over-the-counter meds. There's no way I can work like that. They keep the pain at bay, but barely. Still, I'm back here because, as Ozzy put it, I'm a bulldog. I'm not resting until Cataldi is behind bars. There's no way in hell I'm slowing down for a bruised face and ribs. Plus, once Cataldi is behind bars, I can get back to my life in Boston and out of this uncomfortable-as-hell situation with Ozzy.

"What do you need?" he asks.

"Just Wi-Fi and coffee. Lots of coffee."

Ozzy nods. "Okay. I'll have one of the girls make some food for you, too."

Irritation instantly sparks back to life. "Ozzy, please don't go through the trouble of having your 'bunnies' make food for me," I grind out. "I'll be able to manage just fine." I don't want the woman he's sleeping with one night making food for his ex the next day. That's wrong on so many levels for me.

The asshole smirks. "I was referring to Charlie and Lucy. They'd be more than happy to make a few things and send them over. The bunnies aren't exactly known for their culinary skills."

"So I've heard."

Why does the thought of being around women he's slept with send shots of annoyance through me like this? It's not as though I expected him to be some sort of saint in the last fifteen years. It's not like I have either.

"Listen, you aren't here to judge what any woman does with the brothers inside this clubhouse. It's their lives and their bodies. I won't have you here making them feel inferior because you're some hotshot attorney from Boston. I don't allow that kind of bullshit within these walls. Understood?"

"Hey, I wasn't..." I wasn't what? Jealous? I sure as shit was, but I wasn't trying to be judgmental. I was uncomfortable with thoughts of him sleeping with other women, not the brothers or even the bunnies. God, I really don't want to explain that to him, though.

Psycho ex, party of one.

"You're right," I concede. "I have no room to judge anyone. I apologize."

Ozzy looks slightly taken aback by my one-eighty. "Okay...good. Thank you."

I'm not ready to get into all the reasons why the idea of other women he's slept with being around makes me uneasy, so I let it drop. What would be the point? It's not like Ozzy wants me here to mend fences or anything. I'm here because he owes Liam a favor. Plus, he's right. Having a clubhouse full of armed bikers who hate the Cataldis as much as I do will definitely be more of a deterrent to them than staying with my parents where there's no protection.

"Thank you again for letting me stay. I'm going to head to my room." I stand to leave when he calls after me before I reach the door.

"Freya..."

I turn, and for a moment, the boy I once loved is staring back at me, unsure of what to say but needing to tell me something. The look is gone from his eyes in a blink, and the eyes of an MC president stare back at me.

"Don't leave the property. There's no reason to think the Cataldis know you're here, but considering the recent issues we've had with them, I don't want to give them any opportunity to see you, and I don't want anyone knowing you're here. People will talk if they catch you downtown chatting it up with any of your old friends."

I've never been particularly good at taking orders, and his command grates on my nerves.

"Don't worry, Ozzy. There isn't anyone here I've ever wanted to see again."

I pull the door open and head back to my room, thinking to myself for the millionth time...

This is a terrible idea.

CHAPTER SIX
FREYA

A few days have passed, and physically, I'm feeling better every day. Emotionally, not so much. At this point, I've become accustomed to the awkwardness every time Ozzy and I run into each other, which isn't often. Even though he's been living here, which apparently isn't the norm, I rarely see him. Granted, I spend most of my time in my room. There's still a lot of work to do before the case goes to trial. I refuse to be hit with any curveballs the other side is sure to throw at us, but I'm getting closer every day to being ready.

Living at the clubhouse is slowing things down, though. Every document has to be copied then sent to me, rather than me having direct access. I told my office I had a family emergency and had to be out of town for the foreseeable future. Considering I've never taken a vacation during my time in the prosecutor's office, they didn't push back too terribly hard, but I'm sure there's a shit ton of grumbling going on that I'm not aware of. Hell, there's a shit ton of grumbling coming from me every time I have to wait for one thing or another or have to schedule a phone call with an associate instead of simply running to their office to go over something.

I've been getting up early to make coffee and head back to my room to work, only really popping out to grab something to eat, then work some more. It's typical of what I would be doing back in Boston this close to a trial, except for the added stress of not wanting to get in anyone's way and avoiding any and all conversations with my ex.

I've run into Ozzy a total of three times. Twice when I was up early making myself some breakfast, and once when I was grabbing some lunch the first full day I was here. It was beyond awkward and a little heartbreaking at the same time. At one point, this was a person who I shared every dream, joy, and insecurity with. He knew me better than anyone ever had. To this day, that could still be true. After leaving Shine, I never opened myself up to a man the way I had with Ozzy. There was college, prelaw, law school, internships, then working in the US Attorney's Office. Needless to say, I've been a little busy the last fifteen years. There've been times when I've felt lonely, sure, but those thoughts were quickly replaced with studying then building a career I'm damn proud of. The few fleeting relationships I've been in never came close to the all-consuming feelings I had for Ozzy. I always chalked that up to teenage first love. But the three times we saw each other, awkward as it was, made me wonder if it was me falling into the habit of not having the time or energy to put into a relationship or if it was me knowing no one would be able to live up to the pedestal I'd put him on. Though we crashed and burned in a blaze of heartbreaking glory, there was never a man I'd met since who made me crave his smiles and kisses the way Ozzy did. That's why the end hurt so bad and still stings to this day.

The knock at my door startles me out of my sad musings.

"Come in," I say, scrubbing my hands over my face. I need to get my head back in the game.

Linc dips his head into my room and gives me one of his sweet smiles. I don't know if Ozzy asked him, but Linc has been checking in with me every day, making sure I'm eating and generally doing okay being here.

"Hey, Freya. Charlie and Lucy wanted to come by today and hang for a bit. Charlie mentioned you were interested in some self-defense practice."

Embarrassment washes over me. I've been so wrapped up in trying to get this case ready I haven't texted Lucy or Charlie. Even after Lucy sent some freshly baked bread courtesy of her sister, I never properly thanked her.

"That sounds like fun. Can you let them know I have time later this afternoon?"

"Sure. How are things going?" he asks, looking at the mounds of paperwork I have scattered across the bed.

I shrug. "It would be a hell of a lot easier if I were at my office."

Linc's sympathetic expression makes me feel bad for complaining. I should be grateful for having somewhere to go without having to look over my shoulder, waiting for the next attack.

"I'm sorry. I sound like a bitch. Thank you for checking in on me. Honestly, if I had to pick a hideout, I'm glad it's here where I get freshly baked treats delivered to me." I shoot him a wide grin, and his returning smile lets me know there're no hard feelings.

"I'm sure it's not easy having to uproot everything at the drop of a hat. Especially when you get thrown into a clubhouse full of loudmouth bikers."

"Honestly, I was expecting it to be a little more..." I tilt my head back and forth. "I don't know...rowdy?"

Linc laughs and cocks his head to the side. "It usually is, but Ozzy ordered everyone to keep it low-key."

I shoot him a confused look. "Why?"

"He knew you had a lot of work to get done while you're here and wanted to make sure the noise wasn't keeping you awake at night."

"The other guys must really love me," I groan, rolling my eyes.

"Nah. A little break never killed anyone." A half smile tilts the corner of his lips. "I'm going to let Lucy and Charlie know to come over in a few hours. Holler if you need anything."

Absentmindedly, I nod in his direction while my mind wanders to Ozzy. I've been sitting in here for days on end, keeping to myself, while Ozzy has gone out of his way to make sure I was taken care of, going so far as to have his men keep a low profile so they don't disturb me. The Ozzy I knew back in high school did anything and everything to make sure I was okay in any situation. He was always respectful of me and careful to never push anything beyond my comfort, unlike most guys in high school. But he was never who anyone expected him to be. It's one of the things I always loved about him. I sort of just assumed with him being president of an MC that would have changed.

You should have known better, Freya.

Later in the afternoon, Charlie, Lucy, and a girl who looks familiar show up in workout gear with coffee and a delicious-smelling paper sack from my favorite coffee shop.

"Freya, do you remember Mia?" Charlie asks. "She went to school with all you guys."

That's right. It's coming back to me now. "You were in band, right?" I ask, eyeing the bag in her hand.

Mia gives me a friendly smile and nods. "I was. Good to see you again." Her eyes briefly scan the fading bruises on my neck and face before she hands me the bag. "Treats from Cool Beans. I'm addicted, which is why I jumped at the chance to come over with the girls and get a little workout in."

"I think it has more to do with a certain broody biker but tell yourself whatever you want, sister." Lucy shoots Mia a wink and chuckles.

The red-faced woman turns to Lucy with wide eyes. "Shut up," Mia mouths, looking around anxiously. None of the other bikers are in the main room, but it looks like Mia is afraid someone overheard Lucy.

"Oh, Mia. You know she can't," Charlie starts. "Her brain-to-mouth filter has been broken for years."

Lucy shrugs and hands me a coffee. "I'm an acquired taste. Just ask Jude."

"You're lucky I love you," Mia tells her.

"What are you going to do? Give me a demerit like I'm one of the kids at Shine High?"

I turn to Mia and smile. "Are you a teacher at our old school?"

Mia shakes her head. "School librarian."

"Did you stay here after you graduated?" If there's one thing I remember about this town, it's that most of the kids we went to high school with couldn't wait to leave.

"No. I lived in Arizona for a while. I just came back a few months ago."

"Not many people come back to Shine," I reply—present company excluded.

Mia purses her lips, looking uncomfortable with the direction of the conversation. "Yeah. It's a long story."

She doesn't elaborate, so I don't probe further.

"Alright. Let's get to work, ladies," Charlie says, breaking the sudden awkwardness.

Charlie leads us down a hallway opposite the room I've been staying in and opens a set of double doors leading into a large room with an entire gym setup.

"I didn't know this was here," I say, looking around the space. There are weights and mirrored walls, even a couple of punching bags hanging from the ceiling.

"I figured you'd have the lay of the land after being here almost a week," Lucy comments.

"I've been busy." I set down my drink and the bag from the bakery. Truthfully, every time I leave my room, there's a good chance I'll run into Ozzy. The last thing I want is to deal with the tense and overly polite distance that's between us. I already feel like enough of an interloper, especially knowing he's been enforcing rules the other brothers aren't used to following for my benefit.

"Linc said you're working to take down the Cataldis," Charlie comments.

"I am. We have a real shot at putting Francesco away."

Charlie has a bit of a faraway look in her eye as she nods. "Good." She shakes herself out of wherever she just went in her mind and smiles brightly in my direction. "Ready to learn how to kick some ass?"

"Absolutely."

Thirty minutes later and with buckets of sweat pouring off me, I finally have to tap out.

"I am injured, you know," I tell the black-haired demon trying to kill me. Okay, she's not really, but if I have to try to get out of one more choke hold when I have at least five inches on Lucy, my ego will never recover.

"It's likely you're going to be injured if you ever have to use these moves in real life," Charlie says from across the room as she effortlessly puts Mia in a knee bar.

"Charlie had her own run-in with some men from the Cataldi organization," Lucy tells me in a low voice.

The attorney in me wants to ask questions, but there's another part of me that knows the club would have handled it, and it's a hell of a lot safer for everyone if I don't know any details.

"Alright," I say after guzzling some water. "Let's go again."

A brilliant smile overtakes Lucy's face. "Attagirl."

We grapple for a few more minutes, and I almost make it out of the damn choke hold when a dark figure catches my attention in the doorway.

Ozzy is standing there with an expressionless face, but when my eyes meet his, there's a heated spark in them. It's more emotion than I've seen the last few times we've run into each other. I'm exhausted, sweaty, and sore as shit, but the small flare of pride in his gaze and something else I don't want to even attempt to decode spurs me on. When Lucy releases me, she takes a step back as though she's going to give me a break.

"Nuh-uh, lady. I'm not giving up." I break my eyes from Ozzy's intense stare and get back into position.

Lucy looks at me and nods her head. "I knew I liked you."

When I look back to the doorway, Ozzy shoots me a small, devastating smile before turning and walking away. Without saying a word, the ice between us thaws just a bit, but I'm not sure I'm ready for what that means for my still-fragile heart.

CHAPTER SEVEN
OZZY

I should have known there was no way Freya would have let something like a few bruises keep her from anything. The last few days she's been here have been pure torture, and seeing her sweaty in tight pants and one of those sports tank tops that don't hide anything only adds to the torture.

Every night, lying in bed by myself, I've wanted to knock on her door and just...get to know her again. Have her tell me all about the last fifteen years of her life. Maybe have her give me one of the smiles I used to love when we were eighteen and couldn't imagine ever feeling about another girl the way I felt about her.

Obviously, I haven't been walking around wearing a chastity belt the last decade and a half, but the wall I erected around my feelings when things ended with Freya has yet to be broken through by any other woman. At first, it was because there was no way I was going to put someone I loved in the crosshairs of any of the club's enemies. Then, as the years passed, it became my status quo. I was happy being on my own and having my fun. Why add anything else to the mix?

I forgot why I closed myself off and was happily living my life being president of the Black Roses. Still am. But having Freya here has opened the old wounds that were stitched together with barbed wire and had become second nature to ignore throughout the years.

Watching her power through her discomfort and irritation with Lucy constantly getting the upper hand reminds me so much of the girl I fell in love with.

"I don't get it," Freya grumbles from beside me on the blanket I laid out behind the old, abandoned farm down the way from the clubhouse.

I wanted to come out here and make out with my girlfriend, but she insisted on studying for her AP test.

"What's wrong, pretty girl?" I ask, playing with the ends of her long blonde hair.

"How the hell am I supposed to remember all this stuff? Between cheer and all my other classes, I'm seriously regretting taking AP government."

I sit up from my spot next to her and grab the notes she's been poring over for the last forty-five minutes.

"Hey," she protests, lunging for the notebook, but I hold it over my head. "Ozzy, I need to study." Her little growl is the cutest damn noise I've ever heard.

"I'm going to help you out. Stop trying to attack me." I shoot her a wink as she sits back on her heels with a huff.

Opening the book, I take a look at her neat handwriting and wonder if I'm reading some foreign language.

"Sweetheart, I have no idea what all these words mean."

Freya's light giggle is music to my ears. "Here, let me see."

She proceeds to explain everything she has written in her notebook. I, of course, have no idea what she's talking about, but I don't need to.

She stops speaking and looks at me, her eyes narrowing. "You don't really want to know any of this, do you?"

I shoot her a quick smile then lean in for a kiss. Breaking apart, I tell her, "No, but I did want to do that, so I figured if you had to explain it to a dumb jock like me, it would help you." I kiss her again. "Then it gives us more time to do what I want."

She looks like she's about to rip into me for deceiving her and having less than altruistic intentions. Her mouth opens and closes a few times before she starts laughing. "You know what? I can't be mad about it. That was actually genius."

"Does that mean you're done studying?"

"For today."

I smile widely and lunge at her, causing her to fall back on the soft ground as I nuzzle into her neck with a growl.

"One thing though," Freya says with a laugh. I raise my head and look into her brightly shining blue eyes.

"I won't have you calling my boyfriend a dumb jock." She quirks her brow, and I tilt my lips up in a smirk. Her tough girl attitude is too damn cute.

"Whatever you say, pretty girl."

The rest of the afternoon is spent using our mouths in more creative ways.

I'm startled out of the memory when I hear silence fall over the gym. Freya is looking at me with an unreadable expression. It's the same one I've seen on her face the last few times we've run into each other. There's a divide between us as big as the Grand fucking Canyon, and I hate it. So much so that the last time we ran into each other in the kitchen, I decided to assign Linc to make sure she had anything she needed. It was too much seeing her and not being able to talk about what happened all those years ago and where we can go from here. I'm not a pussy by any stretch of the imagination, but fuck me if I can find the courage to try to make things right with the woman under my roof. So much time has passed. Neither of us are the same people we were fifteen years ago, for better or worse. The way she was when she showed up here four days ago with a chip on her shoulder the size of Liam Ashcroft's ego didn't exactly invite conversation. I wasn't about to push her after what she'd been through, but I thought she would have thawed a little bit by now. The look on her face tells me that hasn't happened. It's not hostile, but it certainly isn't friendly, either. For a moment, I see the girl I fell in love with in high school and smile before turning to head back to my office. It's time I had a talk with the head of the Monaghan family about our Italian problem.

Sitting at my desk, I look over at the pile of paperwork taunting me off to the corner. I have so much to catch up on, but it's been damn near impossible to concentrate. I need to pull my head out of my damn ass and start acting like an MC president instead of the heartbroken puppy I've been the last few days. This shit needs to end.

I grab my phone from my pocket and lean back in my seat before I dial Finn's number.

"Hello, Ozzy," he answers.

"Hey, Finn, how's it going? We need to talk about the Italians." We've been in the business of running guns for the Monaghans for the last few years. The Cataldis have been a problem for both our families for even longer. When we figured Lucy's kidnappers were being assisted by the Italians, I told Finn and he assured me they had plans in motion to take down the Cataldis, but that was months ago.

"Well, I didn't think you were calling me to ask how my day was going." Finn chuckles. "What about them?"

"Are you aware they went after the US attorney that's heading the Francesco Cataldi case?"

"I am. And I'm aware she hasn't been seen in Boston since the attack. My question is, how do you know?"

"Freya Campbell is from Shine. We have a mutual friend"—I nearly choke on the word—"who contacted me after the incident. She's staying here until the case goes to trial."

"I didn't realize you were in the protection game these days."

"Neither did I," I mumble.

"So, what is it you expect me to do about it? If she's there with you, I don't imagine she could be in better hands."

"She's safe. But this isn't the first time someone related to the club has had dealings with the Italians. They aren't outright attacking the club at the moment, but that doesn't mean they aren't a threat. I want to know what you're doing about it."

Finn lets out a huff of annoyance. Men like us aren't used to being called to task.

"Ozzy, you know I like you, and the work our organizations have done together has always been more than beneficial for both parties, yes?"

"It has..." I'm getting the distinct feeling I'm about to be told to go fuck myself.

"But that doesn't mean I answer to you. The Cataldi problem is being handled. You're simply going to have to trust me on that."

"They've been a thorn in both of our sides for a long time, Finn."

"I couldn't agree more, but these things take time and preparation. If we go in with even one loose thread, it could be the end for us all."

Everything he's saying makes perfect sense. I wasn't thrilled when he asked me all those months ago to let him handle the situation, but I obliged out of professional courtesy. We make a lot of money from the Irish, as do they with our help transporting their guns. This situation with Freya is hitting too close to home for me, though. It's now the third time the Italians have targeted someone with ties to the club.

But she didn't have ties until four days ago when she showed up at the clubhouse. No, this was because she found herself in their crosshairs and they thought she was going to roll over and play dead for them. Obviously, they didn't do their research. Maybe it's a sign that the Cataldis are getting sloppy, or they think they're untouchable. I can only hope I'm there when they realize that isn't the case.

"I appreciate that, Finn. Truly, I do. But something needs to be done sooner rather than later if they're ballsy enough to break into an apartment and threaten a fucking prosecutor."

"We're all watching this case closely, Ozzy. Even the Russians are interested in how this all pans out." Of course they are. "It will have an impact on how fast we can make the moves we've been planning."

"So, until this goes to trial, you're telling me your hands are tied?"

Finn lets out a dark chuckle. "My hands are never tied. But there're a lot of players on this board. Not just your club and your girl."

"She's not my girl," I reply.

"My mistake." He doesn't sound like he thinks it's a mistake. "My best advice is to make sure she wins the case. Things will change drastically and quickly if she does."

"She's doing her best." I think about all the times Linc would report back to me after checking on Freya. Every time, he would tell me about the piles of paper scattered all around her when he'd go to her room.

"If there's anything you need from me, let me know," Finn says.

I know Finn well enough to know that isn't a statement made lightly. Finn's help usually comes with armed men who aren't afraid of burying bodies.

"Thanks, Finn. Give your old man my best."

"I will."

We end the call, but I don't feel any more at ease. A war between the Irish and the Italians is definitely on the horizon. I called it months ago, and Finn all but confirmed it. I just hope me and my club don't become cannon fodder.

The next phone call I need to make is to my old man. It's been a few days since we've talked, and he doesn't know Freya is staying here. There's never been anything I've intentionally kept from my dad, Freya staying at the clubhouse being the exception. It was never my plan to *not* tell my dad, but I have a pretty good idea how the conversation is going to go. He was there for the fallout fifteen years ago. Dredging up old memories and feelings isn't something I've been eager to do in the conversation he'll want to have about it. Granted, it's not as though those feelings haven't been at the forefront of my mind since the second my gaze landed on her four days ago. Until now, I haven't had to voice that, but when I call my dad, that could all very well change.

I dial his number and he picks up on the third ring.

"Hey, son."

"Hi, Dad. How's it going?"

"Fine. Just about to go on a ride with Tanya."

"Your hands feeling better?"

"Yup. Tanya makes sure I take my new meds when I'm supposed to so the arthritis doesn't flare up."

Tanya is Linc and Knox's mom. They showed up in Shine when Knox and I were eight years old, and my grandmother immediately wrapped the single mother of two into our fold. Tanya has always been a motherly figure to me, especially since my grandmother passed away when I was a kid. It wasn't until Linc graduated high school that she and my dad moved in together, even though they'd apparently been together for years and didn't tell us. Tanya came from a bad marriage. The man even tried to take her a year or so after they showed up in Shine, trying for a fresh start. That didn't end well for him.

"I need to tell you something," I say.

"Shoot."

"Freya is here. She ran into some trouble with the Italians and needed a place to lie low."

There's a beat of silence on the other end as my dad processes the new information.

"I didn't realize you two were still in touch," my dad finally replies.

"We weren't, but I owed Liam Ashcroft a favor, and he decided to cash it in."

My dad hums into the phone, not giving his opinion on the matter.

"You okay with her being here?"

Part of me wants to answer hell no, considering I've been a mess of emotions—which hasn't been my MO in years. Fifteen, to be exact.

"I'm fine. She'll be gone as soon as her case against Cataldi goes to trial."

"You going to be okay then?"

I know what he's asking. Last time she left, I was a fucking mess and an asshole to be around for months.

"Yeah, Dad. This isn't like last time."

"Maybe not right now, but these things have a tendency to turn on a dime."

It's my turn to hum noncommittally into the phone.

"You know what this means, right?"

My brows scrunch together. "No...what?"

My dad lets out a chuckle. "The second Tanya finds out she's there, she's going to show up with a fucking feast to welcome her back."

"She's not back. She's just staying here for a bit." The statement is as sure as the sky is blue.

Now, my dad laughs outright. "Oh, son. If you think that's going to make a damn bit of difference to my woman, then you haven't been paying attention. Expect us tomorrow for dinner."

"I don't know about that. Freya hasn't really left her room most of the time she's been here. She's been working and keeping to herself."

"You think I can control whether or not Tanya shows up?"

He has a point. I doubt there's a person on this planet who can stand in Tanya's way once she gets an idea.

"Alright, but don't say I didn't warn you. She isn't the same girl she used to be."

Unless she's talking to anyone other than me.

"See you tomorrow, son."

"Bye, Dad."

I disconnect the call and toss my phone on my desk, scrubbing my hands over my face.

Dammit. This is going to bite me in the ass.

Dad called it. Tanya showed up at the clubhouse the next day about four o'clock in the afternoon and instructed us to stay out of "her" kitchen. Not that we needed to be told. The chances any of us are going to be spending time in the kitchen is slim to none.

Figuring it's time to bite the bullet, I knock on Freya's door. I didn't see her after the gym. She made herself scarce once again before I had a chance to talk to her about Tanya coming by today.

"Come in," I hear her call from the other side.

When I crack the door open, I see what Linc was talking about in regard to her turning her bedroom into an office. There are papers all over her bed and more piles on the floor. As someone who deals with mounds of paperwork myself, I can tell her piles are set up with a specific purpose.

"Unless you come bearing coffee, Linc, I'm good," she says, her eyes darting between her laptop and whatever file she has open.

"Not Linc," I reply.

Freya stares at her screen for a brief moment, but I can tell she isn't reading whatever is in front of her.

She looks at me and sends a tight smile my way. "Hey, everything okay?"

My hand goes to the back of my neck with an apologetic smile on my face. "I told my dad you were staying here. Tanya insisted on coming and having a family dinner."

"Oh..." She looks around the room, not meeting my eyes. "When does she want to do that?"

"Umm, she's here now, so tonight. In about two hours."

Freya's eyes widen as she pins me with her bright stare. "When did you find out about her coming?"

"My dad told me yesterday when I talked to him."

"Ozzy," she exclaims. "You just decided to tell me now?"

My eyes swivel from side to side. "I didn't think it was a big deal. It's just Tanya and my dad. Oh, and Gramps will be by in a few. He can't resist Tanya's pot roast."

Freya shoots me an irritated scowl and carefully removes herself from the bed.

"I would have met her out there and helped her. I don't want her to think I'm back here being antisocial."

I'm about to tell her that's exactly what she's been, at least with me, but decide against it. This is the most we've talked since she arrived.

"I need to get out there and help or...something."

"You cook?" I quirk my brow.

"Sometimes." Her voice is unsure and indignant at the same time.

I consider her statement for a moment. "I suggest you stay out of the kitchen. Her roast is legendary around here, and if it doesn't come out perfect, you'll bear witness to a bunch of grown bikers crying."

"What makes you think I'd screw it up?" she asks, obviously offended I'd suggest it.

"I'm just telling you what we'd be dealing with if it did happen, pretty girl."

She sucks in a sharp breath, and her cheeks turn pink at the old term of endearment that slipped out.

"Um," she says, not meeting my eyes again. "I should still go out there and say hello." Thankfully, she doesn't comment on the nickname that used to be as natural for me to say as anything else.

Still standing awkwardly in her doorway, I nod. "Okay. I'll let her know you'll be out in a minute." Offering her a small smile, I close the door and head to the bar. I'm going to need a little—or a lot of—whiskey to get through this night.

CHAPTER EIGHT
FREYA

Walking out into the main room of the clubhouse, I see more brothers in the space than I anticipated. Of course, since Tanya is here cooking, it makes sense they would all show up. I remember Ozzy telling me years ago about how much everyone loved her cooking.

I step into the kitchen and see the woman responsible for the delicious smells emanating into the rest of the clubhouse. Lucy, Charlie, and Tanya have their backs turned, each going about their own tasks while carrying on a conversation about the Thanksgiving dinner Tanya plans on making for the women's shelter.

"Cece would love to make something for them, especially since so many of the women and kids there are from the compound. Matilda has her hands full with all those kids running around," Lucy says.

"Have any of them left?" Charlie asks.

Lucy shakes her head. "No. They don't really have anywhere to go. It's going to take a lot of work with therapists and job training before anyone there is ready to live on their own."

"We should talk to some of the businesses on Main Street and around town about hiring some of the women. The club has done a lot for this town, and it would be nice for some of the business owners to show some support. I'm sure we can find something for most of them when they're ready, of course," Tanya tells the other girls.

That's one of the things I always loved about this woman. She's the type to think of ways to help other women who are in need. If memory serves, she came from a not-so-great situation when she landed in Shine, and Janine, Ozzy's grandmother, helped her out.

"Anything I can help with?" I ask, deciding I probably shouldn't be standing here eavesdropping like a weirdo.

When Tanya turns to face me, I'm taken back to when I first met her all those years ago. Same warm smile and eyes that dance with laughter. And just like the first time, she walks up to me and wraps me in a hug as though it's the most natural thing in the world.

"Freya, it's so good to see you." Tanya gives me a tight squeeze, then leans away, still holding on to my arms. "Let me look at you." Her gaze drifts over my face and body like a loving mother's would, checking to be sure everything is right with one of her children. "Beautiful as ever, honey." She quirks her brow. "But you need some meat on those bones, girl." She laughs and pulls me into another hug. "It's so good to have you home," she says before releasing me.

I don't know why she thinks I'm here, but this isn't a homecoming. Since I don't have the heart to tell her any different, I simply smile.

"It's great to see you too, Tanya. I'm not exactly the best cook on the planet, but I'm here to help," I say with a wide smile.

Cooking can't be that hard, contrary to what Ozzy was trying to imply.

"No, no. You have a seat. We're almost done, then all we have left is to wait for the roast to be done."

I take a seat at the little table set up in the kitchen and watch the three women easily and effortlessly move around each other. The strange pang of jealousy that hits my chest surprises me. One thing I haven't put much energy into the last couple of years is my friendships with other women. Sure, I have Kasey, who I can grab drinks and dinner with when she's in town or I'm in Philadelphia, but that's more and more rare these days. I've become a workaholic. Even being here for the last several days, I've only managed to make time for Lucy and Charlie once, and that was because Linc reminded me about Lucy's offer to work on self-defense with me. It's not the first time I've felt like I should have more of a personal life, but work always got in the way. Now, looking at the three women in front of me makes me seriously second-guess my priorities these last few years.

Mia swings open the kitchen door with several large to-go cups of coffee, looking rushed and out of sorts.

"Sorry I'm late, you will not believe the day I've had." She sets the drink carrier on the table and hands me one. "Hey, Freya." She smiles, then goes about handing out the coffees. "I don't know why the hell teenagers think the corner of the school library is the place to get half-naked between classes."

I blush a little, remembering all the times Ozzy and I did just that. Thankfully, we were never caught, but that was back when Mrs. Bell was the librarian. I think she spent more time dozing off at the front desk than doing any actual work.

"I don't know who was more embarrassed, me or the kids I caught. I had to stay late and write up a report for the vice principal, who is a complete asshole, by the way. He kept going on and on about how young ladies shouldn't be acting that way with boys but didn't utter one word about the boy who had his hand up the girl's shirt."

"Fucking double standards," Lucy mumbles, rolling her eyes.

Mia nods in agreement. "Anyway, I needed coffee after that meeting, so I figured I'd get everyone something."

"Thank you," I tell her, sipping the creamy caramel concoction.

"You haven't missed much, sweetheart. We're all done for the moment," Tanya says, coming to sit at the table with Mia and me. Lucy and Charlie pull up chairs, and we relax in companionable silence for a few moments, letting poor Mia decompress.

Tanya turns to me with a small frown on her lips. "Trick told me about the attack, honey. How are you feeling?"

I let out a long breath. "Better. Still a bit sore."

Tanya's eyes travel to my neck, where the bruises are now a yellowish green. "I hope you put that man away. It's terrible what they did to you back then and now."

Tanya is referring to the night in the clubhouse when several of the men from the Cataldi outfit came in and shot the place up. She was here during the shooting that led to my dad moving us out of Shine and away from Ozzy and the club.

"I'm working on it," I reply with confidence.

Tanya shakes her head as though she's clearing her thoughts about the past. "What have you been doing with yourself over the last decade?"

"Mostly working. I went to UPenn for my undergrad. Then I went to Harvard Law. Studying and working have pretty much been my life since I left Shine."

"No boyfriend wondering where you are?" Charlie asks. Even though we spent some time together the other day, there wasn't much talking. Mostly just me getting my ass kicked.

I can't help the laugh that escapes my throat. "No. One, I don't have time, and two, the only guys I meet are lawyers who work just as many hours as me. Doesn't exactly make time for a relationship."

Not to mention, guys in suits with soft hands that smell like expensive cologne don't really do it for me. I much prefer a man who looks like he could throw me against a wall and kiss the hell out of me to the point I forget my name. I've yet to meet another one of those. The men I dated in college were quiet and a little awkward. Then there was one guy in law school, but he couldn't get over the fact I was more focused on studying than being at his beck and call. My busy schedule was always a bone of contention between us. He would frequently complain about all the things I couldn't do with him, as though he should have been my priority rather than law school. When I told him it sounded like he thought I went to law school to land a rich husband, he looked at me like that's exactly what he thought and couldn't understand why that would be offensive. Fucking idiot.

"Your parents must be so proud of you. If memory serves, your dad won a huge case against some of the Cataldi capos when you were in high school," Tanya says.

"He did and they are. Things were a little rough after leaving Shine, but we worked through it." I don't mention the part where I was a heartbroken zombie for months after the shooting and my dad became increasingly frustrated with me pining over "the biker kid." He wasn't like the other pretentious families in this town that looked down on the Black Roses when I was growing up, but having his only child shot in their clubhouse changed a lot about his outlook on Ozzy and his family.

We chat for a few more minutes about Lucy and Charlie's studies. Charlie wants to be a therapist and Lucy isn't exactly sure what she wants to do but has tossed around the idea that once she's done with her college prerecs, she might take some business classes.

"Jude suggested opening up a gym in town that focuses on martial arts and self-defense. Shine has never had one, so I'm not sure it'll work," she says.

"I think that sounds like a great idea," I tell her. "You seem like a natural teacher."

"There's nothing Lucy loves more than teaching women how to kick ass," Charlie jokes.

"Maybe Jude's dick," Mia volleys.

The two women look toward Mia with shocked expressions.

"Mia!" Charlie exclaims while Lucy looks at Mia with a proud smile.

"Sometimes the zingers that come out of your mouth impress even me, Mia." Lucy holds up her cup as if raising a toast to her friend.

Mia shrugs and sips her coffee.

"Plus, she isn't wrong," Lucy says.

Charlie looks at me and stage-whispers, "It's always the quiet ones." She shakes her head in faux disappointment but can't contain her laugh when Mia sticks out her tongue.

The timer for the roast goes off and Tanya stands. "Better prepare for the stampede of hungry bikers."

The four of us help Tanya cart the food to the main room and set the platters on the tables someone put together while we were in the kitchen. As soon as I lay the first platter on the table, the few men playing pool immediately drop the cues and hurry over.

"Hell yeah, I'm not getting scraps this time around," a man whose name I don't know says.

"Wyatt, I made plenty," Tanya says, carrying out an overflowing tray of sliced meat. "No need to act like a barbarian in front of our guest."

"Sorry, Tanya," he says, leaning over and giving her a kiss on the cheek.

He holds his hand out to me with an apologetic smile. "Wyatt," he introduces.

"Freya," I reply, shaking his hand.

"I figured. We haven't seen much of you since you got here." Wyatt begins loading his plate with meat and vegetables.

I can tell he didn't mean anything by it, but the comment stings a little. I've been a terrible guest since coming to the clubhouse, especially considering these guys are risking a lot by hiding me. Work and my fear of awkward run-ins with Ozzy have kept me hiding in my room.

I turn around to head back into the kitchen, distracted and disappointed in myself, and bounce off a hard chest. Ozzy grabs me by the upper arms before I stumble into the table, shooting me a worried look.

"You okay?"

I laugh a little at my clumsiness and try not to concentrate on the way his hands on me send a riot of flutters through my stomach.

"Fine." I shrug out of his hold, trying to hide what I'm sure are flaming red cheeks.

These little run-ins we've had leave me feeling...flustered and a little angry. With Ozzy or myself, I'm not sure. Especially after talking to Tanya and, to some extent, remembering the last time we were in that kitchen together. It's been a decade and a half since that night, and trust me, I had my fair share of therapy after the incident. The one thing I never truly got over, though, was the fact Ozzy so easily let me go. I never got one phone call or text after he visited me in the hospital. So, while I'm grateful he provided a safe place for me to lie low, my eighteen-year-old heart is still broken, and it's making my thirty-three-year-old brain have some not-so-nice thoughts toward my ex.

What a clusterfuck.

After laying out the last platter, Tanya and I fill our plates. I follow her to her table and see Trick already sitting with a plate of food in front of him and a wide smile directed at me.

"Freya." He stands and walks over, giving me a hug. "Still beautiful as ever. Glad we have a chance to have dinner while you're here." He pulls out my chair and I sit. "Not that anyone would've had a choice once Tanya found out you were back in town."

Tanya smacks the large man in the arm as she passes him to get to her seat. "That's enough out of you, Patrick Lewis."

"She's giving you the full name treatment, son. I'd watch what comes out of your gob next." I immediately recognize Gramps sitting on the other side of Tanya. Even if I didn't know the three men were related, it wouldn't take much to come to that conclusion. They all share the same deep-brown eyes and easy, if not slightly devious, smile.

I send Trick an appreciative smile for pulling out my chair. "I'm happy to see you all again, too. I wasn't sure if Ozzy was going to tell you I was here or not, but I'm glad he did."

And I mean it. I may not have the best memories of being in the clubhouse, but what I do remember vividly is how at home Tanya, Trick, and Gramps made me feel on my first and only visit. There's something comforting about being back and surrounded by their kindness and warmth after what I went through at my apartment. Physically, I've been on the mend. Mentally, though, it's been a little tougher. I've buried myself in work, which tends to be my go-to, but the nightmares when I manage to close my eyes for a few hours at night haven't let up. Being around good people makes the anxiety that much more bearable, at least in this moment.

"This seat taken?"

Take back everything I said about my anxiety being tolerable. It just ratcheted up twenty notches. It would be rude for me to get up and go to another table, right?

Stop it, Freya. You're a goddamn adult.

Ozzy pulls out the chair next to me and sets his overflowing plate down. Knox sits on the other side of him, and Linc and Charlie are across from them.

"This looks great, Mom," Linc says, shoveling a huge forkful into his mouth.

Tanya looks at me and gives me a conspiratorial wink. "Some things never change."

Linc still eats like a caveman all these years later. Even Charlie has a huge plate in front of her. Oh, to be in my twenties again when just looking at a plate like that didn't instantly add three pounds to the scale.

The only chair left at the table is across from Knox. Mia takes it, but I can tell she feels uncomfortable. Lucy and Charlie made a couple jokes yesterday about her having a crush on one of the brothers but didn't mention who it was. I'm pretty sure the answer is sitting across from her.

Ozzy makes conversation with his dad and Gramps, telling stories about when Linc was a kid and he wanted to be a professional, competitive eater.

"I swear, I worked just to keep that boy in hot dogs." Tanya laughs with that motherly affection that says she really didn't mind.

Linc's face has a slight green pallor to it. "I still can't look at a damn hot dog without wanting to dry heave."

Though the conversation is lively and relaxed, I'm having a hard time not concentrating on the fact that my left arm is on fire where Ozzy and I have bumped elbows a couple of times. Or the fact that he's sitting there cool as a freaking cucumber while I'm attempting to calm my racing heart.

Dinner wraps up and the brothers scatter between the couches, bar, and pool table. Since I haven't helped with the food prep at all, I insist on helping with the cleanup. All the brothers have taken their plates to the kitchen, which, let's be honest, probably took years of training from Tanya.

"You really don't have to do the dishes, honey. We can get the bunnies to do it," Tanya tries to argue again as I stand at the sink rinsing plates.

"I'd feel bad. They weren't even out here eating."

Tanya chuckles. "Yeah, they steer clear of me. One of the girls tried to sit on Trick's lap a few years ago and before he could ask her to move, I may have dragged her off." Tanya shrugs, and I chuckle.

"Well, I still feel bad."

"I made enough for them, too. It's in the fridge for them when I leave. I'm not a complete monster. But my reputation precedes me." She shrugs. "What can I do?"

"Does it bother you? The bunny situation?"

Tanya thinks about it for a few moments before answering. "It used to. But it's not my place to judge, either. It's not them I have a problem with or even what they represent. It's when any of them don't respect another woman's relationship. That girl knew Trick was taken. Shit, I was here for chrissake. She tried to prove a point by going after the president like she had some right. I set her straight."

"What happened to her?"

"Trick kicked her out. There's no room for that kind of drama around here. If you decide to roll the dice, you're out. They all know the score when they come here."

That pretty much sums up what Ozzy told me my first day here. "I just don't understand why they're here. Why they choose to live their lives like this."

Tanya shrugs. "Plenty of reasons, I expect. Maybe it's fun for a few years. Not like any of these guys are hard on the eyes. Maybe they left bad situations and being here of their own free will allow them to take their power back. These guys aren't assholes to them, even though the girls are here for entertainment. Shit, Trick and Ozzy have put more than one through school."

Now that surprises me.

"Point is, their reasons aren't black and white, as I'm sure is true for most people. There are all different shades of gray, and unless someone wants to talk about it, it's none of our business. So, I'll just keep my reputation as queen bitch—"

"And keep the fridge stocked for everyone," I interrupt.

Tanya smiles. "Exactly."

CHAPTER NINE
Ozzy

"Let's go to your office," my dad says after we drop our plates in the kitchen.

"Okay." I have a feeling whatever conversation he wants to have is going to lead somewhere I don't want to go. But I left the asshole teenager who thought he knew everything behind years ago, regardless of the fact that having Freya here is bringing up a lot of memories and feelings from that time, especially the ones I had after she left. I'm still shocked Knox or my dad didn't lay me out at least once for being a complete shithead back then.

When we walk into my office, my dad settles into a chair, and I sit behind my desk.

"It makes me proud to see you sitting there, Oz. You've done well as president."

For me, it feels weird not to have my old man behind the desk. Growing up, my dad was larger than life behind this desk. Even when I was a prospect, I never imagined anyone other than him sitting here.

I open the desk drawer and pull out a bottle of Irish whiskey. "Drink?"

"Sure. I'll never turn down Monaghan's fine taste in whiskey."

Smiling, I pour us a couple fingers each and hand one to my dad. We sit in silence for a few moments, enjoying the smoky, rich flavor of the alcohol rolling over our tongues.

"I don't suppose you called me in here just to have a drink."

My dad's lips tip up in a half smile. "Am I that obvious?"

A couple times during dinner I caught my dad's gaze traveling between me and Freya. I'm not sure what he was looking for, but because I know my old man as well as I do, the concern in his eyes was obvious, at least to me.

My dad leans farther back into the leather chair and props his ankle on his knee. I mirror his casual pose, but I can sense this conversation is about to take a turn.

"I don't get involved in club business or how you run things," he begins.

I nod because that's true. Unless I come to my dad for advice, which has only happened a couple of times, he's steered clear of offering his two cents.

"My old man was the same. You and I were raised knowing that if we wanted it and if we could prove we were ready, the presidency of this club would be ours."

I nod again, but my hackles rise a touch.

He must see something in my expression because he puts his hand up in a placating gesture. "You proved to be ready for it, Ozzy. And like I said before, you've done a great job." he takes a sip from his glass. "The biggest regret I had as president was underestimating the Cataldis. Because of that oversight, they came in here guns blazing during a family dinner and could very well have taken us all out. I blamed myself for what happened to Freya."

"Dad..."

He holds up a hand again to let me know he isn't finished. "Ultimately, anything that happens to this club or in this clubhouse falls on the president. It's a heavy responsibility to carry. It's one of the reasons we went after them as hard and as fast as we did. Once the sharks smell blood, they all come swarming. I sure as shit wasn't going to allow the Black Roses to be eaten alive by any asshole trying to rise in ranks."

It was a bloody time in our club. There were many nights the brothers and their families slept at the club-house. It was the only lockdown I remember. We were allowed to go to school, but there were always at least two brothers right outside the gates. The Italians had no problem shooting up a clubhouse full of not only brothers but their wives and kids, too.

"You worried I'm underestimating the Italians?"

My dad's head tilts back and forth. "I don't want you to make the same mistake I did and have it cost you. Freya has a target on her back. How long do you think it'll take the Cataldis to realize she isn't in Boston anymore? Granted, she hasn't been back to Shine in fifteen years, but those fuckers have proved to be slippery assholes.

Who's to say they won't come sniffing around and catch sight of her?"

"She hasn't gone to town and hasn't told anyone where she is."

If I call for a lockdown now, it will definitely set off some alarm bells if the Italians have any clue she could be here. It would mean shutting down our club-owned businesses and canceling the runs we have scheduled with the Irish.

"I'm not telling you what to do. I know you'll make the decision you need to make. I'm simply telling you to not make the mistake I did fifteen years ago."

My dad brings up some good points. The Italians have already proven they aren't afraid to get their hands dirty, even if there hasn't been an all-out attack.

"You have my full support in whatever you do, Ozzy. I want you to know that. Gramps and I may not be the young bucks we were, but we both still have killer aim. If you need us, just tell us where to point."

The last decade and a half has been peaceful. We've had a few issues with other clubs trying to muscle their way in, but nothing that wasn't dealt with swiftly and with extreme force. We've done a damn good job deterring any other would-be interlopers from squeezing into our town or our business dealings. The Italians though? They seem to be trying to come in through the back door. So far, it hasn't cost us any lives, but how long can I expect that to hold?

"Thanks, Dad."

"Anytime, son." He stands from his chair and places his empty glass on my desk. "It's time I got Gramps and Tanya home. Lord knows once Gramps hits the whiskey, we'll be in for a long night of the same stories we've heard a thousand times."

I smile, thinking about the loop of stories Gramps keeps in his rotation. "Well, he does have some fresh faces to corner."

"I better go save them then," my dad replies with a laugh.

"I'll be out in a few minutes."

"Okay, son."

My dad leaves, and I finish off the whiskey in my glass. Maybe staying in Shine isn't the best idea until Freya's case goes to trial. My dad's right. Everything that happens in this clubhouse is my responsibility. If the Italians are keeping an eye on us, it may be in the best interest of the club to take her somewhere they wouldn't know to look.

I pull my phone from my pocket and dial Finn's number.

"Hey, Ozzy. How's the protection gig coming along?"

"Funny you should mention it. I was hoping for a favor on that front."

"Told you before, I'm happy to help. What do you need?"

The next day, I knock on Freya's door.

"Come in," she calls from the other side.

Opening the door, I find her in the same position she was in yesterday, using her bed as a desk with her hair thrown in a bun, wearing an oversized sweatshirt. She looks so much younger. Memories of seeing her exactly like this while she was studying in high school float through my mind. If I'd not been so stuck in my head, I would have thought to pick up a desk for her so she had a proper place to prepare. Hopefully, where Finn is sending us has a better setup.

"Have fun last night?" I ask.

She'd gone back to her room before I made it out of my office to say good night to Tanya and Gramps.

"I did. It was great seeing Tanya and your dad again."

Though the three of them had only met once, Freya made an impression on my family. It's nice to hear they seemed to have made one on her too.

"I talked to Finn last night. I think it may be a good idea to have you hide out in one of his safe houses rather than here. The Italians have been somewhat of an issue for the last several months. They haven't outright attacked us, but they've been poking the bear. I'd rather not have anything happen in Shine while you're here."

Freya's spine visibly stiffens, and she looks at the screen of her computer, refusing to look at me. "Did you call Liam?"

"No...why would I?"

Her brow quirks as she meets my gaze. "Well, someone needs to take me to the new safe house. I'd hate for you to put yourself in any potential danger by transporting me to wherever the hell I'm going next."

I stand in her doorway, confused for a moment, before it dawns on me what the hell she's going on about.

"I'm taking you to a new safe house and staying with you, Freya. I'm not about to trust one of Finn's men to keep an eye on you," I grit out. How the hell could she think I'd just drop her off with some asshole hours away from me?

Her cheeks redden when she sees how offended I am that she would think that.

"Oh," is the only thing she has to say.

"Yeah. Oh." I shake my head and look toward all the files she has spread throughout her small room. "Pack everything up. We have a long drive, and I want to get on the road."

"Ozzy," she says as I turn to leave. "I'm sorry for assuming you were just going to dump me on someone else's doorstep."

I don't bother to look behind me. "I know we haven't been together for fifteen years, but there isn't a universe in which I wouldn't be here when you need me, Freya. Maybe someday you won't question that."

I close her door behind me and head to my room to pack a bag.

Fuck, I hope this gets wrapped up soon. I don't know how much more I can deal with.

The ride to the Irish safe house in upstate New York is quiet. The only time we speak is when I ask her if she needs to stop for a snack or something to drink. Otherwise, she's working, and I'm listening to some country station at a low volume so it doesn't disturb her.

The ease I began to feel toward her last night at dinner is long forgotten, replaced with the tension that's been there since she first arrived. Has it only been six days? It feels like a hell of a lot longer.

I opted to take my old truck for two reasons. One, it blends in better than my bike, and two, the weather up here can turn on a dime. It's November and those nor' easters are no joke. There's also the fact that I'm pretty sure I have Freya's entire office packed up in the back of the truck.

Pulling up to the address Finn gave me relaxes me somewhat. I didn't want the brothers following us up here. If we are being watched by the Italians, a convoy leaving Shine would be a dead giveaway there's something important in the truck. It would also signal that the clubhouse is unprotected. Since my dad brought up the shooting, visions of that night have been tumbling through my head over and over. I don't want to make the same mistake my dad did. If the Italians were to try something, having any of the brothers away from the clubhouse would give them the perfect opportunity to take several of us out in one fell swoop.

I stop in the gravel drive in front of the cabin. We're about twenty minutes from the little town we drove through on our way here. Close enough to get supplies when needed but far enough away that the only people who would come out here would be someone who owned property in the area. No one would be aimlessly driving around this far out. Perfect for a safe house.

Getting out of the truck, I stretch my arms over my head. Fuck, that was a lot of hours on the road, and my back is paying the price.

Freya exits the truck and walks a few feet from where I parked. I follow her and take a look around. The house is on a hill, and from here, we can see the main road and where the little turnoff is to get to the long driveway.

"Finn said there were cameras set up so we can keep an eye on the turnoff," I say, pointing in that direction.

"That's handy," Freya says in a tone that implies she isn't interested in any conversation with me.

She walks back to the truck without sparing me another glance and unlatches the tailgate, pulling out the plastic totes holding all her files. I had one of the brothers run and grab a few so she could load them in the back, then put a tarp over them. I wasn't expecting

rain on the way here, but figured we can't be too careful, especially considering what the boxes contain. The
sooner her case goes to trial and that son of a bitch is
behind bars, the better for everyone.

"Here, let me help," I offer, walking up to the back of
my truck.

"I got it." She brushes past me and sets the tote on the
porch since I haven't unlocked the door.

"Did you get a code?" Freya is waiting at the bottom
of the stairs, looking at me expectantly.

"Yeah." I stomp up the stairs and use the access code
Finn told me to memorize and not write down anywhere. He's one cagey asshole when it comes to his safe
houses.

She slides past me and mumbles a "thanks," setting
the first tote in the house. We walk back down the
stairs, each grabbing a tote from the truck. We're surrounded by picturesque hills and trees as far as the eye
can see, but the tension in the air is fucking stifling.

After dropping the last tote on the floor inside the
house, I march back to the truck and grab our bags.
I tend to pack light and Freya only brought one large
suitcase. She's behind me when I turn around, staring
at the bag in my hand, not meeting my eyes. Again.

"I can take my bag."

"I got it," I reply gruffly.

"No, let me." She reaches for the bag, but I turn,
blocking her from taking it.

"Jesus Christ, Freya. Let me carry your fucking bag."

She rears back with wide eyes and puts her hands up. "Fine."

Moving past her, I hear her mumble, "What crawled up your ass?" under her breath.

I've had enough. Dropping both bags to the ground, I plant my fists on my hips.

"Turn around right now, Freya."

She spins on her heels and meets my furious gaze. "What?" she bites out with all the attitude of a petulant teenager.

"We're having this out once and for all. What the hell is your problem?"

The anger radiating from me does nothing to scare her away. I'm gearing up for a fight and she isn't far behind.

"Seriously, Ozzy?"

"Yes, seriously, Freya. From the second you walked into the clubhouse nearly a week ago, you've acted like I'm the dirt on the bottom of your shoe. Is this because I broke up with you fifteen years ago in an attempt to keep you away from this life after you were shot?"

Freya's hard gaze sears into me as though she could light me on fire with her eyes alone. A lesser man would back down from the heat in her stare; maybe even a smarter man would, too. I am neither and refuse to shy away from this long overdue confrontation. Her jaw clenches like she's holding words back before she fucking erupts.

"Yes! I don't know. Maybe I didn't process how badly you broke my heart or something, but seeing you again made all those feelings come back. And you didn't even care. I was devastated when you walked away from me when I was in the hospital, and you never tried to make it right. So, I'm *sooo* sorry that seeing you again has been hard. A lot harder than I thought it would be." The volume of her voice doesn't exactly make it seem like she's particularly sorry. "You never came after me, Ozzy. You threw me away after I was shot and didn't even try."

"I was eighteen fucking years old, Freya! I had no idea what I was doing. The only thing I knew was my fucking girlfriend had been shot while she was with me, and her dad blamed me for the whole damn thing. And I did try, Freya. After you were released, I went to your house to take it all back. To tell you I'd made a stupid mistake out of fear, but you weren't there. You know who was, though? Your dad." Her head jerks back in shock. "Yup, your old man was there and told me if I came near you, he'd see me six feet under."

"My dad would never threaten your life."

"Oh, sweetheart, I assure you he did. And the look in his eye told me he meant every word. He also told me that you never wanted to see me again. That you agreed the entire thing was my fault and you were done with anything having to do with Shine, the Black Roses, and me. He made it clear you thought we were the trash half the town told us we were."

Freya scrunches her eyebrows and shakes her head back and forth as though she doesn't believe what I'm telling her.

"I have never lied to you. Not once. Two weeks later, I tried to call you. I thought maybe you just needed time to cool off. Lo and behold, you'd blocked my number."

"What are you talking about? I never blocked you. My dad got me a new phone after mine was lost and..." She closes her eyes as she trails off. "Shit."

I don't give her a chance to finish her thought before continuing. "Then, all day in the fucking truck, you barely acknowledged my presence."

"I was working!" she yells, pinning me with a glare.

"Bullshit, Freya. It was more than that."

"You know what? It was. You just came into my room this morning and told me we were leaving. Don't you think it was a little presumptuous of you to expect me to trust that you would take care of me after fifteen years of radio silence? You've barely said five words to me since I came back, then all of a sudden I was supposed to trust you wouldn't just hand me off? You had no right to get mad at me for assuming you'd get rid of me the second things got hard."

"Are you fucking kidding me? It's been hard since you showed up at my clubhouse. You have no faith in me, and that's a real problem."

"You've never proven I could have faith in you. You"—she points her finger at my chest—"bailed on me, Ozzy."

"Once again—I was eighteen *fucking* years old! There's not a person alive who doesn't make dumb-as-shit mistakes when they're eighteen. Are you going to hold that against me for the rest of my life? I tried to make it right and couldn't get to you. I thought everything your dad told me in front of your house was gospel. Especially after you blocked my number."

"I didn't do that. I don't know what happened, but it wasn't me," she yells.

I'd bet my life it was her old man, and that leaves me what?

Deflated. That's what it fucking leaves me.

She was mad as hell because she thought I left her high and dry. I was mad because I thought she'd done the same. Sure, her attitude has been shit, but I can understand it now. We've both been operating under false pretenses for fifteen years over something that could have been cleared up if I'd somehow been able to get to her. But at eighteen, I didn't know how.

At thirty-three, I won't make that mistake again.

I look at her and see all the time we lost, all the time that was stolen from us. Freya was the first and only girl I ever loved, even after fifteen years. I hate the reason she was thrust back into my life, but goddammit, I'd be a damn fool to waste another moment of my second chance.

CHAPTER TEN
FREYA

All this time. All this time, I thought he had thrown me away, but he didn't.

Our breaths come out in rapid pants. My pulse is pumping through my veins so hard I'm certain he can see me vibrating. It feels as though I am, at least. What an absolute mindfuck. And I can't even think about my dad right now. That's something I'm going to have to table. I hated Ozzy. Hated him for breaking my heart. Come to find out, it was my dad that broke both our hearts. My eyes fill with tears. Tears for the eighteen-year-old girl that left Shine shattered and heartbroken. Tears for the eighteen-year-old boy who was willing to defy my father to be with me but was told he was worthless and was made to believe I thought that, too. Tears for the wasted years and the wasted days I spent in the clubhouse being so damn angry.

My shoulders slump as the first watery trail washes down my cheek.

Ozzy takes three purposeful strides in my direction and stops in front of me, cupping my cheek. His thumb swipes under my eye, but I'm too ashamed to look at him.

"Don't cry, pretty girl. You know it kills me." His voice is thick with emotion, which only makes the tears fall faster.

"I'm sorry. I didn't know you came to find me. I didn't know you tried to call. I thought..." I shake my head. "It doesn't matter. I didn't have faith."

"Freya, I didn't give you a reason to. I meant what I said in the hospital. The fact this life touched you the way it did fucking broke me." I look up into his heartbroken brown eyes. "But when I pulled my head out of my ass and realized I was a fucking idiot for letting you go instead of the million other things I should have done, you were gone."

The tormented look in his gaze continues to break my heart.

"I'm sorry I never reached out to you," I say, wrapping my hand around his wrist. "I was shattered when you left the hospital, then everything happened so fast with us leaving Shine and transferring schools. I wish I would have—"

"Shh. We were kids, Freya. A lot has changed in fifteen years, namely the fact we both grew up. I'd never hold anything you did or didn't do against you now."

"Like I did?"

His mouth tips up in a small smile. "You always were a stubborn one."

I roll my eyes, and a small chuckle escapes my throat. "I call it tenacious, thank you very much."

"Regardless of what you call it, I've always admired that about you. Still do."

He leans down and kisses my forehead. This is the closest we've been in fifteen years. The smell of leather, spice, and warm vanilla envelops me. I inhale a deep breath, committing it to memory. It will always remind me of the day my eighteen-year-old heart finally began to heal.

Moments pass before either of us moves. When I find the courage to look Ozzy in the eyes again, what I see in his gaze nearly knocks the air from my lungs. The sound of our labored breathing and my erratic heartbeat echo through my head. I tilt my face toward his and lean in, never breaking eye contact. There's no doubt this decision could have consequences I'm not ready to deal with, but Ozzy and I have always had a magnetic connection. Then and now, it's been impossible to deny. Even through my haze of hurt and anger, I've felt it every time we've been in the same room. Now that there're only inches separating us, I don't think I could stay away from him if I tried.

When he lowers his mouth to mine, the kiss is tentative at first. Just a light brush of his lips. It reminds me of the first time Ozzy kissed me, a little unsure as he waited for my reaction. I didn't make him wait long then, and I don't now.

My hand glides to the back of his head, and I run my fingers through his short, dark hair before molding myself to the front of his body. His arms immediately band around me, holding me tightly as my mouth opens for him. With my permission granted, he deepens the kiss, our tongues playing and exploring. Ozzy's moan vibrates throughout my body, setting off what feels like thousands of little fireworks low in my belly and even farther down as he lifts me, wrapping my legs around his waist.

With one hand tangled in my hair and the other under my ass, he stalks toward the house, breaking the kiss so he can see where he's going. As soon as we make it inside, he slams the door with his booted foot and looks around.

"I hope like fuck Finn doesn't have cameras set up in here or someone's about to get the show of their life."

I laugh and trail my lips down his neck.

"Fuck, pretty girl, that feels so good," he says, rocking me against the bulge in his jeans.

The moan that escapes me is loud and needy. If the last few days have proven anything to me, it's that I'm far from immune to the attraction Ozzy and I had for each other all those years ago. It's still there, though the flame may have dimmed in my head. It had to, otherwise how could I have ever attempted to move on from him? But it's back now, and more than just a tiny little spark. It's a full-blown inferno holding my entire body on the cusp of igniting.

"Bed...or fuck, anywhere," I plead, desperate for some relief.

The house isn't big by any stretch, but Ozzy and I didn't have a chance to explore before we got to this point. He walks us toward a closed door, still holding me with my legs wrapped around his waist and opens it.

"Shit," he murmurs. "Bathroom."

He turns to the other door and tries the handle, but nothing happens. There's a keypad on the wall next to it.

"I don't even want to know," he says, pressing me against the wall and taking my mouth in another brutal kiss.

"Third time's a charm?" I ask, breaking the kiss.

When he tries the third door in the hallway, it opens up into a large bedroom.

"Thank Christ." Ozzy walks to the bed and lays me down gently on the king-size mattress.

I take a quick look around the room. It's a plain space with a dresser and a large bed but nothing else. It's obvious no one lives here. The room is impersonal and cold, unlike the eyes of the man standing in front of me. There's fire and need in his eyes, but something else is there, too. It's a feeling I've only ever had with Ozzy.

Home. Ozzy feels like home.

He closes his eyes and lets out a breath in a huff before rubbing his hand over his face.

"What is it?" Confusion and insecurity rear their ugly little heads.

"I didn't think this would go the way it did," he replies.

"Okay..."

"I didn't bring anything with me. It didn't even occur to me."

"I'm not following," I say, furrowing my brows.

"Protection. I didn't bring any condoms."

I sit up, and he has a seat next to me.

"It would have been a bit presumptuous if you had, I suppose." I chew my bottom lip and peer at him through my lashes.

"If I thought for even a second this was a possibility, trust me, I would have."

Swinging my leg over him, I settle myself onto his lap with my arms draped around his broad shoulders. His hands find their way under the thick sweater I'm wearing to ward off the cold November air. My nails trail over the short hairs on the back of his neck, loving the shiver that runs through him at my touch.

"I just had my annual before the...well before," I finish, not wanting to bring up the attack that resulted in us being reunited. "And I'm on birth control."

"Same. Well, not the birth control part, obviously."

I've never had sex without a condom. Even Ozzy and I used protection the first—and only—time we were together.

"I've never been with anyone without a condom," I admit.

"Neither have I." His lips tip up in a smile. "Another first for us to share."

Fuck, but what this man does to my heart. I press my lips to his. Even though I'm on top, he's controlling this kiss as his tongue sweeps in, tangling and caressing mine. I love how our mouths and bodies move so effortlessly together. It's always been this way. He gives, I take. I take, and he gives. It's a dance we'd perfected years ago and still remember the steps to.

Ozzy breaks the kiss and whips the sweater off me, throwing it to the ground. His eyes roam the expanse of bare skin on display and stop at the bruise covering my ribs where I thought the asshole who attacked me had broken them. His large palm covers the still discolored skin, and he closes his eyes as though he's trying to regain his composure.

"I hate that this world touched you, Freya. You have no idea the terror I felt when Liam called and told me about the attack."

"I'm sorry, maybe this was a bad idea." Suddenly, insecurity washes over me at what he must see as something ugly on my body and breaks through the haze of lust we were in only moments before.

"Stop," he commands when I try to extricate myself from his hold. "Talk to me."

God, this is so embarrassing. "I must look awful with a giant bruise covering half my side."

His eyes soften as his fingers trail up the back of my neck to hold me in place. "There isn't an inch of you that looks awful to my eyes. When I see that, I see another time I wasn't there to protect you."

"We weren't together when it happened. We hadn't even spoken in years."

"Doesn't matter, pretty girl. It's still a reminder you were attacked. On my watch or not, I fucking hate the thought of you being hurt or scared."

I relax in his hold. Does what he said make rational sense? No. There's no way he could protect me when he didn't even know where I was or what was going on, but that's Ozzy. His need to protect everyone he cares about and loves is at the core of who he is as a person.

"I can't help wanting to wrap you in bubble wrap so no one can touch you," he says, tightening his grip on the back of my neck.

"Oh, sounds kinky."

Ozzy lets out a snort of laughter and the somber mood is dispelled. "Come here." He pulls my head to his and dives in for another heart-stopping kiss.

I'm the one to break it this time, pulling away to unclasp my bra and let the material slip off my breasts. His eyes flare when he sees my hardened nipples in front of him. The hand that was at my waist strokes up my side and he cups my naked breast in his palm, sweeping his thumb over the tight bud. The featherlight touch elicits a moan from me before he dips his head, running his tongue over and around the sensitive flesh, never breaking eye contact.

He wraps his lips around my nipple and sucks hard. My back arches and I rub my center over the large bulge encased in the rough denim.

"Fuck," I cry when he bites down for a brief moment before releasing me with a pop.

"You still taste just as sweet as I remember, pretty girl."

His mouth moves to the other side as his fingers find the button of my jeans, popping it open.

When he releases my nipple from his mouth, he lifts me from his lap and settles me on my back. His fingers trail gently over my skin, touching me everywhere but taking his sweet time, studying every inch of naked skin he hasn't seen in fifteen years.

"I never thought..." His voice is thick with emotion before he shakes his head a bit and clears his throat. "I never thought I'd be lucky enough to be with you again. Even if all I get to do is kiss you and worship you with my mouth, it would be enough for me. I'm a goddamn lucky son of a bitch to have you here again. Don't think I'd ever take that for granted."

"Well, it might be enough for you, but not me." I quirk a brow and run a meaningful glare from his covered chest to his booted feet. "You're still far too overdressed for what I have planned."

He shakes his head and stands, pulling his dark Henley from his body and dropping it to the floor.

"Better?"

I shake my head back and forth and point at his pants. "Those too."

Ozzy chuckles but complies, unbuttoning the denim and slowly unzipping his pants. His cock springs free, and my eyes widen in surprise.

"No underwear?"

His lips tip up in a smile as he pumps his fist over himself a few times. Ozzy toes his boots off then removes his jeans before standing in front of me in all his naked glory. Goddamn. I never thought about what he would look like when he was older the one time I saw him naked all those years ago, but there's no way my imagination could have prepared me for the man in front of me. His skin is smooth except for the small patch of hair on his broad chest and the muscular physique he had when playing football never went soft like so many others probably did. Just the opposite, in fact. His hard muscles are tight like he's ready to attack at any moment. In a word, the man is fucking magnificent. Okay, that's two words, but goddamn, he looks that fucking good without a stitch of clothing on. If I had known what lay beneath his clothes, I may have been more inclined to work or shit out sooner and spend our time wrapped up together instead of avoiding each other.

"I like you looking at me like that, pretty girl," Ozzy says, breaking me from my obvious ogling. "But you're the one overdressed now."

Ozzy lifts my foot and pulls my boot off, then does the same to the other. His fingers find the zipper of my jeans and pull it down before grabbing the waist of my jeans and working them down my legs. When he removes them from my body, he kneels on the floor in front of the bed, trailing his fingers up my calves and over my thighs until his thumbs are on either side of my hips. Ozzy yanks me down to the edge of the bed and spreads my legs in front of his face before gently trailing a finger over the wet spot on my panties.

"Soaked through," he growls, removing my thong and throwing both my legs over his shoulders. "Let's see if this tastes how I remember."

His tongue parts my lower lips as he sweeps it through the center, bottom to top. A loud groan escapes both of us, and he repeats the motion several times before lifting his head.

"Even better, pretty girl."

He lowers back to where I desperately need him and swirls his tongue around my clit, teasing me mercilessly. He knows damn well what he's doing by not giving me enough to make me come. Hell, the man chuckles when I grab his hair and let out a little snarl of frustration.

"What's wrong?" he asks, looking at me through his dark lashes.

"You're torturing me," I growl back.

"Does my woman need to come?" His head cocks to the side as he circles his fingers over my wet opening.

"Yes. Please," I beg, not ashamed in the least at the neediness in my voice.

Lowering his mouth back to my pussy, he begins flicking his tongue furiously over my clit. Two of his thick fingers enter me, and he immediately curls them, reaching the small bundle of nerves inside of me. I arch my back from the bed and cry out as an orgasm slams into me, stealing my breath. Holy shit. When Ozzy pushes me over the edge between his fingers and tongue, I have a near out-of-body experience. My entire body is shaking with the intensity of the orgasm. He follows me down, slowing his fingers but still licking my clit, every movement making my core clench.

"Stop." I laugh, and he lifts his head with a wide smile on his damp mouth.

"Watching you unravel will always be my favorite sight in the entire world, pretty girl," he says as he crawls up my body, kissing along my flesh as he moves. When he reaches my mouth, he plunges his tongue inside, and I taste myself there.

"I can't wait to have this mouth on my cock," he pants, breaking the kiss.

"I'm happy to oblige," I reply, trailing my fingernails up and down his back, loving the feel of the goose bumps that erupt over his otherwise smooth skin.

"Not yet. I need to be inside you."

Ozzy props himself on his elbows to keep his weight off me. I would love to feel his skin on mine, but the weight would probably irritate my ribs.

"Is this okay?" he whispers, checking in with me.

I nod. "Yes," I breathe out, opening my legs wider to cradle his hips. "Please."

Ozzy enters me in a slow thrust, watching my face for any signs of discomfort.

"So good," I whisper.

He pushes in a little deeper, his gaze still locked on mine.

"Yes, more," I tell him, pleading with him to give me what I need.

"I don't want to hurt you," Ozzy grinds out through a tight jaw.

I reach my lips to his and kiss him before I press my forehead to his. "You won't."

He grabs one thigh and lifts it, opening me up to him as he moves in and out with every roll of his hips. God, he's reaching places inside I've never felt before.

"You feel so fucking good, Freya," he pants as sweat beads on his forehead, his eyes traveling from my face to where we're connected. "Too good."

His pace quickens and my hips meet his thrust for thrust. I watch a drop of sweat travel down his temple, and I swipe it away before I guide his mouth to mine, kissing him with everything I have, hoping he feels the meaning behind it. *This is it. I'm yours. Don't leave me again.*

I break the kiss and a loud moan escapes me. "I'm coming," I cry out, my back arching as fireworks explode behind my eyes.

"Open your eyes, Freya."

I do as he commands and lock my gaze to his as he releases inside of me, filling me and setting off aftershock after aftershock with every jerk of his hard cock inside me.

Ozzy slows his movements, peppering my face with kisses and making me laugh.

"Goddamn, pretty girl," he groans, pulling out and collapsing next to me. "Come here." Ozzy waves his hand, motioning for me to lie across him.

"I'm all sweaty," I protest, even though I wrap an arm around his waist and rest my head on his chest.

"You think I give a shit?" His hand strokes the long strands of my hair. "I'm just as sweaty."

He is, and I love it. Our slick skin gliding over each other's sends thrills of excitement through me. I love the sweaty afterglow mess we're in. And now that Ozzy and I have worked out at least some of our old baggage, I plan on being here like this as often as I can for as long as I can.

Chapter Eleven
Freya

After the sweat has cooled from our bodies, Ozzy leans his head down and kisses the top of my hair. The action is sweet and familiar, as though we've done it a hundred times. But that's Ozzy and I in a nutshell. There's a familiarity and comfort I find in his arms so unlike anyone since him. The word home runs through my mind again.

"I'll be right back," he says, gently removing my arm from around his waist.

I settle back into the bed and watch him walk out the door, completely at ease with his nudity. There's something so enticing about watching his muscles flex with each step. From the wide set of his shoulders to his tapered waist down to his round ass that flexes with every step. I get the sudden urge to jump up and bite one cheek just because I can.

I'm laughing at the ridiculous impulse when he returns with a half smile and a washcloth in his hands. "What's so funny over there, pretty girl?"

"I want to bite your ass." The look on his shocked face makes me laugh even harder as he rests a knee on the bed, leaning over to kiss me.

"Never took you for a sadist, sweetheart."

"You wouldn't like it?"

"Never said that either." He winks and kisses me again before running a hand to my thigh and spreading my legs apart.

When he runs the washcloth through my center, I let out a small moan.

"That feel good?" he asks, staring into my eyes.

"Mmm."

Ozzy's eyes search my face. For what, I'm not exactly sure. "I love taking care of you." He gives his head a slight shake. "I never thought I'd be able to again."

I rest my palm on his cheek and run my thumb back and forth over his high cheekbone. He closes his eyes and leans into my touch, letting out a sigh of contentment.

"We're moving forward, Ozzy. What that means and exactly what that looks like, we'll figure out."

He opens his dark-brown eyes, locking his gaze with mine. "Abso-fucking-lutely we will. If you think I'm not above chaining you to a bed and torturing you with orgasms until you agree to be with me, then think again."

A bark of laughter escapes me. "That's not really a threat, though, now is it? Countless orgasms? Sign me up."

"Oh, you misunderstood, sweetheart. You won't be having any. I'll take you to the edge over and over until you can barely see straight."

"Well, that's just mean." I pout even though the idea of being edged within an inch of my sanity has my belly tightening with excitement.

My thighs rub together and Ozzy notices, shooting me a rueful smirk. "Yeah, I can tell you hate the idea."

He leans down and kisses me all too briefly before standing from the bed and holding out a hand. "Come on. Let's get cleaned up."

I rise and take his hand, letting him lead me to the bathroom. What I see there brings a soft smile to my face. Ozzy found some candles and left the water running in the bathtub. Earlier, when he kicked the door open looking for the bedroom, I didn't have a chance to look inside the bathroom. The rest of the house has a rustic feel to it and the bathroom is no exception. A giant claw-foot tub rests against a wall with a huge window overlooking the forest beneath the hill that the house is situated on. There's an antique vanity with a standing sink and a little water closet across from it. The flame from the candles paints a warm glow over the space, inviting me to rest my tired body in the steamy water.

"Ozzy," I breathe out. "This is amazing,"

Ozzy turns off the taps to the bath and holds out his hand to help keep me steady as I place one foot, then the other, into the steaming water.

"I could get used to this," I tell him, sinking into the water.

"That's my plan," he says with a wink. "Be right back."

Exhaling a deep breath, I feel my body relax beneath the hot water. God, the last week has been a train wreck of emotions. The quiet of the house and the water are washing away anxieties I didn't even realize had been having such a profound impact on my muscles. The orgasms didn't hurt either.

Ozzy reenters the bathroom with two glasses of amber liquid.

"No wine, but leave it to Finn to have plenty of whiskey on hand." He hands me a glass and we clink in a toast. The whiskey hits my tongue with notes of citrus and rich vanilla, lighting up my taste buds. Ozzy sets his glass on the floor next to the tub and steps into the water, settling himself at the opposite end.

"I talked to Finn for a minute. There are no cameras in the house." He shoots me a wry smile. "And the locked room is a little arsenal he has set up here. Gave me the code, just in case."

The thought we would need more guns than what I know Ozzy brought with him instantly ratchets up my anxiety again. Damn, I was finally relaxing for a minute.

"Hey," Ozzy starts, lifting my foot from the water as he begins kneading the sole. "What's that look?"

"The reason we're here just kind of slapped me in the face again, I guess." I shrug, taking another sip of the whiskey in my hand.

"Having a safe house with an arsenal isn't something that's out of the ordinary in this life, Freya."

"The life of being on the run from the Mafia?"

"No, pretty girl. The life of being connected to the Mob. Italian or Irish. Or being in an MC."

Ozzy's gaze spears me. He's trying to tell me, or maybe warn me, this is what life will look like if we're together.

"How many times in the last fifteen years have you had to deal with stuff like this?" I ask, genuinely curious.

Ozzy tips his head back and forth before answering. "The Italians seem to be ramping up. I don't know if it has anything to do with your case or not. We had an issue with them when Charlie first came to Shine, and I'm pretty fucking sure they had a hand in what happened with Lucy. Before that, they kept out of our way after that night at the clubhouse."

"So, you can't say this is the normal way of life for you?"

Ozzy shoots me a serious look. "Sweetheart, I'm not going to lie to you. Is this the norm every day? No. But shit like this happening is always a possibility. And we don't wait for Johnny Law to take care of it."

Reaching over the edge of the tub, Ozzy grabs his glass and takes a long sip of whiskey.

"Are you trying to scare me?" I ask, a bit confused as to why he's so adamant about making sure I understand this.

"Of course not. But if you're going to stay with me, I need you to know what you're getting into. You made a joke when we were in high school about the brothers being a group of guys who like to work on bikes and ride around. That's not who we are, Freya. I need that to be clear."

"What is it about then?" I never gave much thought to what the club really stood for. Obviously, I know they aren't a bunch of bike mechanics who like to wear matching jackets. That was made clear the night I was shot in their freaking clubhouse.

"We believe in brotherhood and loyalty. We live life on our terms and that doesn't always line up with the definition of the law."

"I know that, Ozzy."

"It's one thing to know it in your head. It's another to be in this life."

Irritation spikes for a moment. It's almost as though he expects the danger of our situation to suddenly dawn on me and send me running.

I lean back and look out the window at the beautiful scenery surrounding us and remember why we're here. This isn't some vacation for two old lovers to become reacquainted. I'm here because the Italian Mob is after me because I'm trying, and likely succeeding, at putting their boss in prison for the rest of his life, which could possibly crumble their entire organization.

But the men helping me aren't really any better, are they?

"There're rumors the Cataldis are involved in trafficking women. Nothing concrete, obviously, or the US attorney and the feds would be all over it, but I've heard rumblings." I look Ozzy straight in the eye. "Is the club or the Irish involved?"

"Fuck no. Everything the club stands for, what I stand for, is completely and wholly against anything that hurts women or kids. And I sure as shit would never do business with anyone who doesn't feel the same way. The Cataldis are scum."

"Do you know if they are?"

"Are you asking me as a US attorney?"

I shake my head, this conversation taking a turn I didn't see coming and am not prepared to deal with. If that makes me some lovesick fool for wanting to bury my head in the sand, then so be it. For now, at least.

"Never mind. Honestly, I just want to enjoy my whiskey and my bath with the hot-as-fuck man in here with me."

I send Ozzy a coquettish grin as I run my foot along his thick, muscular thigh. "Can we table it for now?"

"Yeah, sweetheart. I'm good with that."

I've always been good at compartmentalizing. You have to be in my line of work. I don't want to worry about things I can't control right now. I don't want to think about the fact that Ozzy is a criminal in the eyes of the law. I see him as a man who I'm wildly attracted to, even all these years later. He's the man who took me in to protect me from the real bad guys, the ones who murder and possibly traffic women. Those are the ones I take off the street. He may have a different way of looking at the law, but that's something for future Freya to worry about. Right now, in this moment, it's just me and Ozzy alone in a cabin for the foreseeable future, and I plan on making the most of our time away from reality.

"You know," I say, making my way across the tub to his lap. "You said something earlier, and I can't seem to get it out of my head." My hands are on either side of his hips as I lean up and take his mouth in a wet kiss.

"Oh yeah? What's that, sweetheart?"

The whiskey is making me bolder than I usually am, or maybe it's the man in the bath with me.

"You said you couldn't wait to see my mouth wrapped around you." My voice is low and husky as our gazes hold.

His eyes flare for a moment before a delicious smile stretches his lips.

"I did," he says, trailing his wet thumb across my lip.

I open my mouth and suck his thumb in, never breaking his lust-filled gaze. His eyes darken, his pupils widening to the point of almost drowning out the deep brown around them. When I lean my head back and let his thumb go with a pop, Ozzy grabs me by the back of the head and smashes his mouth to mine.

"Fucking hell, Freya," he growls when he breaks the kiss. "You have no fucking idea what you do to me."

I shoot him a devious smirk and slide one of my hands to his hard cock under the water and slide it through my fist. "I have some idea."

Ozzy's head leans back and he sucks in a hissing breath.

My tongue licks from his damp neck to his ear.

"Sit on the edge of the tub," I tell him, gently pulling on his earlobe with my teeth.

Ozzy slides out of the bath and water cascades down his body as he positions himself on the edge of the tub, leaning back against the wall for more support. He's positioned in front of me with his legs spread wide, hands clasping the tub's edge on either side of him and his steel cock pointing straight up. I stare for a moment at the man in front of me. His gaze is intense, causing shivers to run through me despite the warm bath as he waits for me to make a move.

My hands rest on both of his muscular thighs before I dip my head and run my tongue along his length from root to tip. Ozzy's fingers flex on the edge of the bathtub, turning his fingertips white from the hard grip.

"Fuck, pretty girl," he hisses out through clenched teeth.

My eyes find his again, and I slowly lower my head, sucking just the tip into my mouth, swirling my tongue over the smooth head. The salty taste of precum explodes on my tongue, and I moan loudly, taking the rest of his length inside.

"Better than I imagined," Ozzy moans as I bob my head slowly up and down his shaft, hollowing out my cheeks and creating a tight seal around his thickness with my lips.

"Goddamn, Freya."

I can tell he wants to move his hips, but if he does, he'll likely fall back into the tub. I have the man at my mercy, just as I intended.

"Can you take me all the way, baby?" he asks as he reaches for my nipple, running it between his fingers before he twists the hard bud.

I let out a deep moan. I'm so fucking turned on from sucking Ozzy's cock and the way he's toying with my nipple.

"You like that?"

He twists again, and another moan vibrates around his cock.

"Are you going to let me come in that pretty mouth of yours?"

I nod slightly and let out a long moan. There's nothing I want more than to swallow everything he gives me.

"Suck me deeper, baby. Take me all the way. I'm so close."

The moment Ozzy's dick hits the back of my throat, I swallow around the head, and he loses it.

Ozzy comes down my throat on a roar, praising me with every breath. "That's a good girl, Freya. You look so good with my dick in your mouth. Fuck, you take me so well, pretty girl."

I follow him to the end, never breaking the seal around his length. When he's finished, I move my mouth back to the head and swirl my tongue over the ridge before releasing him with a soft pop.

Ozzy slides back into the water, a blissed-out smile covering his face. He grabs me by the back of the head and yanks me toward him, smashing his mouth to mine. His tongue invades my mouth, and there's sincere appreciation in his kiss.

"That was fucking mind blowing." The tip of his finger trails from my breast to below the water. When he reaches my center, his index finger parts my lower lips, and he gently rubs my clit.

"I think one good turn deserves another."

I let out a half giggle, half moan as his finger continues to gently rub me.

"I didn't do that so you would return the favor."

"Trust me, pretty girl, eating your sweet cunt is far from a hardship for me. Besides, I need a minute before I can fuck you again, so what better way to make use of the time between now and then?"

I mean, when he puts it that way...

"Turn around and lean over the tub," he directs. "I want that perfect ass in my face."

When I'm positioned how he wants, bent over on my knees with my arms resting on the edge of the tub, Ozzy blows on my damp skin. A high-pitched squeal escapes my throat when the cold air hits me, and the man behind me lets out a deep chuckle. It's strange being so on display for him without being able to see his face, but it adds a level of excitement at the same time.

Ozzy takes a finger and runs it over my opening, dipping it in and out a couple of times.

"You're so wet for me," he murmurs, sliding his finger from my entrance to my clit and back again. After he circles the digit around my opening again, he spreads the wetness to my tight pucker and swirls around it with his slick finger.

"You gonna let me in here, too?"

I shiver at the sensation I've never felt before.

His dark chuckle tells me he notices before his finger enters me again.

"I fucking love playing with you, Freya. Watching how your body reacts to me, pretty girl...you have no idea."

Ozzy's finger finds my clit again, and he continues torturing me with not quite enough pressure to push me over the edge.

"I'm going to make you come on my tongue, then we're going to go back to that big bed and I'm going to bury my cock so deep in your pretty pussy, you'll feel me inside of you for days. How does that sound?"

"Fuck, Ozzy. Please." I'm not above begging at this point.

He doesn't make me wait before he begins circling my clit harder and faster with his finger. His tongue spears my opening, lapping at the juices dripping from me.

"Fuck. You taste so good." He groans, pulling away for just a moment before he reconnects his mouth to my wet center.

When he pulls away the next time, he begins pumping two fingers inside me, all the while increasing the pressure with his other hand on my swollen clit. I'm right on the brink, my entire being feeling like it's about to break apart with every thrust of his fingers. When his tongue circles my tight pucker, I come completely undone, the sensations of him being everywhere at once throwing me over the edge. My loud scream echoes through the small bathroom as pleasure pulses through my body. Ozzy slows his motions as I come down, and he bites my ass before sucking the flesh into his mouth, surely leaving a dark-red mark on the spot.

"Hey," I protest. "I thought I was the sadist," I laugh out.

"Sorry, pretty girl. You can't honestly expect me to have this ass in my face and not take a bite."

I giggle and turn around, sliding back into the cooling bath before I wrap my legs around Ozzy's waist.

We sit for a few more minutes, laying soft kisses on each other's bare skin while running our hands over each other like we're reacquainting ourselves with every inch of skin on display. It's soft and sweet, an unhurried luxury we can make the most of while we have the time.

"I think I made a promise to you a few minutes ago," Ozzy says, trailing soft kisses over my shoulder.

"Mmm, you did," I reply, moving my head to the side so he can continue his trail up my neck.

Ozzy moves me off his lap and steps out of the bath, grabbing a towel and drying off quickly. He holds out his hand to help me out with a smile on his face like the one he had when he helped me in. I'll never tire of those dimples that come out to play when he looks at me like that.

He grabs the other towel and dries me, taking particular care with my breasts and ass.

"Perv," I say with a light giggle.

Ozzy sits back on his haunches and winks before standing up and throwing me over his broad shoulder.

"Hey," I cry out. A slap lands on my ass as Ozzy exits the bathroom.

When he gets to the bedroom, he tosses me on the mattress and falls on top of me, kissing me soundly on the mouth.

"Time to make good on my promises, pretty girl."

CHAPTER TWELVE
OZZY

Being that it was last minute when I called Finn and asked to use the house, it wasn't stocked with anything other than whiskey—most likely a staple of all the Monaghan safe houses—and some frozen beef and buns in the freezer. The pantry didn't contain anything other than spoiled potatoes and a can of beans, so Freya and I didn't exactly dine like kings last night. Considering I'm not sure how long we're going to be here, we need to stock up on a few supplies.

The closest town is small; it has a general store and a couple little cafés and bars, but it's far enough off the beaten path that they don't get any sort of tourism or random visitors. Even though I opted not to wear my cut and Freya is dressed casually in jeans and an oversized jacket, the fact that we're strangers has everyone taking second and third glances in our direction. Thankfully, it's cold enough to be bundled in large, nondescript winter wear, which hides the normal identifiable features that could be traced back to Freya or myself. Being strangers in the tiny town has us standing out enough. If anyone were to come looking for either of us, though, they'd have a hell of a time getting a description that would lead back to us or the cabin we're staying in. I even went so far as to change the license plate on my truck to a New York plate. Living the life I do comes with some handy tricks when you're trying to fly under the radar.

Freya and I wander through the old general store, me pushing the small cart, her arm linked with mine. She stops every so often to look at something on the shelf, then she places it in the cart without ever taking her arm from mine. I don't know if she's doing it on purpose or if it's subconscious, but her body has been touching mine in some shape or form ever since last night.

My mind keeps going back to the night we spent wrapped in each other after years of being apart. There's a certain calmness I've seen on my brothers' faces when they're with their old ladies. It's in the permanent small grin they wear. I'm wearing that same grin now. We have about a million things to think about and talk about before we can dive into our future, but after last night, there's no way I won't try like hell to make sure she knows that I'm willing to do anything and everything it takes to be with her. Last night wasn't about closure for me. Last night was about solidifying the fact that there has only been one woman for me, and I'll be damned if I let her walk away a second time.

Freya has been under a tremendous amount of stress. Who wouldn't be after everything she's been through the last several days? That was one of the reasons I drew her a bath last night. Of course, the biggest reason was so I could lie naked in a tub with the stunning woman next to me. I've never claimed to be completely altruistic in any area of my life, and last night was no exception. I woke up several times throughout the night, never having been the deepest sleeper, and watched Freya finally get the sleep she desperately needed. I'm not sure if it was the orgasms or feeling safe with me next to her, but once she succumbed to her exhaustion, she slept like a rock. Every time I woke, for one reason or another, she would be plastered to my side or draped over me like the softest blanket I could imagine. Our naked skin touching during the night quieted something inside of me that never seemed to feel settled. Something until last night I didn't realize had a name. There was a Freya-sized hole inside my chest, but sleeping with her and seeing her peaceful face every time I woke up filled that hole, and for the first time in fifteen years, the weight I carried with me every damn day and night eased. Now, something as simple as walking through a store with our arms laced together while we discuss dinner ideas like any normal couple replaces the heaviness in my chest with an almost giddy lightness.

I chuckle to myself while Freya reads the label of some pasta sauce.

She turns and quirks a brow. "What's so funny over there?"

I shake my head and let out a sigh. "Laughing at myself, pretty girl." I'm being a fucking sap over running errands. "You plan on cooking for me tonight?"

"I plan on cooking, yes. You can have some, too, since I'm stuck with you." She sends me a teasing wink, and I lean in for a brief kiss simply because I can.

"I'm nowhere near Tanya with my culinary skills, I'm afraid. But I can zhuzh up a jar of sauce like nobody's business." She finds the pasta she wants to use, throws it in the cart, and we continue down the aisle.

"I'm not going to judge your cooking, sweetheart. I've never had a beautiful woman make me dinner, so I'll eat it all with a smile on my face. Then, to show you my appreciation, I'll eat you for dessert. Fair?"

The blush that covers her skin is fucking adorable. Freya's pale complexion has never allowed her to hide her embarrassment or desire. It's one of the things I loved when we were eighteen, and I'd whisper all the ways I wanted to make her scream in her ear.

"I find that hard to believe," she responds, attempting to regain control of herself.

"That I won't eat you out on the kitchen table? Trust me, sweetheart, it's all I can think about since getting a taste of you last night."

She playfully smacks my arm. "No, about never having a woman cook for you."

"You forgot the beautiful part," I reply.

And there's that blush again.

"You know what I mean."

Freya continues to scan the shelves as though she isn't invested in my answer, even though she was the one to bring it up.

"I haven't had a girlfriend or any woman trying to feed me in years."

"How many?" she asks, aiming for nonchalance but missing the mark. It's cute she thinks I can't tell she's digging for information about my past.

"Fifteen. Not since a cute-as-hell cheerleader used to leave brownies in my locker on game days."

Yes, there have been women. I've hardly lived the life of a monk, nor have I expected her to. But it was never more than a night or two or a couple women through-out the years who I had an understanding with. It was never about emotion, candlelit baths, or home-cooked meals. It was always just sex.

She looks at me with a sweet smile after I bring up the treats I used to find in my locker from her. I loved playing football, but I loved her baking something spe-cial just for me even more.

"I think we have everything," she says, and we turn toward the front of the store and head to the checkout.

There's only one register, which is probably all that's needed in a store this small. The woman scans our items with a friendly, albeit curious, smile.

"Where are you folks headed?" she asks as she scans and bags each item.

"My wife and I are headed to her family's cabin about two hours west of here. Celebrating our ten-year wedding anniversary." I look at Freya and send her a soft smile. "Figured we should stock up now. There's not much else out that way."

Freya smiles at the woman and, without missing a beat, says, "It's our first weekend away from our kids in two years."

The cashier nods and smiles back. "Well, good for you." She tells us the total, and I hand over some cash.

We leave the store with our bags and head back to the truck.

The small grin playing on Freya's face has me curious.

"What are you smiling about over there, pretty girl?"

"It was kind of fun playing at being an old married couple, even for a few seconds."

"Well, I figured if anyone came asking around and showed a picture of either of us, I sent them in the opposite direction."

Her smile dims, and she looks out the window as I drive from the store. "That makes sense."

"Have you ever been married or close to?" I ask.

Freya laughs loudly at the question. Good. I'd rather have her laughing than see the expression that was on her face moments ago.

"God, no," she chokes out. "Never even came close."

"I don't know much about your life since you left Shine."

Freya shrugs. "Not much to tell, really. When I left, things were...rocky at home. My dad and I weren't getting along, and I was still dealing with the shooting.

I was so fucking mad at everything. My mom finally convinced me to go to therapy for PTSD. It helped, I guess, but my dad and I didn't get along for a few years. I went through a bit of a rebellious phase."

I chuckle, thinking she couldn't have been that rebellious if she still graduated from Harvard Law.

"What did that look like?"

"Well," she draws out. "I went to UPenn instead of UMass." She shoots me a scandalized look then erupts in a fit of laughter. "Thought I was really sticking it to him when I declined the offer from UMass."

"You little rebel." I laugh along with her.

"Honestly, I'm glad I picked UPenn. That's where I met Kasey Hayes."

"Hayes sounds familiar," I comment.

"Her husband is the senator of Pennsylvania. It was Kasey who hooked me up with Liam."

Now I remember the name. Senator Hayes provided a plane when we rescued Lucy from that insane compound in the desert a couple months ago. It was listed on the invoice Liam sent me. Fucking prick.

Freya turns and smiles at me. "She's how we came into each other's lives again."

"I'll be sure to send her a fruit basket to thank her," I say, bringing her hand to my lips and softly kissing the back of it.

"She'd probably appreciate a nice bottle of wine more."

"Uh-oh. I sense a few stories there. Were you two winos back in your college days?"

Freya laughs, her gaze going distant as though she's remembering the nights shared with her friend.

"We were, but the wine was a hell of a lot cheaper than what we can afford now. Thank God. There's a reason a lot of what we drank back then was called gut rot." Freya releases an exaggerated shiver. "Kasey and I are the only two from our friend group who really keep in touch. She was busy with her family, then with her career, like me. And, of course, now being a senator's wife is a little time consuming."

An unpleasant thought creeps into my mind when Freya refers to her friend's husband.

"Is that the type of guy you saw yourself settling down with? White-collar, cushy job?"

Freya stares at the side of my face as I drive the truck up the windy mountain road toward the safe house.

"No, Ozzy. That wasn't my type then, and it certainly isn't what I want now."

I pretend the idea doesn't kill me inside, but it wouldn't matter anyway. Now that I have her in my life, there's no way in hell she'll be taken from me again.

"So, from UPenn to Harvard?" I ask, changing the subject.

"Yeah, my rebellious streak ended in Philly. I may have wanted to defy my dad, but I wasn't an idiot. There was no way I was going to turn down Harvard Law. Even though I was still carrying around so much anger, I worked my ass off to get into law school."

"When did the anger start to get better?" For me, it never entirely left.

She lets out a humorless chuckle. "I don't know if it did. Law school and the US Attorney's Office kept me so busy, I just sort of forgot to be mad." She shakes her head. "That sounds weird when I say it out loud. But it's the best way to describe what it was like at the time. I put it in a box and shut the lid, concentrated on school, then started working my ass off. Having the goal of putting away as many men as I could in the Cataldi organization didn't hurt, either."

"Ahh, revenge is a powerful motivator."

"It wasn't just for me, though. What would have happened if there were kids in the clubhouse that night? I doubt those assholes would have stopped what they were doing and walked out. Any organization that condones breaking into a family event and opening fire needs to be wiped off the face of the earth."

I have a feeling her version of getting rid of the Cataldis and mine are vastly different.

We pull up to the cabin shortly after our conversation and unload the groceries in the kitchen. Such a mundane task, yet I can't keep my eyes off Freya as she puts everything away. In the store, then in the kitchen, we've been working around each other like couples do, with simple touches and silent communication. It's astounding to me that after all these years apart, we can fall into a simple routine. I've never experienced anything like it, never given myself a chance to, but I doubt it would ever be this easy with anyone other than Freya.

"You know, Finn gave me the key code to the locked door in the hallway. Also had some interesting information about the house," I say as the last of the food is put away. "How are you at handling a gun?"

Freya tilts her head back and forth, considering her answer. "Better than I am at hand-to-hand self-defense. I've gone shooting a couple of times, but I don't own a gun or anything like that. I'm still not entirely comfortable with being around them."

"You live alone in a big city. What do you use for protection?"

"Jeez, Ozzy, you sound like my dad," Freya laughs out.

I'm not the biggest fan of her father at the moment, but we can both agree Freya needs something.

"It's not funny, pretty girl. Your safety is important to me."

Freya sighs and turns to me. "I have a Taser and some pepper spray in my nightstand drawer."

I nod. "Okay. That's a start." Not a great one, but I plan on remedying that. "Let's check out Finn's collection."

"Ozzy, I have a ton of work to do. Can't this wait? It's not like the Italians are going to come barreling through the door any second."

I fix Freya with a hard stare, remembering my old man's advice about not underestimating what the Cataldis are capable of. "I'm not trying to scare you. Yes,

I do think we're safe where we're at, but I need to know how capable you are with a firearm, and learning that in the middle of a gunfight isn't ideal."

She purses her lips but nods in acknowledgment. "I suppose work can wait for a few hours."

Walking over to where she's leaning against the counter, I bend and press my lips to hers. "Thank you."

Placing my hand in hers, I lead her to the locked door, typing in the code Finn gave me. The door opens to a set of dark stairs leading to a basement that, until this morning, I didn't know was here. There are no windows along the bottom of the house to suggest a lower level, so I assumed it didn't have one. Should have known better, considering this is an Irish safe house.

I feel along the wall and find a light switch that illuminates the staircase, but nothing past that.

"Creepy," Freya comments as we begin our descent. "This isn't some secret murder room or anything, is it?"

I chuckle and shake my head. Little does she know this basement may have very well seen its share of torture and death. The Irish didn't get to where they are today by being Boy Scouts.

When we get to the bottom, I find the basement is shorter than the rest of the house, with a brick wall sectioning it off. I enter the key code for the other room and when the door opens, the space illuminates automatically.

Finn not only has an arsenal of weapons stored down here, but he also has an underground gun range that extends well past the upper level of the cabin.

I turn around and look at Freya, noting her shocked expression.

"Wow," she breathes out. "I was not expecting this."

"I doubt this is in the building plans."

Moving to the wall where there are several rifles and pistols hanging, I look at Finn's selection and find a smaller pistol for Freya.

"Here you go," I say, handing it to her.

She takes the gun from my hand in a gentle grip.

"Okay, what's the first thing you do when someone hands you a firearm?" I ask.

"Check the chamber to see if it's loaded."

I nod, impressed she knew that.

"I did take a gun safety course. I just haven't bought the gun yet," she says with a huff.

"My apologies, pretty girl." My lips tip up in a small grin at her sass. I love that shit.

I select one for myself, check the chamber, then we head to the folding tables with unused paper targets.

Freya loads the clip herself as I hang the target on a metal clamp and send it about twenty yards back.

"Okay, sweetheart, let's see what you've got."

She fires off two rounds and I nod. "Not bad. Can I help you with a couple things, though?"

She turns from the target and smiles. "Are we about to have a *Ghost* moment?"

My brow quirks, not understanding what she's talking about.

Freya laughs and shakes her head. "Never mind. Show me what you want."

I step behind her and raise her arms. "You're too tense when you're holding the gun. Relax your shoulders a bit. Don't seize up like you're waiting for the kickback to knock you on your cute ass."

Freya smirks but stays silent.

"Widen your stance just a bit."

She does and I step away. "Okay, try again."

This time, she hits closer to center mass, so it's some improvement.

My eyes travel the length of her body as she fires round after round at the paper target, reloads, then starts again. I always thought Jude was slightly unhinged when he would talk about how much he loved watching Lucy at target practice. Considering the way their relationship started and the fact Lucy can outshoot most of my men, I thought he was off his rocker being turned on by her handling a gun so well. Shit, half the time, I thought she was liable to turn it on him. Now, watching Freya, I see the appeal. She carries herself with a confidence that comes to a person when they're holding a weapon they know how to use. She only needed a few pointers, and in just the fifteen minutes she's been practicing, I'm seeing improvement in her aim and comfort level with handling the gun. Maybe the British asshole was on to something. Not that I would ever tell him that.

Freya finishes with the handgun, checks the clip to make sure it's empty then sets it on the table.

"That was fun," she says with a wide smile.

Not ready for this little excursion to be over, I smile and place a kiss on her lips. "Ever fired an AR-15?"

CHAPTER THIRTEEN
OZZY

After another hour of target practice, Freya decides to call it quits.

"Are you satisfied? I have a ton of work to do and need to get back to it."

I smile and take one of the rifles she was practicing with. "Yeah, I think we're good here."

Honestly, I'm impressed with her skill level. I figured she would have been as bad as Charlie was when she first learned to shoot, but once again, Freya surprises me. She has a natural tenacity that simply won't allow her to quit when things are hard, and I know handling a gun is hard for her. But if she sees an obstacle, she's more likely to charge through it like a raging bull rather than throw in the towel.

"Later, I'll wow you with my culinary skills," she laughs out as we make our way up the stairs.

I close the door and reset the alarm, glad to know this is here, just in case. There isn't a way for the Cataldis know we're here unless Finn has a mole in his outfit, but I can't be too careful, especially when Freya's safety is a concern.

The file boxes are still in the entryway from yesterday since we'd been busy with more pressing issues at the time. She grabs her laptop and drags the boxes to the living room, making herself comfortable on the couch.

"Is it going to bother you if I take up the living room?" she asks.

"Not at all." I send a smile in her direction. "Let me know if you need any help."

She laughs as she opens her laptop. "Like you used to *help* me study in high school," she replies dryly.

My gaze travels past her, and I'm silent for a few moments. "Those were good times. I seem to remember getting a lot done."

"Funny. I seem to remember a lot of making out and not a lot of studying."

I shrug and throw her a smirk. "Exactly. Good times."

Freya rolls her eyes, and within a few minutes, she's lost in her work.

There isn't much for me to do here, unlike if I were back at the clubhouse. I'm usually loaded down with paperwork or any various things needing my attention on a daily basis. Grabbing my phone from my pocket, I decide to text Knox and check in.

Me: *How's everything going?*

He answers right away.

Knox: *The place hasn't burned to the ground without you here.*

I shake my head and send a reply.

Me: *Good to hear. Maybe I can finally take a vacation.*

Knox: *Isn't that what you're doing now?*

It kind of is, in a weird sort of way. Out here, there's no business to take care of. It's just me and Freya. The reason we're out here certainly isn't for a weekend getaway, but on days like today, when it's quiet and peaceful, it's easy to pretend.

Me: *Let me know if you need anything.*

Knox sends me a thumbs-up, and I set my phone on the table next to the overstuffed recliner I'm lounging in. Looking back at Freya, I see she's in her own world. Instead of sitting here staring at her like some lovesick kid, I grab a book from the shelf and head back to our room. It isn't long before my eyes become heavy and the words on the page are blurry. It's not often I get to indulge in an afternoon nap, so I allow my eyes to close and drift off with thoughts of what a calm life filled with days like today would look like with the woman sitting in the other room.

Soft hands travel under my shirt, waking me from a dreamless sleep. My mouth quirks in a smile, feeling Freya's warm body press into my back before she touches her lips to my neck.

"Mmm, how long was I out for?" I ask, noticing the sky has grown darker since lying down.

"You've been in here for a couple of hours," Freya replies.

"Did you get your work done?"

She releases an unamused and almost sad chuckle. "It's never done, but I found a stopping point and decided to come check on you."

I turn around so we face each other on the bed and pull her to my front.

"Glad you did, pretty girl," I say, my voice thick from sleep.

She studies my face for a few moments, tracing her slim fingers over my brows and down the bridge of my nose.

"You don't get much rest, do you?"

"Define much."

She looks me in the eyes, studying me like she's trying to unlock some mystery that resides in my head.

"You're always the one taking care of everyone else."

I let out a noncommittal hum and close my eyes, relishing the feeling of having Freya in my arms.

"It's part of the job."

"No. It's who you are. When was the last time you took a break?"

I think about her question. When was the last time I went on a long ride just for the hell of it? Going because I wanted to, not because we were making a run for the Irish or handling any sort of business. For a lifestyle that's supposed to be about freedom and living by our own rules, I haven't done much of that in the last few years.

"You don't remember, huh?" she asks with an almost sad lilt to her voice.

"I could ask you the same question, pretty girl." I pull her closer to me. "When all is said and done here, how about you and me get away, just the two of us? I could take you to a little beach town I know in South Carolina. We'll stuff ourselves on crawfish and lie in the sand. Walk around without anywhere to go."

She smiles and looks down. "This is the first time we've talked about anything 'after.'"

"You good with there being an after? I certainly wasn't planning on having all this blow over and going back to how it was before you came back to Shine."

"It's a lot to think about."

"Define a lot," I say, using her word from earlier.

"For starters, I have a life and a job in Boston and you have your life in Shine. I can't exactly uproot myself and move to Shine, and I don't think you can be a president of an MC without actually being present."

"No, I can't," I agree.

"So what does an after look like to you?"

"It looks like days like today. Us together, just *being*."

"That sounds great, Ozzy, but it's going to be hard *just being* when we live hours away from each other and have lives that don't exactly intersect."

She's referring to her job as a federal prosecutor. I suppose "on paper," our lives look to be polar opposites.

But wasn't that always the case? She was from an upper-middle-class family on the "right" side of the tracks and I was the biker kid who was good at football but was never going to leave Shine. I was convinced we could make it work back then, and I'm even more determined to make it work now.

"We haven't been together in fifteen years, Ozzy. A lot has changed for both of us. Melding our lives isn't going to be easy."

"Nothing about us has ever been easy, Freya. But I refuse to believe we won't figure it out. I'm not going to spend another fifteen years wondering where you are or missing you just because it's hard. I've lived that life, and it made me miserable."

"Please don't tell me you expect me to give up my career. I'm not anywhere near ready to do that."

Anxiety and something I can't quite put a finger on is radiating from her. I hate that any conversation about our future would scare her like this. It's in her nature to want all the answers right away, but figuring everything out in one sitting isn't something she can simply check off some to-do list.

"I'd never ask you to do anything that's not in your heart, pretty girl. All I'm asking is that you make room for me in there, too, and we'll figure the rest out. I know there's a lot to think about. There's no rush to sort it all out tonight."

This conversation is far from over, but it's all I have at the moment, considering we're still in a sort of limbo waiting for her to get her conviction.

I lean in and kiss her pouty lips, trying to ease some of the tension that's slipped in. It's then her stomach lets out a loud rumble.

"Well, before we think about it much longer, it's probably a good idea to get you fed."

Freya laughs and buries her head in my chest.

"No rush," she whispers almost to herself.

I'm not sure if the words were for her benefit or mine, but I answer anyway. "None at all."

We head to the kitchen, even though the only thing I really want to do is keep her in bed and strip her naked.

Freya pulls out the ingredients for some creamy chicken pasta thing and bustles around the kitchen, pulling out various pots and pans, a cutting board, and a knife.

"Can you cut up the chicken while I get the sauce ready?" she asks, handing me the pack of raw meat.

"You got it."

We work in companionable silence and just like earlier at the store, I'm hit with the blissful domesticity of our movements. What would it be like if this was something we did together every night in my house? The idea of coming home to someone and having somewhere soft to land when all the bullshit that comes along with being an MC president gets to be too heavy never appealed to me. I'm happy as hell a couple of my brothers have been able to find that, but I'd accepted long ago it probably wasn't in the cards for me. Never bothered me, either. But being here with Freya is making me realize it wasn't because I didn't want that. It was because I never thought I'd have that with her. If the last twenty-four hours, shit, the last week, have proven anything, it's that I've never gotten over her, never gotten her out of my system.

Freya finishes up the pasta, and I set the table, feeling completely out of my depth. There's never been a time in my life when I've set a table for a meal cooked for me by a woman other than my grandmother or Tanya. And mealtimes in those days consisted more of trying to get a plate and shovel in as much food as we could before running back outside to play some football or baseball before it got dark.

Freya pours the pasta into a giant serving dish and sets it on the table between us. Sitting down, she looks over to me and catches the smile on my face.

"What?" She seems a little self-conscious, like maybe this is a little out of her wheelhouse, too.

"Nothing. This looks great, sweetheart."

We dig in and enjoy a simple meal together, just the two of us. We reminisce a bit about people we went to high school with. She wasn't at all surprised to learn that Trevor Adams got caught with his pants around his ankles in his office at his dad's dealership.

"His divorce was the talk of the town. She took him to the cleaners," I say with a laugh.

"God, too bad I'm not a divorce attorney. I would have loved to help his ex-wife with her case. Hell, I probably would have done it pro bono just because he's still a complete douchebag."

Trevor wasn't well liked in high school, but he was popular. He was part of the jock crowd who thought they were God's gift. Knocking him to his ass at his own damn party senior year was one of the highlights from my high school days.

"Did you keep in touch with anyone from Shine?" I ask, having a feeling I already know the answer.

Freya shakes her head. "No. I wasn't really interested in talking to any of the girls after we moved. Plus, I was afraid they'd tell me how you'd moved on and were happy without me or something."

I pin her with a stare. "That wasn't the case at all, Freya. I was a miserable asshole after you left." I shake my head, remembering that time in my life. "I nearly knocked Knox on his ass when he questioned why I was being an asshole. Coach threatened to cut me from the team if I missed one more practice, and I couldn't be bothered to give a shit. It took years before I stopped looking for you any time I passed Cool Beans or when I drove past your street. I'm pretty sure the only reason my dad let me prospect for the club was that he hoped it would give me some sort of purpose instead of working on my bike or fighting anyone who looked at me wrong. I was an angry kid hell-bent on making everyone around me feel as bad as I did. So no, pretty girl, no one was going to tell you I'd moved on."

The sad look in her gaze has me refraining from telling her that after graduation, her "friend" Michelle came into the shop and tried to put the moves on me. I hated that bitch in school and wasn't about to thaw to her then. I told her exactly what I thought about her advances and never heard from her again.

"Ozzy," she whispers, covering my hand with hers. "I had no idea."

"There was no moving on for me once I'd had you, Freya. There never will be."

I lift her hand to my mouth and place a soft kiss on the back of it before setting it in my lap, effectively ending the conversation when I dig back into the plate of pasta in front of me.

We've nearly licked our plates clean when Freya stands from her chair and begins to collect the dirty dishes from the table. Before she passes me on her way to the kitchen, I grab her hand and pull her toward me.

"Set the plates down, pretty girl."

She gives me a quizzical look, but there's no way she misses the heat in my gaze.

"I told you what was going to happen after you cooked for me and how I plan to show you my appreciation."

We don't have answers about our future, and we can't change our past. The present is all we have, and I plan to spend as much of it as I can making Freya scream my name.

Freya laughs and tries to pull away. "I didn't think you were serious, Ozzy."

I yank her toward me and grab the plates from her hand, laying them on the floor. "I'm never *not* serious when it comes to eating your pussy."

She flushes at my words, and I pull her to my lap and lay a breath-stealing kiss on her mouth before she can protest any further. Positioning her so that she's facing me, I drape her legs on either side of mine, feeling the warmth from her center over my aching cock. It only takes moments with my lips on Freya's to have a raging hard-on like a damn teenager.

I rise from the chair and place Freya on the table, standing between her legs without removing my mouth from hers. My hands find the bottom of her thick sweater and I whip it over her head and feast my eyes on her round breasts encased in the lacy fabric of her bra. The bruise on her side is still there, but I try not to let my gaze linger on it too long, knowing Freya is a little self-conscious about it. A sudden burst of anger travels through me, but I tamp it down. Those bastards will pay for what they did to my woman, one way or another.

"You're everything," I whisper, brushing my finger-tips over the lace. "Every inch of you was made for me, Freya. And I'll be damned if I ever let you go again."

She whimpers at my touch and molds her mouth to mine, kissing me as though her life depends on it. I know mine does.

My hand travels to her back and with a flick of my fingers, I unclasp her bra and watch as the straps trail down her arms, revealing creamy, perfect skin beneath. My mouth latches on her dusty-pink nipple, and I suck it in deep. A loud moan escapes her as she clutches the back of my head, sending a thrill straight to my dick. I knew what my plan was when I set her on this table, but I didn't realize how much restraint it was going to take to not rip the jeans from her body and sink deep inside her.

I move to her other nipple, laving it with the same attention. Freya leans back on her outstretched arms and raises her face to the ceiling while wrapping her legs around my waist, pulling me closer to her.

When I release her nipple from my mouth with a loud pop, I trail my hand down the center of her chest and unbutton her jeans before slowly pulling the zipper down.

"Lift up, baby," I command. When her ass rises from the table, I rip the denim from her body and toss them on the floor next to the forgotten plates.

Once she's naked in front of me, I sit down in my chair and lean back, admiring the insanely tempting view in front of me.

Freya and I lock gazes before she notices my cock straining to get out of my jeans and fucking smirks at me.

"Baby, I'm going to wipe that smirk off your face when I have you begging me to let you come."

"What are you waiting for then?" she teases.

"Just getting my fill of seeing you wide open for me." Spreading her knees apart, I catch the mouthwatering sight of her glistening pussy. "So fucking needy," I say, swiping my finger through her center before sticking the digit in my mouth and sucking. "And so damn sweet."

She bites her bottom lip as I scoot my chair closer to her wet opening.

"I think you're my new favorite dessert," I say after taking one long lick from her entrance to her clit. Freya lets out a shuddering breath as I stroke her clit with my finger, not giving her the pressure she needs to come.

"Ozzy," she moans out. I fucking love that sound coming from her mouth. "Stop teasing me."

If my dick wasn't so damn hard right now, I'd play with her some more, but I need her to come on my tongue at least once before I give in to temptation and give her my cock.

My head lowers to her pussy, and I suck her clit into my mouth, spearing her with two fingers. I pump them in and out, swirling my tongue around her clit, taking her high as fast as I can. Her shouts of pleasure as her walls clamp around my fingers are fucking music to my ears. Before she comes down from her peak, I pull away from her body and undo my belt and button of my jeans, quickly lowering them to my ankles, not bothering with my boots. I need inside my woman right fucking now.

I grab her hips and set her on my lap, filling her in one swift motion.

"Oh fuck," she screams as I let out a groan of satisfaction at finally being in her tight heat.

"Too much?" I ask, hoping like hell I didn't hurt her.

She shakes her head back and forth, moaning as she bounces that perfect pussy on my lap. "No. Fuck, you feel so good inside me," she groans out.

My eyes travel to where we're connected, watching my glistening cock move in and out of her.

"Goddamn. Look how perfect you take me, baby."

She presses her forehead to mine as we both watch me slide in and out of her.

"I'm going to come, Freya. Fuck, I can't hold back." It's too good, having my cock sink into heaven over and over while her tits bounce in my face.

"Yes, Fuck. I'm right there. I want to feel you," she pleads.

The mouth on my woman when she's in the moment has always been a fucking turn on like I can hardly believe.

I slam into her twice more before holding myself as deep as I can, releasing inside her. Her slick walls strangle me as she tightens around me, screaming out her second orgasm of the night. There's no chance in hell there's a more beautiful sight on this planet than seeing Freya come apart on my cock, mouth, or fingers. She's a fucking goddess, and I can't wait to spend the rest of my days worshiping her.

It takes a few moments for us to catch our breaths as I trail my fingers up and down the damp skin of her back. Freya groans as she moves off my lap, letting my cock slip from her. Then the little vixen drops to her knees and uses her tongue to clean our combined releases from my sensitive dick. I nearly jump out of my skin when she sucks the head into her hot mouth, swirling her tongue before she releases me.

"Mmm," she moans, licking her lips.

I swoop down and take her mouth in a bruising kiss, turned the fuck on all over again.

"You fucking shatter me, Freya Campbell. Every. Damn. Time."

What I want to say is I *fucking love you and can't imagine spending the next fifteen years anywhere without you.* Instead, I take her to bed and spend the rest of the night showing her what I'm too afraid to say.

CHAPTER FOURTEEN
FREYA

We're woken at some ungodly hour by the shrill sound of Ozzy's ringtone. I don't know what time we finally fell asleep last night, but it's still early enough that there's only a faint blue hue coming from behind the blinds of our bedroom.

Ozzy's hand smacks the nightstand, blindly fumbling for his phone.

"'Lo?" he groans out when he answers. "No, It's fine. What's going on, Finn?"

His eyes pop open and his jaw clenches as he listens to whatever Finn is telling him.

"Okay." He's silent for a beat. "Let me call Knox before you do that." Silence again. It's killing me not knowing what Finn is saying to him on the other end. "I'll let you know. Appreciate the heads-up."

Ozzy disconnects the call and we both sit up.

"Finn got word from his inside man in the Cataldi organization. They know you're with us." Fear ricochets through my chest as Ozzy continues. "Finn's guy doesn't know if they plan on making a move or not. He wasn't able to catch the entire conversation."

"What did he say?" I ask, anxiety clawing at my throat.

"Just that they know we're hiding you. Finn wanted to call in some reinforcements to meet us here."

"Do they know where we are?" I ask—terrified someone could be on their way here to finish what they started at my apartment.

"I'm not sure. Finn says, as far as he knows, we're safe up here. The extra manpower was more of a precaution than anything else."

"But they could go to the clubhouse," I say, hating that even though I'm not there, I'm still bringing danger to Ozzy's family.

"I need to call Knox. It's time to go on lockdown."

"We need to go back, Ozzy. We can't stay here knowing everyone you care about could be in danger because of me."

Ozzy looks at me, then at his phone. It's evident how torn he is over bringing me back to a potentially dangerous-as-hell situation, but at the same time, not being at all comfortable with leaving his brothers on their own.

"Look at me, Ozzy." He turns his head and meets my gaze. "Your family is in Shine. God forbid the Cataldis make a move without you there and someone gets hurt...or worse. I know you well enough to know if that happened, it would eat at you for the rest of your life."

"Losing you would more than eat at me for the rest of my life, pretty girl. It nearly killed me when you left the first time, but I knew you were safe." His hand cups my cheek and the fear shining in his eyes makes my breath catch in my throat. "If we go back to Shine, I'm scared they could take you from me for good."

I cover his hand with mine, attempting to reassure him. "Considering how this all started, I'd say I wasn't as safe as you thought. But we both know, with you, I am. And the safest thing for everyone now is to be with your brothers and the rest of your family. At least until I put the old man away and we can move on with our lives. I trust you to protect me wherever we are."

Ozzy stares into my eyes. The fear I saw is replaced with pride and something else I can't quite decipher.

"I'll call Knox and let him know we're on our way back."

I nod and move to get off the bed before Ozzy grabs my arm and pulls me in for a brief kiss.

"Thank you," he says quietly, pressing his forehead to mine.

"For what?"

"Understanding me."

A soft smile touches my lips, and I get up, pulling out a fresh pair of jeans and panties from my bag.

"Let's take a shower and get on the road," I tell him, ready to get back to Shine because if I know anything about the man in front of me, it's that he won't be able to relax until we're safely inside the clubhouse gates.

After our shower, which understandably doesn't lead to anything more, I make us some coffee and fill two giant travel mugs.

Ozzy's just finished carrying the last of our things to the truck. "Ready?" he asks as I'm rinsing out the coffeepot.

There's a nervous energy flowing through me. Like, as soon as we get back to Shine, things are going to change, and I'm not sure if it'll be for the better. We're about to walk out of the little bubble we created only two days ago. God, has it only been two days? It feels like a lifetime has passed and no time at all.

"Yup," I reply, walking past him.

Ozzy locks the door and sets the alarm, following me to the truck and helping me in.

When he gets in on the other side and begins driving away, I watch the house behind us get smaller and smaller in the side mirror. There's a selfish part of me that wishes Ozzy would have insisted on staying here. I know it probably makes me sound like a total bitch, but I can't help but feel if only we'd had a few more days, hell, a few more *hours* without the outside world coming here, we wouldn't be on such shaky ground.

If we had still been at the clubhouse, he never would have confronted me like he did the first day we got here. There would have been too many distractions, too many places for Ozzy and me to hide from each other. He would have skirted around his feelings, not wanting me to be uncomfortable in his clubhouse. I would've run back into the safety of my room like I'd done any other time we'd had any sort of interaction if he'd tried to bring it up. Being out here with nowhere to hide from each other forced us to face the pain from fifteen years ago. It gave us the space to just be Freya and Ozzy, not MC president and the injured woman his club is protecting. That wouldn't have happened had we stayed in Shine.

I was the one who insisted we needed to go back, and I still completely believe that to be true, but something happened yesterday between us. There was a calm I hadn't felt before. A rightness. We have more to decide on and figure out, but one thing that's certain is we're both in this and ready for a future neither of us thought was possible. I just wish we could have talked about it more and been on sturdier ground before being thrust back into the real world.

"Did you get a hold of Knox?" I ask, needing to get the hell out of my own head.

"Yeah. He and the rest of the guys are getting everything together and letting everyone know they're taking a little impromptu vacation for the time being."

"What exactly does lockdown entail?" I'd heard it mentioned before but never asked about it.

"Basically, we shut down the club businesses, and all the brothers will stay at the clubhouse, where we'll have prospects or brothers constantly guarding the gate and patrolling the property. Anyone associated with the club, like our employees, will be offered a place to stay if they need it. Last time, when my dad was president, he was afraid the Cataldis were going to target our businesses or employees. We'd heard they'd done that in the past with rival organizations." Ozzy lets out a humorless chuckle. "There were kids running around driving everyone up the wall. Even Tanya, who is a fucking saint when it comes to rambunctious boys, was at her end."

"So when the businesses get shut down, what happens to the people who aren't in the club? Do they just have to wait until this is over to continue making a living for themselves or their family?" It hits me that because the Black Roses were tasked with my protection, everyone associated with them could potentially be affected, too.

Ozzy shakes his head. "We'll still pay them their normal wage. Like I said before, the club takes care of family and everyone working for us is part of the extended family."

I nod, glad Ozzy has a plan in place. The wave of guilt washing over me, knowing people were going to have to go without a paycheck because of the situation I put them in, lessens slightly. People are still going to be displaced because of all this shit. That's a crappy thing to be responsible for. I need to get back to my work. It's the one thing I can do to put an end to the nightmare everyone is finding themselves in because of this case.

The rest of the ride back to Shine is quiet. We only make one quick stop for snacks and a bathroom break before we continue our drive. Ozzy is constantly glancing in his rearview mirror and the side mirrors.

"Are you afraid someone could be following us?"

"I'm making sure we aren't caught unaware, pretty girl. Finn didn't know how the Italians found out you were with us, and that isn't sitting right with me."

He has a point. The only way that seems logical is there's a mole somewhere. It would be one of three groups. The Black Roses, which is highly unlikely considering I was there for over a week, and nothing happened. One of Liam's guys, which is also unlikely. The Monaghans could have a leak, considering Finn didn't catch wind of it until we were at his safe house.

"How much do you trust Finn?" I ask Ozzy while he continues constant eye movement between the mirrors and the road in front of us.

His eyes narrow slightly while he considers the question.

"I trust him to keep quiet about our whereabouts if that's what you're worried about. He's helped us out in the past. Usually, I wouldn't trust anyone outside of my brothers, but he's proven himself trustworthy on more than one occasion. When shit went down with one of Cataldi's capos, it was his guy that tipped him off, and he and some of his guys went in with us to take care of it. There's not a lot of trust to go around in our life, but Finn is one person I don't question."

I don't ask any more questions. Ozzy's confident in Finn's trustworthiness, and he's mentioned more than once he wouldn't work with people like the Italians who'd sell out their own grandmother for more power. He also doesn't seem particularly keen on giving me any details, which is understandable. We haven't talked about how my being a US attorney is going to affect his role as president of an outlaw motorcycle club. I can't deny that, at some point, it could cause some tension with his associates.

Ozzy begins speaking again. "Another reason he has a vested interest in keeping you safe is you're trying to put away the old man."

"Not trying. I'm going to," I reply with confidence. Francesco Cataldi will not die a free man.

Ozzy smirks. "My bad. You're taking out his competition for him. When Cataldi goes away, there's likely to be a power vacuum. It'll take time for the Italians to sort through it. There's nothing better than leaving your rivals to deal with the chaos that's going to follow his conviction."

I remember my dad saying something similar when I was younger, and he won his case. It's when they eventually rebuild that we have to tear it down again. God, it's like this endless cycle, and I feel like nothing more than a cog in the proverbial wheel—and not for the first time. We get a big conviction, they scramble to rebuild, they rebuild, then ten, fifteen, or twenty years later, we do it all again.

"I'm not sure how I feel about that," I say. "Helping another criminal empire."

"We're all criminals in the eyes of the law, Freya."

He's right. Ozzy doesn't follow the letter of the law by any stretch. Obviously, I don't know exactly what he does, and I'm not going to ask. Partly because I don't think he'd tell me. Or he'd feel obligated to lie so I wouldn't be in any sort of compromising position with my job. But also, I don't think I want to know. I've spent the better part of the last fifteen years working to put away criminals. Even when I knew, at eighteen, that the Black Roses weren't some club filled with guys who just liked to ride motorcycles, I never thought of Ozzy as a criminal. Maybe I'm burying my head in the sand.

Not maybe.

No, I absolutely am.

But I'm not ready to take it out quite yet.

The Italians hurt innocent people. Hell, maybe the Irish do too, just not to the same extent. The Black Roses, though? I don't believe they do. That has to count for something. It definitely counts for something with me.

I stay quiet for the rest of the drive. It's not that I'm angry or afraid of what we're about to walk back into. I'm thinking about the man sitting next to me, tracing his thumb in circles against the inside of my thigh because he can't stand to not touch me in some small way. I'm thinking about all the ways he's tried to keep me safe. First, by breaking both of our hearts when we were teenagers. Then, by giving me somewhere safe to land after I was attacked. My mind is filled with the dichotomy that is Ozzy Lewis. He's an MC president, a criminal who's respected by other criminals. But he has a soft yet fierce heart. He protects the people he loves.

Respects the brotherhood his father and grandfather created. Callous with one hand but gentle with the other. And I'm pretty damn sure I'm in love with him. What that means for me, or my life, is anyone's fucking guess.

The clubhouse is bustling with people when we get back. It reminds me of the first time Ozzy took me here, although it was under completely different circumstances.

"I'm going to check in with Knox," Ozzy says before bending down and kissing me soundly on the mouth. When he pulls back, he winks then walks away.

"Looks like a few days away did you two some good," Lucy says, walking up with a wide smile on her face.

"That kiss," Charlie says, fanning herself.

I feel the blush creep up my neck, knowing everyone in the vicinity must have noticed.

Another woman with a young boy walks up before either of the women can embarrass me further, and Charlie turns to her.

"Freya, this is Maizie. She works with Lucy and me. And this little guy," she says, mussing up the boy's hair, "is Colby."

I shake the woman's hand and smile at the shy boy holding a toy car.

"You like cars?" I ask.

"Oh yeah. I'm going to buy one like this when I'm big," he comments, pretending to race it around himself.

"It's nice to see you again, Freya," his mom says.

I look at the woman for a beat before remembering we went to high school together. She was a few years younger than me, a freshman when I was a senior.

"Hi, Maizie. Sorry, it's been a long time. I didn't recognize you," I say, embarrassed by my mistake.

She waves her hand. "No worries. We were only in school together a few months before...you left."

I'm sure my leaving Shine High and why were the talk of the school for some time.

"I'm so sorry about all of this," I say, looking down at her son, then around the room filled with bikers and other people I haven't met.

"It's not your fault," Lucy interjects. "Don't take the blame for what those assholes are doing."

Charlie nods. "It's time they were stopped. One way or another."

"Mommy, I'm hungry," Colby says, looking up at his mom.

"What's new, little man?" Maizie replies with a chuckle.

"Come on, Maiz. I'll help scrounge something up," Wyatt says, walking up and nodding his head in my direction.

They turn and head to the kitchen, and I feel like shit as I look around the busy clubhouse. I don't even know all the brothers' names and here they are going on lockdown just in case the Cataldis decide to come looking for me. My first week here was spent holed up in my room, working on the case instead of getting to know the group of men who are protecting me.

"What's that look?" Lucy asks.

I shrug and let out a sigh. "Just realizing what an asshole I've been."

"Well, you're in good company, then. Have you met my old man?" she asks, laughing at her own joke.

"Are you talking about me, Lucifer?" Jude asks, walking up behind Lucy and laying a kiss on the top of her head.

"You heard Freya say 'asshole' and assumed it was you?" Lucy volleys back, blinking rapidly and smiling at the man behind her.

"That mouth is going to get you in trouble," he growls.

"Don't threaten me with a good time."

Charlie and I laugh at the couple who are clearly in love and obviously live to give each other shit.

Lucy turns to me with a wide smile. "How are you at pool?"

I shrug. "Okay, I guess. I played a bit in college when we went to bars, but it wasn't often. Why?"

"How much cash do you have on you?" she asks.

Charlie and Jude groan and Lucy laughs. "I'm kidding, I'm kidding."

"Lucifer here is a bit of a pool shark," Jude tells me.

"Hey, I never pretended I couldn't play to try to swindle you. You just assumed you were better and I proved you wrong. Over and over again." Lucy rolls her eyes, and Jude smacks her ass.

"They'll be at each other all night," Charlie remarks, turning toward the kitchen door. "I'm going to see if Tanya needs help in the kitchen."

"I'll come, too," I say.

We head in that direction, and I spot Gramps and Trick sitting at a table with cups of coffee in front of them.

"Hey, Freya," Trick greets.

"Hi. I'm so sorry about all this," I reply, stopping at the table.

"This isn't your fault, sweetheart. Those bastards have been a thorn in our side for too many years," Gramps reassures, and Trick nods.

"I'm glad you're here and safe with us, Freya," Trick tells me. "We take care of family, and by the looks of things, that includes you now, too."

So, Trick saw the kiss along with everyone else.

The man smiles as though he's reading my mind. Not that it would be too hard to figure out where my thoughts drifted.

"I'm going to go help Tanya," I say, pointing at the kitchen door.

"I'm sure she'll appreciate that." Trick smiles again and sips his coffee.

When I walk through the door, there are several women making sandwiches, chopping vegetables and mixing various things in giant bowls.

"Not too much pepper, Tiffany. Gramps gets heartburn and the last thing we want to listen to is him whining all night."

The girl nods at Tanya and puts the pepper back on the counter.

"Hi," I say, walking up to Tanya. "What can I help with?"

"Hi, honey," she says, enveloping me in one of her warm hugs. She releases me and looks around the space. "Nothing in here. A couple of the girls are freshening up the guest rooms. You and Charlie could help with that."

"Who are all these women?" I ask, looking at the unfamiliar faces.

"The bunnies."

My head jerks back in surprise. "I thought they were all scared of you."

Tanya shrugs. "Our conversation the other night got me thinking. Since we're all going to be here together for the next while, it isn't fair for them to feel like they have to walk on eggshells when I'm here. It's their home too. And we had a talk about making sure they're only here for the single men, right, ladies?"

"Yes, ma'am," choruses throughout the kitchen.

"It's kind of like being a housemother at a sorority or something." Tanya smiles as her eyes take in all the helpers she's put to work.

I look around at the scantily clad women in full hair and makeup at eleven in the morning.

"Okay, maybe it's completely different." Tanya laughs and turns to Charlie. "You two go find Cece. She was helping the other girls with the rooms."

Charlie and I find Cece in a room as she's finishing making the bed.

"Hey, Ce. This is Freya," Charlie introduces us.

The stunning woman's face lights up when she sees me and she holds out her hand.

"Hi. I've heard so much about you from Liam and my sister."

"Nice to meet you," I say, shaking her hand. "How are the throwing stars coming along?"

Cece lets out a light, tinkling laugh. "Good. I'll be up to my sister's standard in no time."

Charlie lets out a groan. "Great. Now there'll be two of you with an affinity for sharp objects," she says playfully. "Where do you want us, Ce?"

There's only two more bedrooms to tidy up then we're done back here," Cece replies.

Charlie and I head to the other room.

"Are Cece and Liam together?" I didn't think Liam had a girlfriend, but Cece spoke about him with affection in her tone.

"Oh God, no. Liam's taken on the big brother role. It was just he and Jude growing up, so Lucy and Cece are his honorary sisters now. Besides, I think one of the brothers would have one hell of an issue if it were anything more."

That piques my interest. "Who?"

Charlie pretends to zip her lips. "Trust me, you'll see for yourself while we're all staying here."

God only knows how long that's going to be.

CHAPTER FIFTEEN
OZZY

I kissed Freya in front of the entire club, well, at least everyone who was in the main room when we walked in. One, because I can't look at her and not want my lips on her, and two, it was a claiming. Lockdowns are hard on everyone, and tempers can flare when you're stuck in close quarters with other people. If anyone would've thought to blame Freya for the situation, they'll damn sure think twice about it, knowing she's with me. Doesn't matter who it is, brother or employee, they all answer to me, and they all know I don't deal with bullshit or complaining. It was my way of trying to keep her out of the line of fire just in case someone got mouthy. Not that I think anyone would, but with everything I do, I always look at all possible outcomes and try to prepare for them.

I find Knox in the basement, checking weapons and ammo.

"Hey brother," I say, clasping his hand.

"Hey. Glad you're back."

"Aww. Miss me?"

"Fuck no. I just don't want to be doing all this shit myself." He looks around at the cases upon cases of ammo he's going through.

I smirk and start pulling out magazines and ammo. Knox doesn't give a shit about having to take inventory. He's almost as anal with all the details as I am.

"How was New York?" He asks.

"Cold."

"And Freya?"

"She's fine."

I feel like he's either fishing for information or gearing up to tell me something I won't like. When he sets down the ammo box and turns to me, I realize it's about to be the latter.

"She's bringing a lot of heat to the club."

"She didn't bring shit, Knox. The heat has been here since Charlie got here, hell, even before that. The Cataldis have been fucking with us for a long while, brother."

"Maybe, but this is the first time we've had to go on lockdown because of it. At least since Gramps and Trick took care of them last time. That has everything to do with your ex-girlfriend."

"Not ex," I reply.

Knox's eyes widen for a moment before he schools his expression. "Can't say I saw that one coming." He shakes his head. "She's not the same as us, Ozzy. Her life is the complete opposite, in fact. She's built her career on putting guys like us away."

"We're nothing like those Cataldi fucks."

"No. But we're not Boy Scouts, either. Have you two talked about what's going to happen when her case goes to trial? When she gets her conviction, who's gonna be the next one on her list? The Irish? That would be one hell of a conflict of interest for her and you."

Freya and I didn't talk about specifics, but we're on our way to figuring out what our future will look like. But Knox brings up a good point. Her profession could cause problems in that future we've only just started planning.

"We'll cross that bridge when we come to it," I tell my VP.

"I just hope the bridge doesn't blow up in all of our faces."

Lockdown can be tough on even the most seasoned biker, but Freya is handling it like a fucking champ. She holes up in our room—I may have lied and told her she needed to stay with me because we needed the space—while working on the case; although she didn't buy my reasoning for shacking up together for a second, she still obliged.

If she isn't in our room, she's helping Tanya and the girls with whatever needs to be done around the club-house. As for me, it's been sleepless nights worrying about being attacked any minute. There haven't been any signs of the Cataldis in Shine. We have plenty of friends of the club who would call us if they saw anything out of the ordinary in our little town. One thing my dad was always adamant about when he was president was maintaining a good relationship with the town as a whole. We keep a lot of shit out of Shine that has destroyed other small working-class towns.

I'm sitting in my office going through the books and looking for where we can move money around to pay the employees. They're out of work right now because of the lockdown, but I'll be damned if they struggle with bills because of it.

There's a knock at my door, and Freya peeks her head in. I smile at the welcome distraction.

"Hey, pretty girl."

She steps in and shuts the door behind her. "Hey, yourself," she greets and takes a seat across from me. "It seems like forever ago we were in here after seeing each other again for the first time."

"You knocked me on my ass that day. Just like you do every time you walk into a room."

She shoots me a soft smile. "You seemed so mad at me."

"I wasn't mad at you. I was furious when I saw what those monsters did to you." Just remembering the bruises on her neck has my blood pressure rising. "Come here," I tell her, motioning for her to sit on my lap. I've found that having Freya in my arms, touching her and feeling the heat from her skin takes away my anger and frustrations better than anything else I've tried.

She sits across my thighs and her soft hand caresses the side of my face. "The best thing that ever happened to me was coming back to Shine."

I lift my face and kiss her sweet smile.

"But we need to talk about the next few days," she continues.

My eyes close, and I let out a deep sigh. Her trial is right around the corner.

"I can't stay here while everyone prepares in Boston, Ozzy." Her voice is quiet, but she doesn't leave room for argument in her tone.

"It's not safe for you there right now." I had a feeling this conversation was going to come up.

"It's not really safe for me anywhere, is it?"

"That's not true. You're safe here where we can protect you if they come after you."

"Ozzy, I can't do my job the way I need to hours away from the rest of my team. With the trial being this close, staying in Shine isn't feasible anymore."

"Maybe you should find another job." The words are out of my mouth before I realize what a colossal mistake it is to say that out loud, remembering her reaction at the safe house when she thought I was suggesting she quit her job.

Freya stiffens and moves to get off my lap. I allow her the space because I'd rather not lose a certain appendage if I try to stop her. When she sits back in the chair across from me, it's as though a wide canyon has opened between us.

"You cannot be fucking serious, Ozzy. I've worked my ass off to build an airtight case even Houdini himself couldn't wiggle out of. Putting Cataldi away for life is what I've wanted since I was eighteen, lying in a hospital bed because a bunch of his goons came in here guns blazing."

The stark reminder of where her need for revenge against the Italians came from sends a shot of pain to my heart. I've never been more fucking scared in my life. Not until two minutes ago, when she came in here and told me she wanted to go back to Boston, where they got to her again. I knew this day was going to come. It had to, but that doesn't mean I was as prepared for it as I should've been. It's been easy burying myself in Freya every night and not thinking of anything except the feel of her wrapped tightly around me. But I'm not the president I am because I've spent the last several years burying my head in the sand.

"Freya, the only concern I have is keeping you safe. Can you really blame me for wanting you to stay here? For having your team handle the case?"

"It's not that simple. Shit pops up all the time in trials. I have to be there, just like when we came back from New York, because you had to be here. I have a responsibility to my team and to every person who that man has been responsible for hurting or worse. This isn't just about me."

Goddammit, I fucking hate what she's saying because it makes sense.

"I want the record to show I am not in favor of this decision."

Freya's mouth quirks in a smile. "Have you been watching *Law and Order* or something?"

"No, pretty girl. I'll leave the lawyering to you." My breath leaves my lungs like a deflated balloon. "If you believe the best place for you is Boston so we can put an end to this, then to Boston we'll go."

"I can't ask you to leave Shine," she says. "I'll request protection. It's a high-profile case, so it's not unusual for prosecuting counsel to have a police patrol."

"You never even told them what happened in the first place. Won't they question why you feel the need to have protection now?"

"How do you know I didn't report it?"

I shoot her a wry smile. "Because I know you and how stubborn you are. If you thought, for a second, this was going to have any effect on you being on the case, I know damn well you would have kept your mouth shut."

"Fair," she concedes. "But it's too close to trial for them to make any changes to counsel. And I don't have to say anything about the attack. I'll just tell them I've been getting threatening phone calls or something."

It might work, but it still doesn't sit right with me.

"Like fuck I'm going to trust some beat cop to keep you safe. I'm going with you. I'll call Liam to see if he can spare someone for surveillance so the other brothers can stay at the clubhouse while I'm gone."

Freya nods. "Is Knox going to be okay with it?"

The bastard has been more standoffish than usual, and everyone has noticed.

"It doesn't matter. He'll have to deal with it."

I'm not the type of president who hands out orders without a vote in church, but I'll make an exception for my woman.

"Okay, I'll get everything ready."

I nod and curl my finger, beckoning her to me. When she leans forward across the desk, I stand and lay a kiss on her lips. Just because I need a taste.

"I'll talk to Knox and give Liam a call," I tell her, reluctantly pulling away from her lips.

Fucking joy.

The ride to Boston is tense. I'm still not sure how Cataldi found out Freya was in Shine, but now that she's leaving, I'm on the lookout for a tail. Liam was able to send one of his guys to Freya's brownstone to set up some cameras he assured me couldn't be hacked. He'll personally see to it that they're monitored around the clock and have someone close in case anyone tries something. Knox was, well, Knox. Meaning he wasn't thrilled with the idea of me taking off to Boston with Freya but kept his mouth shut.

When we pull up in front of her apartment, I'm reminded of how different the last several years have been for us. I couldn't imagine living on top of my neighbors like Freya has. I like my privacy and my space. Not much of either around here.

"Come on in," Freya says as she opens her apartment door.

The space is tiny compared to my house or the clubhouse. There's a small living room with a couch and TV and an even smaller galley kitchen. A short hallway is visible from her entryway with two doors, which I assume are her bedroom and a bathroom.

Even though the space is small, it looks comfortable and screams of Freya. Eclectic yet elegant, just like the woman standing next to me.

"Home sweet home." A rosy blush covers her cheeks. "I know it's tiny."

"I like it," I tell her, hating that she takes my silence as judgment. "It suits you."

"I like seeing you here," she says, coming to stand in front of me. She wraps her arms around my neck and leans up on her toes to kiss me.

"I have a couple hours before I meet with everyone." Her voice dips low with a husky rasp.

I smile down at my girl. "I think we can come up with a few ideas to pass the time."

Lifting her up, her legs around my waist, and my tongue delves inside her mouth. Before I can take a step toward the hallway, a buzzing sounds in the apartment.

"You expecting someone?"

Freya shakes her head and walks to the small intercom next to her door.

"Yes?" she says into the speaker.

"It's me," a male voice replies.

Freya whirls around and meets my gaze with wide eyes. Who in the fuck is the man at her door?

"It's my dad," she says in a loud whisper, like he can hear us through two doors and up a flight of stairs.

Well, shit.

"Buzz him in," I tell her.

She looks from me to the front door and back to me as though she's not sure how to proceed.

"Freya, he's going to find out about us eventually. We're not kids anymore."

Forget the fact I'm starting to sweat like one. I couldn't give a flying fuck what her old man thinks of me or my family, but I know Freya is close with her parents. I hate the idea of our relationship causing any sort of wedge between them. Not enough to end things with her like I did fifteen years ago, but still, I hate seeing her torn.

She presses the buzzer, allowing him access to the building, before opening her door.

"Hey kid, I was in town having lunch with a buddy," I hear Mr. Campbell call as he stomps up the stairs.

"Your mom wanted me to stop by. You really need to call her. Texts aren't—" He stops abruptly when he sees me standing in the middle of his daughter's apartment.

"What the hell are you doing here?" he asks, fists instantly clenching at his side.

"Mr. Campbell," I say, attempting to sound civil out of respect for Freya.

He looks to Freya with disbelief in his gaze. "Is this why you haven't called us in almost two weeks?"

I never asked Freya if her parents knew where she was. Guess I don't need to now.

"Dad, some stuff happened, and I didn't want you and Mom to worry."

"I'll say." The man lets out a derisive scoff.

"Listen to your daughter, Mr. Campbell. Please."

His disbelieving look turns to me, but there's a hell of a lot more anger thrown in my direction than there was at Freya.

"Don't you dare tell me what to do. You shouldn't even be here. We left Shine and the dangerous life you were trying to drag my daughter into behind years ago."

"Dad," Freya attempts again. She's trying to stay calm, but her voice is rising as she continues. "I was attacked by Cataldi's men. They threatened to come back if I didn't lose evidence and find a way to make the case disappear."

"Honey," he says in a softer tone than the one he was using with me. "Why didn't you come to us? Mom and I could have taken care of you. We could have called the police and had them patrol or hired private security or something."

"I took care of it myself. I didn't want you and Mom to be in danger with me at your house. Who knows what they would have done to you two?" She takes a breath and lets it out slowly. "Kasey has a friend who works in security, and he knows the club and knew they would protect me, keep me hidden away until the trial."

"Did he know they were the ones that almost got you killed to begin with?"

Mr. Campbell is making it really fucking hard to keep my composure.

"That's not fair and you know it. It was the Cataldis that came in that night and shot the place up. It wasn't anyone's fault but theirs. What happened after though, that's entirely on you." My girl straightens her spine as though she's gearing up to give her dad the dressing down of his life.

Mr. Campbell's head rears back in surprise. "What are you talking about, Freya? I know we had a hard time for a while there, but you were dealing with having been shot and starting a new school in a new town—"

"I'm not talking about that," Freya replies, her tone growing icy. "I'm talking about you not telling me that Ozzy came back. Then you went so far as to secretly block his number from my phone. I'm talking about you hating him and looking at him like a criminal when he was only eighteen and scared out of his mind."

"He nearly got you killed! I did what I thought was best, and you know what? I'd do it all again. Not that it would matter. Apparently fifteen years later, you still can't see straight when it comes to him and that damn club. He's a criminal who deserves to be locked away, not some lovesick teenager who can give you the life you deserve. The safety you deserve."

"That's my decision to make!" she yells. "It always was, and you went out of your way to take that from me. You saw what losing Ozzy did to me. You were there every day and saw how much pain I was in."

"I knew you'd get over it and move on, Freya. You were just kids. It was a high school romance," he says with a sneer.

"I never did, Dad! I never got over him and because you thought you knew better than everyone else, I lived with a broken heart for fifteen years," Freya cries. "And all this time later, thinking I threw him away like the trash you wanted him to believe he was, he still took me in, still kept me safe."

"You were never going to see the situation for what it really was, Freya. I wasn't about to let my daughter, my smart, beautiful daughter, be made into a club whore."

Freya gasps and I see red. "That's enough," I bellow. "You aren't going to speak to her like that. Father or not, no one talks to her like that."

"Or what?" he turns his hateful gaze to me. "Go ahead, prove to her what men like you and your *broth-*

ers"—he says the word as though it tastes sour on his tongue—"are really capable of."

I shake my head. This man is so off base with who he believes us to be.

"He's not going to do anything to you, Dad. Jesus. The only thing happening here is you're showing your true colors. Turns out, the man I always looked up to is as big of a self-righteous, stuck-up prick as everyone else in Shine."

"How dare you speak to me like that? I'm your father. I gave you everything to make sure you could grow up and make something of yourself instead of being tied to a criminal who would have dragged you down."

"Yeah." A grim laugh escapes her. "You gave me everything except the one thing I needed. You made sure that was taken away." Freya crosses her arms over her chest with her head held high. She isn't backing down.

"Freya, you aren't seeing reason. You never did when it came to him," he states, pointing at me.

"Wrong," she replies, pointing at him. "You never saw reason. You only saw what everyone else did. You let them tell you who Ozzy and his family were. They aren't the assholes you believed them to be. They were good men. Men who took care of the people they cared about and the town they lived in. Instead of making your own decisions, you listened to everyone else and ripped the only man I ever loved from my life."

"He's got you twisted just like he did back then. He isn't a knight in shining armor. He's a damn plague on society, just like every other criminal out there."

Freya shakes her head. "We're done here. I'm not going to allow you to stand in my home and speak about Ozzy like that."

"You've got to be kidding me. You're going to choose him over your own family?" he asks with disbelief.

"I'm choosing us over my family," Freya says, pointing her finger from herself to me. "I will always choose us."

Mr. Campbell shakes his head and spins on his heels. Before he walks out the door he turns back to Freya. "You're going to regret this. This isn't who you are."

"This is exactly who I am, and I won't regret a damn thing," she replies, standing close to me. "I'm making the decision for myself this time, Dad."

With nothing else to say, he walks out the door, slamming it for good measure.

We stand in silence, staring at the front door for a few quite moments. "So...that went well," she says, blowing out a long breath.

I am in awe of the fiery goddess in front of me. I've never had anyone go to bat like that for me. Actually, that's not true. Freya always has.

I bend down and press my forehead to hers, clasping her cheeks in both of my hands. "Fuck, pretty girl. I don't think I've ever been more in love with you."

CHAPTER SIXTEEN
FREYA

"Fuck, pretty girl. I don't think I've ever been more in love with you," Ozzy says, holding my face in his strong hands.

Tears fill my eyes, my emotions all over the place. The fight with my dad, being back in this apartment, hearing Ozzy say he loves me, it's all so much.

"I love you, too," I choke out, trying to focus on his touch rather than the vortex of so many different feelings slamming into me at once.

"Why are you crying?" he asks, looking slightly nervous that I'm about to have the emotional breakdown that's probably long overdue but I haven't had time for.

"I'm so...mad." Not what I thought was going to come out of my mouth, but it fits. "How could he say those things to you? About you? All these years later, and even after telling him you're the one who kept me safe after the attack, to have him stand here in my apartment, in front of you, and still act like you're some hardened criminal who doesn't give a shit about me or anything else infuriates me." Hot, angry tears pour down my face. "It wasn't even you that put me in danger. They broke in here because I'm damn good at my job, the job I've wanted to do since I was a kid because I looked up to my dad. I've gotten so good at it they know damn well Cataldi isn't getting out of it. Yet somehow, all he can think about is you're here instead of back in Shine, where he thinks I left you all those years ago. I'm about to win the case of my damn career, and he called me a club whore, like being with you or loving you is something to be ashamed of, something useless and stupid. So yeah, I'm fucking pissed right now."

The louder my voice gets, the wider the smile on Ozzy's face gets.

"Why are you standing there smiling?" I ask, out of breath and confused with his reaction to my angry tirade. But there's no denying how his radiant smile somewhat calms my frayed nerves.

"I like seeing you fired up. The fact that it's to defend my honor? That's hot as fuck, pretty girl."

I bark out an incredulous laugh. "Anyone ever tell you that you have a strange idea of what's sexy?"

"It's all you. Everything about you is sexy. When your temper flares, it's everything I can do not to throw you down and fuck the anger right out of you."

My core clenches with the idea of him doing just that. How the hell do I go from as angry as I've ever been to wanting whatever salacious ideas he has in his head?

"You're mine, Freya." He leans in and kisses me. "No one threatens that. You just made damn sure he never thinks he can again."

I smash my mouth to Ozzy's. I *am* his and I want him to claim me. My anger and frustration need an outlet, and it looks like Ozzy is the lucky recipient.

Leaning back, I tug the bottom of the dark Henley he's wearing, ripping the soft cotton over his head.

"Show me," I say, meeting his heated gaze with my own. "I want you to prove I belong to you."

Ozzy tangles his hand in the back of my hair, wrenching my head back so I can't move and am completely at his mercy.

"You want to know what it feels like to be fucked by a criminal? To have your pussy owned by someone like me?"

God, he's never been so crass, so vulgar, with me. The intensity in his gaze should frighten me. This isn't going to be gentle or sweet, but that's not what I want or need. He looks like he's ready to devour me, and I am here for it.

"Yes," I moan. "Please."

The anger that was coursing through me moments ago has turned into a fierce need to be thoroughly fucked by the man standing in front of me.

Ozzy's hand clasps around my neck. Not enough to hurt or scare me, but just enough to show me he's taking control. "This isn't going to be sweet, pretty girl. You good with that?"

"Fuck me, Ozzy."

Something in his eyes changes, and he gives me an almost feral smile. His hand moves from my neck to the collar of my white button-down shirt. I wasn't sure how much time we'd have between getting home and meeting with my team, so I figured business casual was the way to go when I dressed before leaving the clubhouse. When his other hand grasps the other side of the collar, he rips the shirt open in one fluid motion, buttons flying off and scattering on my wood floor. His hands squeeze my lace-covered breasts harshly before he bends and latches his mouth to my hard nipple, biting down. My fingers claw through his short hair as a cry escapes me, which only seems to spur him on. He moves to the other side, biting one nipple and roughly twisting the other between his fingers.

"You still sure about this?"

"You're not going to break me, Ozzy."

He smirks and smashes his mouth to mine, our tongues vying for control. His hands wander to the back of my thighs before hoisting me up and wrapping my legs around his waist. In three long strides he moves from my entryway to my couch and drops me on the soft cushion.

"If you don't want me to cut that bra from your tits, I suggest you take it off now."

I do as he commands. These things aren't cheap, after all, and drop the lacy fabric next to me.

"Goddamn, your tits are fucking perfect."

Ozzy drops to his knees in front of me and undoes my slacks, tearing them down my legs as though the fabric offends him. I'm left with nothing on but a pair of nude underwear and a wide smile.

Ozzy's gaze travels to my lace-covered pussy and he swipes his finger over the wet spot in the center. "So ready for me. You need me to fill you? Make you scream?"

"Yes," I moan, plumping my breasts in my hands and twisting the sensitive peaks.

"Naughty girl. I didn't say you could touch yourself."

"You didn't say I couldn't," I sass.

He cocks his head to the side, a smirk playing on his lips. He grabs my bra from next to me and takes both of my wrists in his large hand.

"The only one giving you pleasure is going to be me. My mouth, my hands, my cock."

He uses my bra to tie my wrists together over my head.

"We clear?" he asks.

I nod obediently, absolutely loving this side of him. I love the sweeter side too, the one that made sure I wasn't in any discomfort while the bruises were still fresh. Now that I'm mostly healed, it looks like I get to see an entirely different version of the man in front of me.

His face moves to my breasts, and he flicks his tongue over my sensitive nipple, swirling around, then biting down. His heated gaze meets mine before my eyes roll back from the stinging sensation I love. His teeth scrape the tender flesh before he blows cool air across my skin.

"I love how you taste. Do you like having your nipples sucked?"

I emphatically nod my head. They've always been a pleasure point for me.

"Do you think I could make you come just by playing with your perfect tits?"

"I don't know, but we could give it a shot." If anyone could make that happen, it would surely be Ozzy.

He squeezes both of my breasts together tightly and nips at each peak, licking and sucking while grinding himself against my drenched pussy.

"What about if I slid my dick between your perfect breasts? I'd love to see your tits covered in my cum."

"Fuck...yes. Anything you want."

"Mmm, pretty girl. That could be a dangerous invitation. You sure I can do whatever I want to your body?"

"I trust you." And I feel that to the bottom of my soul. No matter what he has in store for me, it will bring me nothing but immense pleasure. He may like to be a rough lover at times, but he would never truly hurt me.

"Right now, the only thing I want to do is put my face between your thighs and eat your cunt."

I moan with desire and anticipation. The man has me so fucking worked up right now I can barely think straight.

His hands grip the elastic sides of my panties, and in one hard tug, he snaps the fabric from my body. Fuck, I suppose none of my clothes are safe from his destruction.

Ozzy's hands travel to my thighs, and he spreads me wide, gripping the backside of my legs and lifting my pussy to his mouth. His tongue spears me before his lips latch on to my clit, sucking it in his mouth, then moving back to my opening. It feels as though his mouth and tongue are everywhere at once, licking, then sucking, then moving inside me.

He lifts his head and kneels in front of me, my wetness coating his lips.

"You taste fucking delicious."

Ozzy positions himself at my entrance and thrusts his cock inside me, hard and deep. When he retreats, he stands and holds my chin. "Open."

When I do, he thrusts his length inside my mouth and stills himself. My tongue swirls around the head, and I taste his salty precum mixed with my own desire.

He pulls out and slams his mouth to mine, kissing me deeply, then pulls back and licks over my lips. "Delicious."

He kneels again and sucks my clit into his mouth, this time spearing me with his two thick fingers and curling them, hitting the spot inside that causes me to see fucking stars. It takes mere moments before the walls of my pussy clamp down and wetness explodes from me. Ozzy moves his tongue from my clit and circles my entrance, lapping at every last drop he wrings from my body.

"You come so perfectly for me, pretty girl."

I'm a sweaty, tangled mess of pleasure and euphoria, but he looks at me like he's never seen anything more beautiful.

"I need another one," Ozzy says, throwing my legs over his shoulders and sliding into me hard and fast.

I haven't even come down from my first orgasm before he bends me nearly in half and drives deep inside. My moans are incoherent words while Ozzy praises me with every thrust.

"You're doing so good. Look at how perfectly you take my cock. Your pussy was made for me to fuck."

Again, I feel my walls flutter then tighten around his length, sending me over the edge once more and into a state of total and utter bliss.

"That's it, pretty girl. Fucking strangle me."

Ozzy throws his head back and bellows out his orgasm, and I feel his hot cum filling me with every last twitch.

He slows and looks at where we're connected, sweat dripping from his hair down his reddened face before his gaze collides with mine.

"You're fucking perfect for me, pretty girl," he says as he pulls himself from me. His hands go to the bra around my wrists, and he releases my hands before falling onto the couch next to me.

"Come here," he says breathlessly, pulling me onto his lap.

We're silent for a few moments, with me tucked into his damp chest as he trails his fingers lazily up and down my back, both of us trying to catch our breaths.

"You okay?"

"Perfect," I purr, running my fingers through the soft patch of hair on his chest.

"I wasn't too..." His voice trails off, a touch of nerves running through his words. "I've never been like that with you."

I look into his dark eyes and give him a soft smile. "I loved it. I loved seeing this other side of you."

Ozzy smiles back, all uncertainty wiped from his face. "What time do you have to be at your meeting?"

I look at the clock hanging on my wall. "About an hour," I groan, so depleted of energy and wanting nothing more than to slip into bed with the man whose lap I'm currently curled up on.

"Let's get you cleaned up, pretty girl."

Instead of making me walk on my own, when Ozzy stands, he lifts me in a bridal hold and looks down my hallway.

"Which door is the bathroom?" he asks.

I can't help but giggle. We couldn't even make it past the living room before we tore each other's clothes off.

"Right," I reply, pointing to where he needs to go.

Ozzy sets me down in my small bathroom and starts the shower.

"I don't think the tub is big enough for both of us to take a bath in," Ozzy notes as he holds his hand under the stream, waiting for it to heat up.

For being an old building, I've never had a problem with having hot water after only a few seconds. When he's satisfied the temperature is warm enough, he holds my hand, helping me step in. Ozzy positions me under the spray, tilting my head back and running his hands through my hair. I turn and let the water wash over my face, clearing away the sweat from my sticky skin. He places featherlight kisses over my shoulders before turning and grabbing my shampoo bottle. When he massages the lather into my hair, I let out a groan of satisfaction.

"Forget my nipples; I could come just from you washing my hair."

"Don't give me any ideas, pretty girl. We have a schedule to keep."

I give him a little pout and he chuckles, tilting my head back into the stream of water.

"We'll have plenty of time later to explore all the different ways I can make you come."

"Sounds like a plan to me."

"Have I turned you into a sex fiend, pretty girl?"

"You've turned me into an Ozzy fiend."

He smiles and presses a soft kiss to my lips. "I'm okay with that. I mean, I'd be okay with you being a sex fiend too, but—"

I cut him off with a smack to his hard abdomen.

When we finish our shower, I have just enough time to throw my hair in a bun and put on some light makeup.

"That was my favorite shirt, you know," I say, referencing the destroyed article of clothing still lying in my entryway.

"If you expect me to apologize, you're going to be disappointed," he replies, lacing up his boots. "It was in my way."

"Your way of what?" I ask, standing in front of him.

He grabs the waist of my pants and jerks me toward him. "Your tits."

A laugh escapes when he smiles up at me and winks. "Fair."

Ozzy lets out a hum and stands, shrugging on a thick flannel, then his cut over it.

"Ready?" he asks, holding out his hand.

I nod and take it. Time to get back to the real world.

The real world sucks.

Well, that's not entirely true. I'm just a little cranky. In the four days Ozzy's been here, we've barely been able to spend any time together. Sure, he's with me every second of the day, sitting in my office while I work or just outside if I have a meeting. Since the Cataldis already know I've been hiding out with him and the club, there's no reason to hide that fact anymore. Ozzy is a constant presence at the office. He's gotten a few sidelong looks, being a big guy with an even bigger presence. Add in the president patch on his cut, and it's expected people are going to wonder what the hell he's doing here.

The Black Roses haven't put themselves on the US attorney's radar, though. The only time they found themselves in trouble with the law was when Linc went to prison in Minnesota. It's strange to think how that could change, that my boyfriend could one day face charges my office would be responsible for prosecuting. I shake the thought out of my head. The only thing that needs my focus is the case in front of me. Putting Cataldi away is the priority. Everything else can wait.

"The trial starts tomorrow."

Ozzy and I are lying in bed, each of us on our sides facing each other with nothing but a blanket draped over our naked bodies.

He nods. "You nervous?"

I shake my head. "Not really. I know we're going to win."

"So cocky." He laughs lightly, trailing a finger over my arm. Goose bumps erupt, making him smile that self-satisfied smirk he gets every time he sees what his touch does to me.

"Not cocky, confident." My brow arches and his smile widens before he kisses the tip of my nose.

"I've liked watching you work. You get this cute little crease right here"—his finger grazes the spot between my eyebrows—"when you're concentrating. I'm excited to see you in action tomorrow."

"You're coming?"

"Of course, pretty girl. I wouldn't miss it."

It's not a closed courtroom, but I haven't had anyone come to see me try a case since my first when my dad sat in the back.

"You can't bring any weapons. They'll have you arrested if you even try."

Ozzy scoffs. "I know that. I'm not as dumb as I look."

"I didn't mean anything by it. Just...okay, maybe I'm a little nervous."

"Hey, what happened to the confidence from a second ago?"

"Not about the trial. About after the trial," I reply.

"Oh, well, after the trial, I'm going to take you out to celebrate, then when we get back here, I'm going to tie you to the bed and torture you with orgasms."

I laugh. "Your idea of torture and mine are two very different things."

When my laugh fades, I look into Ozzy's deep-brown eyes, which I could easily get lost in if I let myself.

"I meant with us. After the trial and Cataldi is put away, I won't need to hide or have protection anymore. It would be useless for them to come after me."

"I'll wait for confirmation about potential blowback before I make a decision on that, pretty girl." His hand brushes a lock of hair behind my ear. "What do you want to happen?" Ozzy asks, not giving any indication of what he wants.

"I don't want to be away from you. I know that much. I also know you can't leave Shine and my entire life is in Boston."

"Are you happy here?"

I think about his question for a beat before I answer. "I was. I never imagined moving anywhere else. Now, though..." I trail off, not ready or able to put words to my scattered thoughts.

"Freya, the only thing I want you to worry about tonight is kicking ass tomorrow. The rest we can figure out when you get that piece of shit off the streets."

He leans in and kisses my forehead before looking me in the eyes. "Yeah?"

I smile and nod. "Yeah."

Before I fall asleep in Ozzy's arms like I've done since the first night at the safe house, I wonder, and not for the first time, if I've just been hiding in Boston and burying myself in my cases instead of actually living the life I want.

CHAPTER SEVENTEEN
Ozzy

We walk into the courthouse and per Freya's unnecessary instructions, all of my weapons are at her apartment. I don't remember the last time there wasn't at least a knife attached to my hip. I called Liam because I was a bit concerned with the Cataldis pulling something in front of the courthouse, but he assured me he had it handled. When I take my seat in the back of the courtroom, I look over and spot a familiar face standing guard in front of the closed doors. Abel. I recognize Liam's man from the night we rescued Lucy from the compound she was being held captive in. Except this time, instead of wearing army fatigues, he's dressed in a courthouse security uniform with a gun at his hip.

Huh. Liam really does have connections everywhere. I doubt Abel took a second job as a security guard for the federal court system.

Though Freya was a ball of nervous energy this morning, she's calm and collected as she discusses something with her team while they shuffle around files at the table in front. I'm so fucking proud of my woman. It took a lot to get here today, and now that the day has come, she looks ready for battle.

We rise when the judge enters, and she instructs everyone to sit except the jury. They're sworn in and have a seat.

Then Francesco Cataldi walks in.

My vision tunnels to the man as he takes his seat at the table with several attorneys surrounding him. The bailiff removes his handcuffs before he leans back in his chair and surveys the room around him. It's not the first time he's seen the inside of a courtroom, but it is the first time he's been sitting where he is as the one on trial. There's a certain satisfaction I feel seeing him being held accountable for the crimes he's committed. In this life, you usually end up in prison or six feet under. I'm not opposed to seeing either happen.

The man has aged and not well since the last time I saw a picture of him. Still, seeing the man responsible for hurting Freya fifteen years ago and then again just a few weeks ago has my blood absolutely boiling. I look at Abel standing in front of the door. A sudden and insane thought enters my mind. It would be so easy to launch myself at the man dressed as a security guard, grab his gun, and shoot Cataldi between the eyes. It's only a fleeting image, but fuck, I can almost see the entire scene play out in my mind like a movie. Abel looks at me and must see the bloodthirsty expression on my face. He narrows his eyes and gives me that *don't even fucking think about it* look. My jaw clenches before turning back to the front of the courtroom to watch the show.

Freya stands without a trace of nerves. Not that I've seen any from her when she talks about this case. Any time she spoke of putting the old man away, it was with the same confidence she exudes in front of the jury now. They hang on her every word as she lays out the case she and her team are going to present. She lists his crimes and the devastation he's wreaked as the head of a criminal enterprise. When she sits to allow the defense their turn to speak, I catch more than one glare cast in Francesco's direction from the jurors.

After the defense has concluded their opening statements, the real fun begins. Freya calls witness after witness to showcase the crimes Cataldi has committed. Expert witnesses and forensic accountants detail the money laundering and tax evasion that the criminal organization committed. I sit in my seat, completely enraptured by Freya and the way she handles each witness and the jury at the same time. I'm in awe of not only her assuredness but her intellect as each objection that's called by the defense is swatted away with her poised and practiced rebuttals. No matter what's thrown at her, she doesn't waver. Doesn't show any amount of nerves or hesitation. She knows damn well she has the evidence and the law on her side. It's a sight to behold, and I'm so fucking proud watching her as she obliterates the defense.

Each night after court, I draw her a bath—I'm still unhappy the tub isn't big enough for two—and worship her the way she deserves. I haven't been as rough with her as I was the first day back in Boston. Instead, every time I move inside her, I whisper how fucking proud she makes me and how watching her every day has me half-hard sitting in a room full of people. I tell her I love her and how much she means to me. Then I make her come so hard her eyes roll back in her head before I hold her throughout the night.

It takes three days for her side to present their case against Cataldi. If I thought Freya was amazing present-ing all of her evidence, she's even more impressive as the defense tries to paint Francesco as some retired businessman who wants to live out his golden years playing Parcheesi or some shit. They try to lead each witness they call on the old man's behalf in a cunning, underhanded way, but my girl is too smart for that nonsense. Her objections are held up by the judge and the frustration from Cataldi's lawyers is palpable in the room. The small twitch of her lips every time the judge rules in her favor wouldn't be noticeable to the casu-al observer, but I've been studying every inch of her face for the last two weeks, hell, since I was eighteen and could hardly keep my eyes off of her. She's damn proud of herself, as she should be. What's even better is, judging by the jurors' faces, they aren't buying any of the bullshit the other side is trying to peddle. After Freya presents an airtight case, there's not a spin big enough the defense could put on her evidence to sway the twelve people sitting up front.

On day seven, when closing arguments finish and the jury is led away to wherever they go to deliberate, Francesco Cataldi scans the audience behind him. I'm not sure who he's looking for, but his gaze lands on me, sitting in the back with a smirk on my face. The old man holds my stare for a few moments before a sinister grin spreads across his mouth. Does this fucker think he got away with it? He must not have been in the same courtroom as me if he thinks he'll ever see the light of day as a free man again. The look only lasts a second before the bailiff is escorting him out of the courtroom to his jail cell.

I exit the courthouse and wait for Freya on the steps. When I see her through the glass door, it takes an insane amount of willpower not to run up and crush her tightly to my chest. I want the entire world to know she's mine and I'm so fucking proud and lucky to be able to say that. Considering where we are, though, I temper the impulse and patiently wait for her at the bottom of the stairs.

Freya and I don't feel the need to keep anything secret, but this isn't Shine, and I know how hard Freya's worked to gain the respect of her peers. Her boyfriend hollering and spinning her in circles in front of the courthouse may not be welcome in her eyes. It reminds me of when we won the game in high school that secured our place in going to state. I wanted to rush off the field and celebrate by smashing her sweet lips to mine. Back when we were kids and Freya wore those little cheer skirts that drove me fucking wild. Now, it's tailored slacks and tight pencil skirts, but I have the same reaction as I did back then. The same reaction only this woman has been able to pull from me.

"You know what I could use?" she asks, stopping in front of me with her heavy bag hanging over her shoulder.

I slip the strap off her and hold the monstrosity of a briefcase in my grip while sliding my hand through her blonde waves, not able to stop myself from touching her.

"What's that, pretty girl?"

"A steak. A nice big fat slab of meat cooked medium rare and a cold beer to wash it down with."

I bark out a laugh at her decisive and very specific request.

"Come on, sweetheart." I throw my arm over her shoulders and begin walking to the parking garage. "I know just the place."

CHAPTER EIGHTEEN
OZZY

After taking Freya to the hole-in-the-wall dive bar I know that makes the best damn steaks in Boston, I hand her a glass of red wine as she lies in the bath, as per our nightly ritual the last week and a half. Sitting on the edge of the tub with a beer in my hand, I watch the stress of the day melt from her as she sips her wine.

"I've done all I can do. It's up to the jury now," she sighs out and leans her head back on the towel propped behind her.

"You did so good, pretty girl. Every day when I thought you couldn't impress me more, you proved me wrong."

"You just liked the tight skirts." She sends me a playful smirk.

"I liked watching you wipe the floor with the defense." I tilt my head to the side. "The tight skirts were an added bonus." I clink the tip of my beer bottle to the rim of her wineglass as Freya laughs then takes a sip.

"So, what happens now?" I ask.

"The jury deliberates. It could take a few hours or a few days." She shrugs.

"Are you nervous?"

She takes another sip of her wine as she considers the question. "Yes and no. Yes, because we've worked so hard on this case and went through so much to get here. Me in particular. It would feel like a slap in the face if he got off scot-free after what he did, not just to his other victims, but to me too."

I don't bother telling her that even if Cataldi gets off, he's not going to get away with shit. If Finn doesn't make sure of it, I will.

She takes a deep breath and continues, "And no because my team and I did the absolute best we could. I'm so damn proud of us, and I have every confidence that we nailed it." Freya laughs and it brings a smile to my face.

"It was something else seeing you up there."

Her face sobers and her bright eyes fall to mine. "Thank you," she says in an appreciative tone.

"For what? I didn't do anything."

Freya shakes her head. "Don't sell yourself short, Ozzy. You took care of me. From the second I showed up at the clubhouse, making sure I ate and had everything I needed when I was there. Then, during the entire trial, you made sure to show me love and support with baths and wine when I got home instead of me passing out on a pile of briefs like I usually do. This is the first time I've had a partner who cared enough to do any of that. You've been amazing."

"Don't forget the nightly orgasms," I tease.

Freya smacks my leg and rolls her eyes.

"Careful, pretty girl. If you want to get handsy, I may have to tie your wrists again."

Heat flares in her eyes, her pupils dilating with the memory of our afternoon on her couch.

"You would like that, wouldn't you?" My voice comes out as a low rumble as I hold her gaze. "If I tied your wrists above your head and didn't let you touch yourself. All the things I could do to make you scream, and you wouldn't be able to stop me." My hand dips under the water, and my fingers glide softly up and down her smooth thigh. "I could sink deep in your tight cunt then have you suck your wetness off me like I did last time. Make you taste yourself from the tip of my cock."

Her eyelids lower and her breaths come out as little pants. She's getting turned on by my simple touch and the filthy words spilling from my mouth.

My finger glides up her thigh again, but this time I lightly caress over her center, doing nothing but sliding along her slit over and over. Freya's hips twitch at the contact, but I'm having too much fun teasing her center rather than allowing her any relief right now.

"You're cruel," she moans when my hand glides back down her thigh.

"Maybe, but you love it." Leaning in, I grab her jaw with my other hand to open her mouth so I can lick my tongue inside.

I nibble on her lips, biting down, then swiping my tongue over the abused flesh as her pants turn into breathy moans. I peer down her naked body and see her nipples are tightened into perfect points, begging for attention. Freya loves having her tits played with, and I love her tits, so it's a win-win.

"Give me your tits, pretty girl."

Her hands lift the mounds out of the water as she arches her back. I dip my head and pull her tight bud into my mouth, sucking deep before I release it with a pop and move to the other one. Freya cries out as I bite down hard then swirl my tongue around the abused flesh.

"Fuck baby, hold them there, just like that," I tell her.

She moans and bucks her hips as I attack each perky breast with my lips, teeth, and tongue. Water is splashing all over her tiny bathroom from her unrestrained thrashing, soaking my jeans. She's so close to coming just from me playing with her. My hand travels to her center once more, but instead of teasing her, I plunge two fingers into her slick heat. My thumb immediately begins rubbing her clit and she comes undone, screaming my name as the orgasm ricochets through her body. I follow her down, slowing my thrusts as she lets out a long sigh. When she opens her eyes, I pull my fingers from her core and bring them to my mouth, tasting her and the bath oils on my tongue.

"This is how every bath should end," she says, tiredly sinking deeper into the tub.

A chuckle escapes me, and I grab her oversized towel from the rack.

Standing, I hold the towel open for her and watch as rivulets of water slide down her naked body when she stands. Getting an eyeful of all that deliciously soft skin on display has my cock trying to punch its way out of my jeans. When Freya wraps herself in her towel, she leans up to kiss me, brushing against my hard-on.

"You know what would make this day even better?" she asks with a sly smile on her face.

"What's that?" My hands rub over her shoulders, arms, and back, drying her with the towel.

"You letting me suck your cock."

My hands stumble in their movements, and I bark out a laugh. "I'd say that's a good way to end any day."

Freya turns to head to the bedroom, dropping the towel on the bathroom floor and I'm treated with the perfect view of her heart-shaped ass before she disappears into her dark bedroom.

Fuck me if I'm not the luckiest son of a bitch in the world.

The night passes in a blur of making love and downright fucking the woman asleep next to me. I know she needs to go into the office at some point today, but she said her boss was giving her and her team a few days off after the trial. He and everyone else think she had a family emergency when she was in Shine. Since she was still working her ass off on the case, no one questioned it. From what Freya told me, his offer of vacation time is practically unheard of, but I plan on taking full advantage of having my girl next to me without the distraction of this case.

Last night was the first night since Freya and I started sleeping together that she didn't toss and turn when we eventually succumbed to sleep. I'd like to think it was due to the orgasms I gave her, but that's been standard the last couple weeks. If I was a betting man, I'd say it had more to do with the case being done. Even if Freya doesn't win—which is highly unlikely—it's over. She said it herself; she and her team did everything they could and presented the most airtight case possible, but she also said juries can be unpredictable. Though I'd be shocked if the verdict came back as anything other than guilty. It's an entirely different experience watching her sleep without the perpetual frown she wore during her slumber.

And here I am, staring at her like a fucking creep. I should get up and make some coffee or something, but I much prefer the view in front of me, and I'm finding it impossible to tear myself away. If only we could shut the world out and spend the next six months or so right here. I may get my fill of her by then. On second thought, that's as likely to happen as pigs fucking flying.

Her long lashes flutter before she peeks one eye open.

"I feel you staring at me." Her voice is rough with exhaustion as she buries her face in her pillow.

I swipe her hair from her bare shoulder and kiss the soft skin. "You're hiding my favorite view, pretty girl."

Freya groans but turns to face me and sticks her tongue out.

"Careful sweetheart, I have uses for that tongue that you may be too tired for this early."

"Sex fiend," she groans playfully.

"Freya fiend." I shoot her a wink and roll to the side of the bed.

"Coffee?" I ask, pulling up my discarded jeans. I turn and catch Freya eyeing my naked backside. "See something you like?"

She meets my eyes, and a sly grin tilts her lips. "Absolutely. To the coffee and your ass."

I shake my head with a laugh and head to her little kitchen. Fuck, I forgot how much fun she and I have together with the simple, mundane things like waking up in the morning and falling into the playful banter we always had when we were kids. Or the way the playfulness can turn into heat and passion with just one look. It's not something I've ever had with another woman or allowed myself to have. Although, I highly doubt it would've been possible with anyone other than Freya.

Her cell phone rings from her room, and she answers with a professional, "Freya Campbell." A beat of silence passes. "Thank you. I'll be right in."

Moments later, Freya emerges from her bedroom, tying the belt of her robe in a knot. "Jury's back. They're ready to render their verdict."

"I'll make the coffees to go."

She scurries off to get ready so we can put this trial to bed once and for all.

The drive to the courthouse is quiet. Freya doesn't seem nervous, per se, but contemplative.

"What's on your mind over there?" I ask, glancing at her then back to the road.

I see her shake her head from the corner of my eye. "I'm just sitting here going over every way I could have possibly screwed up the case," she replies and lets out a humorless laugh.

I grab her hand in mine and raise it to my mouth, brushing my lips over the soft skin. Having Freya trust me to see her vulnerable and insecure when what she shows the rest of the world is the exact opposite is an honor and a privilege I plan to spend every day earning.

"Listen, I haven't watched many trials in my day, but from what I saw in that courtroom, you have absolutely nothing to be nervous about."

"This is part of my process. Don't question it." She lets a small chuckle escape. "It's okay. I always second-guess myself right before the verdict."

"Has there ever been a case you were confident you'd win and didn't?" I don't know anything about her previous cases. Shit, I hardly know anything about her time as an attorney.

"A couple of times, but not often. Sometimes, it's hard when I lose a case. There was one I thought for sure the jury would convict on, but they didn't. Reasonable doubt can be a bitch."

"Have you ever prosecuted a case you weren't sure about?"

Freya shakes her head. "Never, but sometimes the evidence isn't compelling enough to get a conviction. I can't exactly tell the jury to trust my gut feeling."

"I suppose not."

After parking in the garage, Freya walks into the courtroom with her head held high. Her face is stone cold as she sits next to her associates. The nerves she was showing me on the way to the courthouse are long since forgotten. When one of them leans over to tell her something, she barely pays him any mind. Her singular focus is on the door the jury will be walking through. There's no uneasy fidgeting, shit, she barely breathes, waiting for that damn door to open.

Francesco, on the other hand, looks like he doesn't have a care in the world. He's all smiles with his attorneys like this is just another Tuesday afternoon. I still can't get the way he looked at me out of my head on the first day. I texted Finn, wondering if he'd heard anything from his inside man about any backlash from the verdict. He let me know they don't think Freya is going to get her conviction, which seems absolutely insane to me.

The jury is let in through the small door off to the side of the courtroom. I swear we could hear a pin drop. Everyone is waiting with bated breath for the verdict. The only outward sign that Freya is feeling any sort of anxiety is the slight clench in her jaw. It blows my mind how she can look so unaffected, knowing what's riding on this conviction, both professionally and personally.

I'm on the edge of my damn seat as the foreman hands the paper to the judge. The judge reads the verdict, nods, then hands it back to the bailiff. Jesus fucking Christ, could they make it any more suspenseful? This is killing me.

When the foreman calls guilty on all counts, the courtroom erupts in a chorus of cheers and groans. Freya shows no outward emotion except for a small pump of her fist at her side, her professional mask staying perfectly in place. I want to get up and cheer with everyone else, but refrain. That fucking piece of shit is finally getting what's been coming to him. Freya's gaze meets mine in the melee as the judge pounds her gavel, demanding order in the courtroom. A grin splits my face as pride shines from hers. The look between us only lasts a minute before her fellow attorneys get her attention, obviously ecstatic over the verdict. She fucking did it.

I look toward Cataldi and the casual smile he was wearing only minutes before has evaporated. He and his attorneys are in a huddle, still sitting around the table. Everyone is talking in hurried but hushed tones, probably trying to figure out what went wrong and maybe even trying to save their own asses in the eyes of the old man. They just lost him his freedom. Shit, I'd be scrambling to save my ass, too. He doesn't pay me any mind as he listens to his counsel, but I take a moment to absorb the feeling of satisfaction I get watching his world crumble around him. I cast a knowing smile in his direction, even though he doesn't see me. *Take that, motherfucker.*

The courtroom clears and I follow the crowd. Waiting several minutes for Freya on the front steps is worth every second when she emerges from the large double doors with the rest of her team, and I catch the wide smile of victory on her face. Now that she's out of the courtroom, it's impossible not to see how fucking elated she is that she got the conviction. She walks down the stairs to me, and I grab her in a tight hold, twirling her around the sidewalk. Fuck it, I contained myself long enough.

I set her down and bring my hands to her face, crouching enough so we're eye level.

"You fucking did it, pretty girl. I'm so damn proud of you." I pull her in for a kiss in front of everyone and their damn dog passing by.

Pulling away, I squeeze her to my chest. "Where to now?"

Freya looks up at me with bright, excited eyes. "Now, we celebrate."

CHAPTER NINETEEN
OZZY

We meet Freya's colleagues at a bar not far from the courthouse. Everyone in here is in a suit or some sort of business attire except Freya and me. After leaving the courthouse, we went back to her apartment and had a mini celebration of our own before coming to this bar. It strikes me that it's only a block from where I saw her ten years ago. God, what would have happened if I had gone outside and talked to her? No use crying over spilled milk and all that, but it doesn't stop the pang of regret from ricocheting through my chest. So many wasted years.

"Just a few weeks ago, I would have been in here after work, still in my skirt and uncomfortable heels, rubbing elbows with other attorneys and trying to network," Freya says.

"I like those tight skirts and heels," I comment as she scans the bar for her friends.

"I prefer jeans and boots," she replies with a smile.

When we were at her apartment getting dressed—after I pulled two orgasms from her—she looked at her closet filled with her fancy clothes and shoes for a few minutes, shook her head, then yanked out a pair of jeans from her dresser.

She spots one of her coworkers, Brian, and waves. We make our way over to the group and a chorus of cheers erupt. Freya laughs as we have a seat at the long table already filled with empty pitchers and wineglasses. Damn, who knew attorneys liked to party as hard as bikers?

"You did it, Freya Campbell," Brian says, raising a glass to Freya.

"We did it." She smiles and flags down the waitress, asking for a round for the table.

The night passes with talk of the trial, and several other attorneys I'd never met come up and congratulate Freya. She makes sure to point out it was a team effort, and she couldn't have gotten a conviction without the hard work and sleepless nights everyone put in. It strikes me how cutthroat this world can be. Everyone at the table preens and sits just a tad straighter when Freya mentions how tirelessly everyone worked, never taking all the praise for herself.

Two hours and several beers later, it's time to head back to her place. While I love seeing my woman in her element and celebrating her victory, I've had about enough of being out in a noisy bar. Freya looks relieved when I ask if she's ready to leave.

"Please," she groans, kissing the side of my neck.

We cab it back to her place, and as soon as we enter her apartment, my phone dings with a text alert.

Finn: *Your girl killed it. My guy says the Italians are scrambling.*

Me: *Did he say if he heard anything about Freya or the club?*

Finn: *They aren't concerned with her or the club. Carlo said and I quote- I don't give a shit about the bitch lawyer. They're too busy scrambling in a power vacuum.*

Don't appreciate that asshole referring to my woman as a bitch, but I'm certainly glad to hear their focus is elsewhere.

Me: *Thanks, man.*

I pocket my phone and turn to Freya. "I want to take you somewhere."

Freya walks over from the kitchen with another glass of wine and a beer for me.

"To the bedroom?" she asks with a saucy wink and a lighthearted giggle.

"No," I laugh out and take the beer from her hand before looping my arm around her waist, bending to kiss her wine-flavored lips.

"The couch?" she asks, looking in that direction. "I have some fond memories of you and me on that couch."

I bend and kiss her neck. "We'll definitely be reenacting all those. I was thinking we could head to my cabin. Now that the Cataldis are taken care of, I want to spend some time alone with you, away from everything."

"That sounds amazing. Does your cabin have a gun range in the basement like the other one we were just at?"

I laugh again at her slurred question. "No, pretty girl. It's just an old cabin that Dad, Gramps and I use to get away and fish. It's one of my favorite places."

"Then I'd love to get away with you, Ozzy Lewis." She throws her arms around my neck and smiles widely.

After taking her mouth in a deep, passion-filled kiss, we finish our drinks and head to bed, celebrating some more. This time without any clothes.

It's a long drive to the cabin, and I'm itching to get out of the crowded city the next morning. Even though we were up late, my eyes open bright and early.

"Mmm, what time is it?" she asks as I kiss along her naked shoulder.

"Seven. Time to get up and hit the road."

"Sleep sounds better," she moans into her pillow.

"Come on. Up and at 'em." I smack her ass and she growls at me.

"Fine. But only because I smell coffee and bacon."

Since I was excited to get out of here, I got out of bed early and decided to make my girl a nice, greasy breakfast to soak up all the alcohol she drank last night.

When Freya walks into the kitchen she looks a little worse for wear. I can't help the laugh that escapes when I see her disheveled state. "I don't think I've ever seen you hungover."

"Yeah, I may have gone a little hard last night." Freya shrugs a shoulder and grabs the cup of coffee and piles her plate with bacon and pancakes. "Give me thirty minutes and a couple ibuprofen, and I'll be good to go."

I smile behind my cup, excited as a kid at Christmas to see her in the one place on earth I love almost as much as her.

It takes a few hours to drive out to my place by the lake. The entire time, Freya has a small smile playing on her lips as we enjoy the changing leaves around us and some soft country music coming from the truck's speakers. My hand rests on her thigh with her fingers laced with mine. It's such a small thing, holding hands with my woman, touching her any time I please. It's the first time, first woman, I've ever wanted to do this with, to simply exist with someone.

The morning is nearly gone when I pull up to the secluded cabin by the lake. Freya gets out of the truck and stretches, letting out a groan of discomfort.

"As much as I love road trips, I think my ass needs a break from sitting in a truck."

I walk up to her and grab said ass in my hands. "I'll rub it and make it all better."

"I'm sure you will." Freya smiles wide and looks around the property. "It's so quiet here," she whispers, as though her voice would disturb the peace.

"That's why I love coming out here. I can actually think."

"What do you think about when you're here?" she asks, looping her arms around my waist.

"Mostly about the club."

We both laugh, and Freya shakes her head. "You can take the man out of the job..."

"When you left, I came out here a lot. Back then, I thought about you and what a mess our lives turned into. How I ruined us."

Freya's eyes soften when she looks at me. "You didn't ruin us. The Cataldis and my dad were responsible for that," she grumbles.

"It didn't feel that way at eighteen, though."

"No, I suppose it wouldn't."

Freya and I stand next to the truck, holding each other and breathing in the peace I've always found here. It never occurred to me that one day I'd be here with her. I'd thought about it, sure. In the back of my mind, I'd imagined having her here, swimming in the lake or lying in the old hammock I hung between two huge trees with me, but it was a pipe dream. And today, it's my reality.

"Come on. Let's get our stuff inside, and we can make lunch," she says, pulling away and opening the back door of the truck.

"It's nice not having to lug around your files anymore," I say, grabbing the one suitcase she brought with her.

"You're telling me."

We walk into the small cabin and Freya spins, taking in the outdated decor and tiny space.

"I'd say I'll give you the grand tour, but this is it. Bedroom and bathroom are right there," I point to the two doors next to each other. "Kitchen is right there," I point to the left, where the small stove and fridge are visible from where we stand. "And the living room." My hand swings around the room we're already standing in.

"It's perfect." Her face is alight with happiness, this place already working its magic on her.

I bring our things into the bedroom and set them on the floor next to the bed while Freya unpacks the groceries we stopped for on the way here.

"Have you talked to Knox?" she calls as I'm walking out of the bedroom.

"Yup. We lifted the lockdown, so back to business as usual."

Which means back to late nights at my desk and never-ending paperwork.

"I'm sure everyone is relieved."

I nod absently and watch her chop the vegetables and cold chicken for a salad. Don't get me wrong, I'm so fucking relieved the Italians are too busy scrambling right now to worry about the club or Freya, but I'm wondering what comes next. Now that the Cataldis are out of the picture for the time being and Freya just won the biggest case of her career and doesn't need my protection anymore, where does that leave us? She loves me, I have no doubt of that, but her life is in Boston, and mine is in Shine. There're a lot of unanswered questions hanging between us. Neither of us has voiced them, maybe because there's been so much pressure and stress with the trial. Since we finally have a second to breathe, we're enjoying the peace. Or maybe because neither of us is ready for the hard questions and even harder truths. Freya is a US attorney and I'm the president of a motorcycle club. I live my life skirting around the laws she's obligated to uphold. Doesn't exactly make for a match made in heaven.

There's no way in hell I'd ever ask her to give up her career, just like she wouldn't ask me to give up the club. So where does that leave us? We're two people who love each other despite spending fifteen years trying to re-create the magic that's always been unique to us. Or, in my case, ignoring the possibility that there could be someone else out there.

Nah, that was never going to be a possibility, I think as I watch her toss a sliced tomato in her mouth and do a cute as fuck little shimmy with her hips.

"You chopping or eating, pretty girl?" I walk up behind her, sliding my palms under her sweater and around her waist.

"I'm multitasking," she says, popping a cucumber into my mouth.

I quickly chew and swallow the vegetable so I can kiss the side of her neck, then spin her in my hold and plunge my tongue into her mouth.

Breaking the kiss, I trail my lips down her neck as my fingers find the clasp of her bra. "Lunch can wait, yeah?

I haven't been inside you all day, and that's a downright travesty."

"It's salad. Not like it's going to get cold."

I smirk down at my girl and snap the hooks on her bra open.

"Arms up."

Freya complies, and I slide her sweater and bra over her head, leaving her topless. Fuck food. The only thing I want to feast on is all her smooth skin displayed in front of me.

My hands go to her breasts, and I mold the soft flesh in my hands, squeezing them together, then bend to take each hard nipple in my mouth. Her hips buck forward, searching for something to rub her needy cunt against.

A chuckle rumbles from my chest against her flesh, and I release her nipple from between my teeth. After pushing the ingredients for the salad aside, I yank her jeans down and set her naked ass on the counter.

"This seems a little unsanitary," she quips.

"I don't give a shit. I'll clean the fucking counter after I eat your pussy."

Freya leans back, her head resting against the cupboard, with a wicked smile on her face. She spreads her legs wider apart, putting herself even more on display for me.

"By all means, then."

I drop to my knees and a low growl escapes my throat when my face is perfectly aligned with her glistening

center. I couldn't care less about any lingering questions or the damn salad she's making when her cunt
is practically begging for my tongue and fingers.

"Hold on to the edge, pretty girl," is the last thing I
say before attacking her pussy with my mouth.

My tongue goes straight to her clit, and I flick it over
and over while she squirms on the countertop. Next,
I add two fingers in her channel and begin pumping.
Freya wraps her thighs around my head, but I can still
hear her cries of pleasure even though they're muffled
by how tightly Freya is squeezing my ears.

Pulling my head back, she mewls in protest, but
I quickly replace my tongue with the fingers of my
other hand and stand. I need to see her fall apart,
not from between her legs but face to face. I need a
full view of the blush that covers her entire body and
watch her eyes roll back when she comes so prettily
for me.

I kiss her deeply. One thing I fucking love about my
woman is she doesn't shy away from my mouth being
on hers after I've just eaten her pussy. I'd even venture
to guess it spurs her on with the way she attacks my
mouth and sucks on my tongue. Her walls are flutter-
ing around my hand, and just before I know she's going
to come, I pull back and watch her face contort, seeing
the pleasure wash over her. She cries out while my
fingers continue their brutal pace. There isn't a sight
I've ever seen that's more breathtaking than watching
Freya's face as I pull orgasm after orgasm from her.

"I love you," I whisper into her mouth while she comes down, breathless and sated as her body slumps against mine.

There's a strong urge to beat my chest with male pride that I've never felt before. I refrain, but just barely.

Wrapping her legs around my waist, I carry her naked form into the bedroom and lay her on the bed. I strip from my shirt and pants, hurriedly throwing them to the side before lying next to her.

"Get on top of me, pretty girl. I want to watch you ride me." I've taken Freya in every way imaginable in the last week, but having her ride my dick has to be my favorite way to have her. It's a front-row seat to my favorite show that I'll never get tired of watching. What man in their right mind would?

Freya leans up and swings her leg over my waist, leaning forward and shrouding us in her long, dark-blonde hair.

"I love you, Ozzy." her mouth meets mine as she sinks down on my painfully hard erection. The second I'm sheathed in her wet pussy, a sense of rightness, of home, overwhelms me. There's something different about this. Something primal and deep. Maybe it's being here. Maybe it's not having the threat of the Cataldis hanging over us. I'm not going to question it right now. Shit, I can barely think straight as Freya grinds down, taking me as deep as she can. She leans back farther as I pump in and out of her, tilting her head to the ceiling with her eyes pinched shut as her hair tickles the top of my thighs. It gives me the perfect view of my cock sliding in and out of her. I hold her hip in one hand as my other comes to her clit, and I begin rubbing. I need to use everything I have at my disposal to get another orgasm from her because I'm not going to be able to hold back much longer.

Her movements become jerky, and I take over, pumping up hard and fast from beneath her.

"Get there, baby. I want you to squeeze my cock while I come."

"Fuck, fuck, fuck," she chants, and her walls clamp down around me, sucking me deeper into her tight, wet core.

The roar that bursts from me when I let go is loud and deep, probably scaring away any wildlife around the cabin. Freya collapses onto my chest, a mess of tangled hair and damp skin.

"Goddamn, pretty girl. You fucking wreck me."

She lets out a contented sigh. "Same," she whispers sleepily into my chest.

We lie together in comfortable silence as the sweat cools on our heated skin and our breathing returns to normal. Being out from under the weight of the trial and Freya being targeted has lifted something in both of us. We can finally get a sense of what our future together holds.

"Have you given any thought to what happens now that your case is over?"

"I move on to the next one, I suppose." She doesn't sound excited at the prospect. "Get back on the hamster wheel." Freya shrugs.

"That doesn't sound appealing."

Freya lets out a long sigh. "Yes and no, I guess. Don't get me wrong, what I do is important, but sometimes it feels like I'm chasing my tail. I don't think, for a second, there won't be another case against the Cataldis in the next few years. When you cut the head off the worm, it just grows back."

"Why do it then?" I ask, lightly trailing my fingers up and down her smooth back.

Freya is silent for a few moments, mulling over her answer. "What else can I do? I've been living and breathing putting away the bad guys for as long as I can remember. Even before graduating high school, I knew this was going to be my path."

"It doesn't sound like you're finding what you want from it anymore."

"There's disillusionment when you achieve any goal, I suppose. Did you think being an MC president was going to be what it is?"

I can't fault her logic, but I had a pretty good idea. "Some parts are exactly what I thought. The paperwork, on the other hand...that shit sucks."

She lets out a small chuckle. "Not very badass outlaw biker of you."

"I'm still a badass, pretty girl," I say, tickling her waist. "But I'll always take my responsibilities and the livelihood of my brothers seriously."

Freya laughs and tries to squirm away. I decide to show her mercy and end the tickle torture when I place a sweet kiss on her lips.

"Have you ever thought of doing something else?" Like, come back to Shine and stay? Be with me so we can have this every day, not just the odd weekend when neither of us is too busy?

Freya's quiet. Too quiet. Is this where she tells me it was nice reconnecting thanks for the orgasms, but her life is in Boston?

"Honestly," she starts. "No, I never considered not being a lawyer. Lately, though... lately I've been questioning if the path I chose is still what I want."

There's a painfully raw honesty in her quiet voice. She isn't ready to talk about it. It can't be easy questioning why everything you thought was going to make you happy and fulfill your dreams suddenly seems like a chore, draining you of joy.

"You don't need the answers today, sweetheart," I tell her, sensing the turmoil inside her mind.

She smiles up at me. "I love you."

Freya knows I'm letting her off the hook—and she knows why, too. She needs time to figure out if being a US attorney is still right for her, still what she wants. And I'll be right next to her while she does.

CHAPTER TWENTY
FREYA

B efore yesterday, no, that's not right, before Ozzy kissed me in front of Finn's safe house, I never imagined moving back to Shine. In fact, until Liam dropped me on the doorstep of the clubhouse after my attack, I never even considered stepping foot back in Shine. Too many bad memories, or at the very least, good memories that became shrouded in heartbreak.

The disconnect between my job and feeling like I'm making an actual difference has been tickling the back of my mind for the last couple years if I'm being honest with myself. I'm just really good at ignoring the incessant little voice telling me I'm only doing this job for revenge, or because my parents are proud of me for what they see as accomplishments or a myriad of other reasons that don't have anything to do with what I actually want. Now, that voice has gotten louder and much harder to ignore. Especially when I wake up every morning next to a six-foot-three biker whom I've been in love with since I was eighteen.

To his credit, all Ozzy has done is ask the questions I'm beginning to seriously ask myself. Before this case, my doubts were chalked up to exhaustion. Those doubts are easy to dismiss once you've had some rest and are back at it with a shiny new case, especially when the cases become more and more high profile. I've made a name for myself as being a shark to go up against, and I've worked damn hard to earn that reputation.

But at what cost? And is the cost even worth it anymore?

I accomplished what I set out to do, which was to take down a powerful criminal, and I'm so fucking happy I did. But there's always going to be another one, then another, and another. What if what's important to me isn't in Boston anymore? What if it's with the man currently making coffee and toast in the kitchen while I get dressed so he can take me out on his little boat tied to a dock outside his cabin in his own personal slice of happiness?

"Here's your phone," I say, handing Ozzy his cell as I walk into the kitchen to pour myself a cup of coffee.

"Thanks. Reception out here is shoddy, so I never worry about it. We have a landline in case of emergencies, but Gramps always turns the ringer off. Says he likes the quiet too much to be disrupted by spam calls."

Ozzy walks into the living room. "Usually, if you stand in just the right spot..." his voice trails off when ping after ping sounds from his phone. Ozzy stands stock-still as he reads each message, his jaw tightening more and more with every second that passes. He looks up from his phone, his terrified gaze clashing with mine as we hear the sound of multiple cars racing up the dirt driveway of the cabin. Ozzy runs to the window and peeks out the blinds before looking back to me.

"Bedroom. Now," he barks.

"What's going on?" I ask as he stalks toward me, grabbing me by the upper arm and propelling me into the bedroom. He opens the small closet door and sweeps the hanging sweaters and jackets to the side, revealing a removable panel completely flush with the drywall in the back of the closet.

"Ozzy, what the hell is going on?" I'm panicking as someone knocks hard on the front door. Ozzy turns around from the well-hidden hole in the closet with two shotguns and three handguns in his arms. He throws the weapons on the bed and slams the bedroom door. Bringing his phone to his ear, he taps a name and waits for the call to connect.

"Goddammit," he growls, throwing the phone on the bed next to his stockpile of weapons. "The Cataldis are here."

All-consuming terror like I've never felt before rips through my chest.

"Finn was trying to get ahold of me, but this fucking reception is shit."

He walks around to the other side of the bed and grabs the guns on the bed, setting them on the floor next to us. In one swift movement, he flips the mattress so it blocks the one window facing the back of his property. Next, he rushes to the large dresser between the bedroom door and the closet and shoves it in front of the exit.

When he comes back to the other side of the bed, he tugs me down and moves the nightstand, revealing a small black button. He slams his palm against it, then hands me a shotgun and pistol. I immediately check the chamber of the handgun. Seeing it's loaded, I set it next to me and grab the other shotgun, loading it, then setting it next to the other gun.

"That's a panic button," he says, coming to kneel next to me. He flips one of the box springs on its side, shielding us from the bedroom door. It won't do anything to protect us if bullets come flying through the door, but it hides us from plain view.

"Just in case any of your enemies came looking for you here?"

"I told you the reception is practically nonexistent. That just sent a 9-1-1 message to all the brothers."

"Do they know the Cataldis are here?"

"I'm not sure. Finn said he was trying to get a hold of Knox. They're two hours away, and Finn sent me the first text thirty minutes ago."

Hope that the MC was going to come charging up the driveway any second to help save us from the mess we're in quickly vanishes.

"No one is coming?" I ask, holding my breath.

"I don't know, pretty girl." The devastated look on Ozzy's face makes me want to cry, but it won't do a damn bit of good.

The pounding on the front door begins again.

"Ozzy," someone calls. "We know you're in there. Make it easy on yourselves."

Ozzy shakes his head and stays still, listening for God only knows what.

"How about we make a deal? We just want the lawyer."

"Bullshit," Ozzy whispers.

I'm trying to keep a brave face and not shake like a fucking leaf with this shotgun in my hand. Ozzy's face is hard as he listens for any movement. This is the first time I've seen him as the outlaw MC president he is. It reminds me of the look his dad had on his face when the Italians stormed the clubhouse all those years ago.

"If anyone comes through that door, blow a hole through their gut. No head shots. Those are harder. Always aim for center mass."

I nod and stare at the door, clutching tightly to the shotgun. It doesn't escape me that I'm in nearly the exact same position as Tanya was in the clubhouse when I was shot. We made it out then, and I have to have faith we'll make it out of this, too. Of course, the stark difference being there are only two of us, and God only knows how many of them.

Squeezing my eyes shut, I send a prayer to whoever is listening for help to get to us soon. I have a feeling it's going unheard today.

There's a loud crash from the front of the house and heavy footfalls sound throughout the space.

"They're inside," I squeak out.

Someone tries to open the door to the bedroom, but their efforts are halted by the dresser blocking the door.

Ozzy pops up and fires three shots through the door. A yell erupts from the other side.

"Fuck, I'm hit," an agonized voice calls from the living room.

If he's still talking, it means he's not dead. *Fuck.*

"Ozzy, how long do you think you can hold out? Help isn't coming. At least not before we get to you and the girl." The voice on the other side of the door is taunting and dark, sending shivers down my spine.

Two shots pierce the wall above our heads, and Ozzy pops up, sending another four through the bedroom door.

"Okay, have it your way," someone else yells from the living room.

"Who is that? What does that mean?" I ask, staring at Ozzy.

"I don't know. Fuck."

We hear the intruders' heavy footfalls in the house and then silence. I'm sure they didn't leave, but what the hell are they up to?

"We just have to keep them out until the Irish or the brothers arrive, Freya."

"Ozzy, you said it yourself. They're too far away, and the Cataldis know that."

Through the mattress-covered window of the bedroom, we hear stomping boots and liquid being splashed around outside.

"Ozzy?" I whisper.

He doesn't respond, the look on his face telling me he's running through scenarios in his head.

The next thing I smell is the pungent odor of gasoline. Seconds later, I hear the whoosh of flames licking up the outside wall as men whoop and holler.

"Oh my God, Ozzy. They lit the house on fire."

It's not like we can shoot at them through the wall. It would only create holes for the fire to spread faster inside.

Ozzy takes my face in his damp palms and looks me dead in the eye.

"Listen to me, Freya. They're trying to smoke us out, which tells me they want us both alive. If not, they would have come in here, guns blazing. They know we don't have the manpower to fight them off. We have two choices."

I look at him with wide eyes, terrified of what he's going to say but knowing he's right.

"We can either let the fire engulf the cabin and die inside..." If the heat I feel from the fire outside the window is any indication, we aren't far off from that. "Or we can walk out there and let them take us," he finishes.

I frantically shake my head from side to side before he can finish his sentence. "I hate both of those. There has to be another way out."

His gaze softens and the pain behind his eyes is breaking my fucking heart.

There is no other way out of this.

"I wish like hell I had a better option, pretty girl. But there isn't one." He presses his forehead to mine as smoke fills the room, and I let out a hacking cough. "Know this: my brothers will make sure, come hell or high water, that you'll be rescued. They know we're in trouble, and they won't stop until you're safe."

Tears are pouring down my face from the smoke. The realization that this sounds an awful lot like goodbye hits me painfully in the chest.

"What about you?" I croak out.

"I'm not going to lie to you, baby. They'd be stupid to let me live. I'm a threat to whatever plan they're trying to pull off. Taking out the president of the Black Roses would put them at a definite advantage."

"You can't expect me to walk out there knowing they'll probably kill you." My entire body is shaking. Walking out that door and into a world where Ozzy won't exist anymore goes against every fiber of my being.

"Staying here kills us both. I refuse to let that happen. Pretty girl, I've loved you since I was eighteen. That has never and will never change. This is the best option to make sure you survive."

The glass on the other side of the window explodes. Flames and thick black smoke immediately engulf the room.

"We have to move. Now." Ozzy grabs my hand and drags me to the bedroom door, knocking the large dresser out of the way with almost superhuman strength. He opens the door and calls, "We're coming out."

The smoke is quickly filling the cabin from the back bedroom. There isn't a doubt in my mind the entire cabin will be engulfed in flames in a matter of minutes. Tears are pouring from my eyes, and it isn't just from the smoke.

When Ozzy opens the front door, he keeps me shielded behind him as we walk onto the front porch.

"We're unarmed," he says.

Peeking around his arm, I see three black SUVs and at least twelve men with their guns pointed at us.

We never stood a chance.

"I'll come with you. Just don't hurt him," I call to the man in front, who looks to be in charge. None of these men look familiar, so I'm sure I haven't seen any of them in the files from the case.

The men chuckle and the one in front steps forward. "Let's get something straight. You don't get a say in what we do to your boyfriend, puttana."

Ozzy lets out a low, angry growl. I don't speak Italian, but I doubt whatever the man said was a compliment. We make no effort to move, and the man blows out an annoyed breath as though we're somehow inconveniencing him.

"Fine, fine." He waves his hands and the men behind him lower their weapons but still hold them tightly in their grips. "We won't hurt him."

He motions for us to walk down the stairs. Considering the only other alternative is to run back into a smoke-filled house and to our certain deaths, Ozzy and I make our way down the steps with my hand still tightly grasped in his.

Three men walk forward and pass the man giving the orders. One grabs me by the forearm and yanks me away from Ozzy as the other two grab Ozzy's arms. He uselessly fights against their grip, his fight-or-flight instinct kicking in, and I watch him struggle in vain as tears pour down my cheeks. We have no idea what's going to happen, and there's nothing we can do about it. Another large man walks forward and punches Ozzy square in the jaw, knocking him out cold. The only reason he doesn't fall face-first into the dirt is the other two are holding him up. Though he's unconscious, the man wails on his face a few more times before shaking out his fist.

"You said you wouldn't hurt him," I scream.

Everyone laughs at my outrage, and the man in charge simply shrugs. "What can I say? I lied."

It's then I realize I was an idiot for believing for even a second that what Ozzy said wasn't true. There is absolutely nothing and no one stopping these men from killing us where we stand. I have nothing to offer them in exchange for our lives. I'm the reason their boss is going to spend the rest of his life in prison, for God's sake.

The man holding my arm in his tight grip starts digging around in his pocket for something. Swiveling my head toward him, I see him take a syringe from his coat. He uses his teeth to remove the cap of the needle before plunging it into my neck. All the fight leaves me, and seconds later, my limbs give out, making it impossible for me to stand on my own. I desperately try to fight against the drug, but it's no use, and I fall into a black hole of unconsciousness.

Fuck, I'm so cold. Tremors rack my body from lack of heat, the movement making my teeth chatter so hard they're liable to break in my mouth. The smell of smoke is still pungent in my nose. It takes a moment to remember why it's there. My eyes snap open, and I'm met with darkness and a bitter chill. Sharp plastic cuts into the skin around my wrists when I attempt to move my arms. Those assholes have my arms and legs tied to a fucking chair.

Bile works its way up my throat, along with an overwhelming surge of panic.

Keep it together, Freya.

I inhale several long, deep breaths, trying like hell to calm my nerves. The thought almost makes me laugh.

Does it really matter how calm I am? I've been abducted by the Italian Mafia and the man I love is probably lying dead in front of the burned-out shell of the cabin he once loved, the one he wanted to share with me. Who the fuck cares if I go to my death a blubbering mess of fear? I'm still dead either way.

"Shh, I'm right here, pretty girl."

My head whips to the side. It's dark as hell, wherever we are, but my eyes have adjusted enough to see the outline of a man tied to a chair a few feet to the right of me.

"Ozzy?" I croak out.

"It's me. Are you okay? Did they...did they hurt you?"

I know what he's asking, and I shake my head, though I'm not sure he can see it. "No. They stuck me with a needle after that lying piece of shit knocked you out."

Ozzy chuckles, then lets out a pained groan. "Honey, did you really expect them to keep their promise? Criminals aren't exactly known for their trustworthiness, especially these guys."

Now that the panic has receded a tiny bit because Ozzy is still alive, I'm able to focus my eyes better and take in the man next to me. His face is bruised and bloody. A gash is oozing blood from a cut above his brow, over his eye that's swollen shut. A dark bruise has formed over his other cheek. Considering the light is minimal in what looks to be a warehouse they're holding us in, I can only imagine how awful he would look in better lighting.

"Do you know how long we've been here?" I ask,

"Probably a few hours." He nods toward the window in the back corner. It doesn't look to be pitch black outside, but the light has faded considerably since we were standing outside the cabin.

"Do you have any idea where we are?" My voice is still hoarse and painful from the smoke.

"I think we're at the docks. I heard a few ship horns blow."

"So, we're in Cataldi territory," I surmise.

"Sounds like it, but no one has been in since they brought us here."

I don't know if that's a good or bad thing.

As I'm considering my question, a door at the other end of the warehouse opens, but it's too dark to see who's walked in. Unhurried steps are heard as three, maybe four men make their way over to us. My heart rate is through the roof as the men near, not knowing what they want or who they are. All of a sudden, the lights of the warehouse illuminate overhead, momentarily blinding me. I squeeze my eyes shut until the burning sensation lessens. When I open them, four men stand before me. One I recognize instantly.

"So nice to finally meet you. I believe you know my father."

CHAPTER TWENTY-ONE
Ozzy

Motherfuck. Am I surprised? No. Do I think we're royally screwed? One hundred percent.

What was supposed to be a nice weekend getaway for Freya and me to celebrate her victory—and maybe figure out what the future holds for us—has turned into a nightmare of epic proportions. The man in front of us is proof of that.

"Hello, Carlo," I say to Francesco Cataldi's son. "If I'd have known you were stopping by, I would have made myself presentable." Hopefully, by putting the attention on myself, it will take it off Freya and give me a minute to figure out what the hell to do.

Carlo laughs, but it's a hollow sound. "Now, now. Don't worry yourself over it."

I've never met the man in person. He's about the same age as Freya and me with a story not too different from mine. He's been the right-hand man of his father's for longer than I was with mine. I came into leadership long before him, considering I've been president of the MC for the last five years and his father just went away.

Guess the Cataldis aren't scrambling as bad as Finn was led to believe.

Or maybe these assholes were prepared for the inevitable, and Carlo has been patiently waiting in the wings to take over the empire his old man built. We're both the heirs to the throne, except I'm going to make damn sure his kingdom crumbles. He had the audacity to take my girl and leave me alive. Stupid fuck.

"You know, Ms. Campbell," he begins, turning his slimy gaze to Freya. "We could have avoided all this unpleasantness if you would have just played along with what my men asked of you. But no, you had to go full steam ahead. If it was any of your other counterparts, we probably would have let it drop, but you're too damn good at your job."

"Should I be flattered?" Freya asks with an attitude I really wish she didn't have. It's never a good idea to piss off the man who holds your fate in his hands. Attempting to stare a hole in the side of her head does nothing. Freya is too busy staring daggers at Carlo.

"You have fire," Carlo comments. "I like that."

He walks over to her and twirls her hair in his fingers with a sadistic smirk slashed across his face.

It takes everything in me not to roar for him to get his filthy hands off her, but I have to refrain. If I'm injured any further, or if he sees Freya as more of a weakness for me than he already does, who knows what kind of condition we'll be in when my brothers get here. And make no mistake, I believe with every fiber of my being, they will come. Freya and I haven't found each other again to be torn apart like this.

"Our tactics in the past have usually been successful in escaping jail time for our men unless we needed to make a show of being weak." Carlo continues to stare at Freya as he speaks. "Your father's case helped with that."

"What are you talking about?" Freya asks.

Carlo chuckles. "Do you honestly think we didn't plan for that? We wanted to look weak. It gave us time to put some plans in motion. Everyone thought we were dying out. The other families, the Irish, even the Black Roses. No one was concerned with us, thinking we were happy to have what we had left and were too scared to make moves."

He turns to me. "Why did you think we let what your father and grandfather did in retaliation for the shooting at your club go?"

Well, I'll be goddamned. These fucks were a lot smarter than I gave them credit for. Shit, what anyone gave them credit for.

"Sure, we lost some decent men during that time, but they were shortsighted. They didn't see the big picture. I should really thank your dad for cleaning up a mess we would have had to deal with eventually."

"It's nice to know how much you value your men's lives," I bite out, looking at the other three in the room with him. "Hope you're all prepared to be sacrificial lambs."

"Don't bother, Ozzy. These three know exactly what it takes to get where we are. Their loyalty is unwavering."

I didn't expect them to turn on Carlo this instant, but when seeds of doubt are planted, they eventually grow. If any of them make it out of here alive, that is.

"Besides, my men are well rewarded. Aren't you Roberto?"

The big guy, who I recognize as the one who knocked me out in front of the cabin, steps forward with an evil grin.

"You know what I've been doing for the last fifteen years, Ozzy?" Carlo asks.

"Haven't the foggiest," I reply.

"Research and planning. In the last five years, those plans have been coming to fruition. My father didn't have the stomach for a lot of it," he laughs, but the sound is bitter. "Fitting, considering that's where the cancer has been eating him."

Say what now?

Carlo catches my look of surprise and tilts his head. I look at Freya, who's just as shocked as I am.

"Oh, this is so perfect," Carlo laughs out. "You thought he was going to spend the rest of his long life in prison." He points at Freya. "Tell me, would you have worked so hard knowing the man has months, maybe a year tops, to live?"

Freya closes her eyes, the reality of the situation hitting her.

"Doesn't feel so good to know you put a dying man to live the rest of his life behind bars as cancer ravages his body." He's enjoying rubbing salt in the wound.

"Why attack me, then? Why try to get me to lose evidence?" she asks.

"I wanted to see how far we could bend you. It's worked before with your predecessors. It didn't with you, though, so now we find ourselves here. And lucky for us, I get to kill two birds with one stone. At first, I wasn't interested in dealing with you after the conviction, thinking too many eyes would be on me and my organization, but I realized that was shortsighted of me. It's time everyone comprehends how powerful I've made my family. Not my father. Me. I'll make a pretty penny off you and the world will be short one more Black Rose," he finishes, turning his gaze to me.

"Pretty penny?" Freya asks.

"Ah yes, that brings me back to what I've been working on. Alberto, God rest his soul"—Carlo makes the sign of the cross and I have to stifle my laughter—"took care of a lot of the day-to-day operations of the skin trade for me until those Irish bastards put him to ground."

Alberto was the man Charlie's ex had made a deal with trying to sell out the Irish and us. When that didn't work, he tried to sell Charlie to him.

"He's a sex trafficker, Freya. That's how he's been making the family their money," I supply.

And this bastard thinks he's going to put Freya through that. Not a fucking chance, asshole.

"Roberto, come take a taste of our new toy."

The man walks forward, and Freya begins to struggle in her bindings, nearly toppling the chair she's strapped to over onto the dirty concrete floor.

"Oh goody, he likes when they fight. You'd be surprised how many buyers like the feisty ones." He faces me, and I see his smile from the corner of my eye. I refuse to look at him though, my eyes trained on Roberto as he circles Freya. He leans down and grabs her breast in his hand, squeezing it roughly. A tear falls from her terrified eyes and every muscle in my body is tight with rage. If I thought breaking my bindings would get us out of here, this metal chair would be lying in pieces on the floor.

Roberto leans over and licks the tear from Freya's face as she tries to wrench her head away from his disgusting mouth. That motherfucker is going to lose his tongue when I get my hands on him.

"How does she taste?" Carlo calls to the soon-to-be-dead man in front of Freya.

"Like strawberries, boss."

"That means he likes it. Strawberries are his favorite."

Suddenly, loud shouts can be heard from outside the warehouse. Carlo turns to the other two men and nods his head toward the door. Before they can step outside, a loud explosion detonates, and the steel door flies from its hinges in a cloud of smoke. Knox, Linc and Jude file in, followed closely by two of my other brothers, Wyatt and Barrett. Shots ring out and the two men who Carlo sent to check things out duck behind large spindles of cable to avoid the shots.

"We're here," I call to my men so they know where to try to avoid aiming their weapons.

Roberto crouches behind my woman, attempting to use her as a human shield. Fucking coward.

"Kill her," I hear Carlo call from somewhere to my left. The piece of shit went to hide behind a pallet stacked with thick metal tubing.

I watch Roberto raise his gun to Freya's head, and I desperately struggle with the zip ties holding my hands behind my back. A loud shout erupts from me as I yank down hard, breaking the plastic, and I lunge toward Roberto. Before I make it, a gunshot explodes and Roberto crumbles to the ground, blood immediately pooling around him. I kick the gun from his reach and raise my eyes, seeing my dad with a pistol in his grip pointed at the man.

"Jesus, Dad. Little close to Freya."

I'm on my knees behind her as she shakes with fear and adrenaline coursing through her body.

"Excuse you, son, but who taught you how to shoot?"

Dad reaches Roberto as I break the ties around Freya's wrists and ankles.

"Come here, pretty girl."

She collapses into me, wrapping her legs and arms tightly around my middle before I have a chance to get up from the cold concrete floor.

"He's still alive," Dad says with two of his fingers against Roberto's neck.

"Good," I reply.

His death is mine.

My brothers have taken out the other two, their lifeless bodies slumped to the ground.

A moment later, I hear a door open and gunshots ring out outside the building next to where I'd heard Carlo call for Freya's death.

"Motherfucker," my dad curses, popping up and running toward the door with Wyatt and Barrett taking off after him.

Jude and Linc come to stand next to me and Freya, their eyes scanning the warehouse and guns at the ready, just in case any surprises jump out at us.

"How many were here?" Jude asks.

"Four, including Carlo," I reply as I run a hand over Freya's back. "Shh, pretty girl. Let me look at you." I pull away slightly to scan my woman for injuries from any stray bullets. When I'm satisfied she's whole, I wrap her tightly in my arms, cooing and whispering to her over and over that she's okay, that we're safe, that it's over as she sobs uncontrollably into my chest.

Dad and my other two brothers stomp back inside, followed by Finn and two of his men.

"The asshole got away. He had a fucking armored car waiting for him," Barrett supplies.

Goddammit. I wanted to watch that bastard bleed.

"What about him?" my dad asks, pointing to the bleeding man on the floor.

"He's mine," I answer.

My dad nods toward Barrett and Wyatt. They walk over to Roberto, one grabbing his arms, the other his legs, and carry him out the open doorway they came through when they stormed in.

"Come on, son. Cash is in the van."

"I don't want Freya in the same car as that piece of shit."

"Good thing Gramps brought another van."

I nod, and my dad and Knox help lift me from the floor so I don't have to set Freya down. Finn follows us out of the warehouse and stops me before I can get in the back of Gramps's van.

"I want to be there when you question Roberto," he tells me.

"Then you better follow us. He's not long for this world."

Finn tilts his head before I turn to leave. "Understood."

We make our way back to the clubhouse in a few hours, and I pray that Roberto makes the drive. Having him die on the way to his execution would be wholly unsatisfying.

Freya is silent for most of the ride, only letting out little sobs every now and again.

"You're okay now, pretty girl. I've got you." It doesn't matter how many times I reassure her, she doesn't speak. Every time I try to pull away to look at her face, she burrows into my hold even more so. That's fine. If what she needs right now is to hold on to me and not face anything or anyone, then that's exactly what I'll give her.

When we pull into the parking lot of the clubhouse, Tanya, Lucy, and Charlie come barreling out of the door before we can park. The other van with Roberto in it heads to the back of the building. Rather than carrying his bleeding body through the clubhouse for everyone to witness, Cash made the right call to park next to the back door, where there's an entrance to the hallway leading to the basement. Plenty of men have taken their final breaths down there, and Roberto is about to have his name added to that list.

Tanya opens the back door of the van as Freya lifts her head from my chest.

"Oh, honey," Tanya coos, holding out her arms.

For the first time since leaving the warehouse, Freya removes herself from my lap and falls into Tanya's out-stretched arms.

"Let's get you cleaned up, sweetheart," she tells Freya, walking away with my woman tucked into her side.

Tanya looks back to me and I smile, mouthing my thanks as the two women disappear into the clubhouse.

Finn pulls up next to the van and rolls down his window.

"Follow the other van to the back," I direct. "I'll give you a few minutes to get the information you need."

His window rolls up, and he follows my instructions.

There's nothing I want more than to find an outlet for the rage simmering under my skin, but Freya comes first. Always.

Walking into the clubhouse, I spot Charlie and Lucy holding tightly to their men.

"Where is she?" I ask no one in particular.

"Tanya took her to your room to get her cleaned up," Charlie supplies.

I smile in thanks and head back to my room.

Standing at my door, I inhale a deep breath before entering. The adrenaline has worn off, but my soul is tired. So fucking tired. I almost lost the most important person in my life today. She was nearly ripped from me. She had that disgusting man's hands on her, and there was nothing I could do to stop him. I've never felt more helpless in my entire life. No, that's not true. There was one other time. When Freya was bleeding in my arms in the kitchen of this clubhouse.

I open the door to my room and find Tanya laying out some fresh clothes for my woman.

"She's in the bathroom," she says softly.

It takes three long strides to get to the bathroom door, and I knock gently.

"Yeah?" Her small voice can barely be heard through the sound of running water.

Cracking the door an inch, I answer, "It's me. Can I come in?"

"Yeah."

I step into the steamy bathroom and shut the door behind me.

Freya is peeking her head from the other side of the shower curtain. Now that the dirt and grime have been cleared away from her tearstained face, her emotionally charged blue eyes stare at me.

"You okay?" Could I have asked a dumber question?

Freya shakes her head. "No, but I will be."

I send her a small smile. That's my fucking girl. She's a fighter through and through.

"Is he still alive?" she asks.

I work my jaw back and forth, wondering how much I should tell her. She knows he was in the other van. There's no way she could have missed Wyatt and Barrett carrying the huge asshole out of the warehouse.

She must see the indecision in my eyes. "Don't lie to me, Ozzy. I can't take it. Not after everything we've been through today."

I nod. "Okay. Yes, he's still alive."

"Will he be tomorrow?"

I pause and hold her gaze. "No."

Freya lets out a breath and gently shakes her head. "Good." The shower curtain falls closed, and I assume that means I've been dismissed.

I turn to the door, but before my hand twists the knob, I say, "I love you, pretty girl."

"I love you too, Ozzy," she replies from behind the curtain.

There's a resigned ring to her tone, as though it's a fact she's not happy about but can't change. I'm not sure what to do about it at this moment, except let her shower and find comfort with Tanya for a bit while I handle the man who nearly turned her life into a living nightmare. The fact he's breathing the same air as my woman makes me feel like there're a million ants crawling under my skin.

It's time to rectify that situation.

Making my way to the basement, I pass Finn on the stairs.

"You get everything you need?" I ask.

"I did. We'll talk later. Take care of your girl."

"Plan on it."

I shake the man's hand and continue down the stairs to the room we have set up specifically for "questioning" our enemies.

Knox is standing next to the door, waiting for my instruction.

"How is she?" he asks, sounding unusually concerned.

"She'll be fine." And she will be. I'll make damn sure of it. "If you hadn't found us when you did, Knox..." I let the thought trail off, not wanting to think of what that piece of shit in the next room was going to do to my woman right in front of me.

"I'm just sorry we didn't know they were coming after you sooner. Finn's inside guy said Carlo's been really fucking tight-lipped lately. If he hadn't overheard one of Carlo's men on the phone, we wouldn't have known where they took you."

"I could have lost her all over again," I whisper, trying like hell not to break.

"But you didn't." Knox grabs my shoulder and pins me with his stare. "And now you're going to make sure that piece of shit regrets fucking with what's yours."

I straighten my spine and clear my thoughts until my singular focus is on making that asshole pay for what he planned to do to the woman I love.

Opening the door, I step into the room and see the man handcuffed to a chair. Sweat and blood cover his face. Looks like it took some convincing from Finn to get the information he wanted. There's a bandage wrapped around his shoulder, stanching the blood flow from the bullet he took at the warehouse. I walk over and rip the bandage off, the wound oozing when it's uncovered.

"Nasty wound there, Roberto."

He grunts, pale and resigned to what his fate holds.

I walk over to the table in the corner of the room, staring at the implements lying before me.

"You know where you guys fucked up?" I give it a beat, but Roberto doesn't answer. Picking up a pair of garden shears, I turn to the dead man tied to the chair. "You let me live."

To his credit, Roberto doesn't utter a word, but his pale skin goes a shade whiter.

I signal for Knox to come stand next to Roberto and me.

"You thought you could touch my woman. Thought you could put your disgusting hands on her, your mouth on her."

Roberto stares at me. He's trying to hide behind the bravado so many men in this life have, but there's no hiding the true fear in his eyes. It sets my blood on fire, knowing he has no idea how unhinged I can truly be. In the warehouse, I stayed levelheaded instead of shouting useless threats. I never saw the point in telling someone how you planned to make them suffer before snuffing out their useless existence. No, I'd much rather they experience it in the moment.

"Oh Robby, you really should have killed me when you had the chance." I grab the sides of his face in my grip and force his jaw open. He wiggles on the chair. It's amazing the strength an exhausted body can exert when faced with the terror of pain.

"Knox, grab me a clamp."

My best friend saunters over to the table and comes back with the tool in his hand. I shove it in his mouth and attach it to his disgusting tongue, yanking the flesh from his mouth.

"Here, hold this," I direct to Knox.

He takes the end of the clamp from my grip and watches as I line a pair of shears up with Roberto's tongue and snap them closed. Blood pours from his mouth as he lets out loud and obnoxious howls of pain. I ignore his incoherent begging, just like he ignored Freya's.

Roberto's eyes roll back in his head as though he's about to pass out. Grabbing a tube of smelling salts from the table, I wave it under his nose.

"Not so fast there, pal. We're not done."

I walk back over to the table and pick up a recently sharpened pair of large hedge trimmers.

"Which hand was it you grabbed my girl with?" I point the shears back and forth between his fists as though I'm playing eeny, meeny, miney, mo. "Oh, yeah. It was this one." I slide his wrist between the sharp-as-hell blades and, with all my might, yank the blades together and watch his hand fall to the ground.

Roberto screams in agony then promptly passes out from the pain, and this time, I let him. He has minutes before he bleeds out.

"You good, brother?" Knox asks, concern lacing his words. He's never seen me torture a man in such a gruesome manner, but he wasn't with me and Freya in the warehouse. Seeing them touch her, knowing what they had planned, made something snap in me.

"No," I answer honestly. "But I will be."

CHAPTER TWENTY-TWO
FREYA

After Ozzy leaves the bathroom, I continue my shower. There's a man in this building who will be dead by morning if he isn't already. I don't know what to do with that information. I don't know what to do with the fact that I'm happy about it. *What kind of monster does that make me?*

My career has been spent putting killers and horrible people behind bars. Now, I'm justifying that man's murder in my head. In the eyes of the law, it makes no difference. Taking someone's life is illegal. There's no two ways about it. But for the life of me, I can't quite grasp the part of me that says what's happening in the basement is wrong.

Tears fall from my eyes as I attempt to scrub the grimy feeling from my body. I could take a million showers and cover my body with the most potent-smelling soap, and I swear I'll never get rid of the smell of smoke from the cabin or stop feeling the cold from the warehouse we were taken to. Not to mention that disgusting man's hands and tongue on me as he tasted my skin.

A loud cry falls from my lips, and I yell in anger, slapping the shower wall over and over.

"Freya, honey, are you okay?" Tanya calls frantically from the other side of the door.

Why does everyone keep asking me that? No. No, I'm not okay. I was kidnapped and faced a very real threat of being sold into sex slavery. I found out that all the good I thought I was doing as a federal prosecutor was really just a flash in the pan for the organizations I was trying to take down. Sure, I could get more convictions, but at what cost? There is no way Carlo Cataldi is going to let me live if I continue to go after him. He said it himself. I was the one he couldn't get to, and I'm so damn good at my job, I'm a threat.

I wasn't doing the good I'd thought, though, was I? I was just an annoying gnat buzzing in the face of the Italian Mafia.

"I'm fine, Tanya. I'll be out in a minute,"

No use scaring the woman trying to help me half to death by screaming what I really want to. No, I'm not fine. I'm fucking pissed. I'm fucking terrified. I want to go down to that basement and kill that bastard myself, but I'm terrified that if I do, it will make me into a monster I'm not ready to face. I want Ozzy to kill him for me. But I'm scared I won't be able to look at him as my savior anymore and, instead, as someone I should be working to put in jail. But the bastard deserves it. I don't know how to come to terms with knowing what Ozzy's doing is wrong but being okay with it, understanding it, and even wanting it.

I turn the shower off because I'm not going to find the answers under the spray, and I wrap myself in a fluffy towel. When I step from the bathroom, Tanya is sitting on the edge of Ozzy's bed.

"I laid some clothes out for you. I'll give you some privacy." She stands to leave, but panic grips me.

"No," I nearly shout at the poor woman. "Please stay. I...I..."

Tanya looks at me with a soft smile on her face and sits back down. "It's okay, honey. I know what it's like to not want to be alone." She turns so her back is facing me. "I'll just sit right here until you're dressed."

I hurriedly throw on the baggy sweats and thick sweatshirt she gathered for me. When I bring the collar of the soft material to my nose, I smell Ozzy's spicy, leathery scent. Much better than the smoke smell I thought would never leave.

"Okay," I say, and Tanya turns around.

She motions for me to sit on the bed, then grabs a brush from the dresser. "Here, let me brush out your hair."

I do as she says. It's been years since anyone other than my hairdresser has taken this kind of care with my long locks. Tanya has a mother's touch that I desperately need right now.

Sitting on the bed, my gaze meets our reflection in the mirror. My eyes are haunted, while hers are warm.

"Do you wish you had daughters?"

Tanya laughs. "Good Lord, no. There was enough drama with two boys growing up in the house. A girl..." Her voice trails off. "I would have been scared for."

Her response is...odd.

"Why scared?" I ask.

Tanya gets up and sets the brush on the dresser. She walks back over to the bed, pulls the heavy winter comforter down and motions for me to get under the warm blanket. She then proceeds to tuck me in like I'm six years old and a burrito. It's a silly little thing, but there's no denying the comfort it brings, nearly making my eyes well with tears again.

"Did you know I was married before I came to Shine?" Tanya asks as she swings her jean-clad legs on the bed and props herself up next to me against the headboard.

"I know you came from a bad situation, but I don't think I've ever heard Linc or Knox talk about their life before they came to Shine."

A small, sad smile tilts her lips. "No, I suppose they wouldn't. I never married Knox's dad. Got pregnant right out of high school, and he didn't stick around long. I was broke with a baby living in Tennessee, and my parents were less than willing to help me out." She lets out a huff and shakes her head. "I met Linc's dad when I was cleaning hotel rooms. Seemed like a nice enough guy. He was traveling for work, and I caught his eye. I thought I'd won the jackpot having a handsome man interested in me who had a good job and was kind to me and my kid." Tanya shakes her head and looks toward the ceiling. "When he got offered a job in Nebraska where he wouldn't have to travel so much, he took it and wanted me and Knox to come with him. Knox was a baby, and I was convinced my ex would make a great dad. Not long after we got to Nebraska, I got pregnant with Linc." The love she has for her boys shines brightly in her smile when she talks about them.

"Two boys under two. You must have been going crazy."

"I was." She chuckles. "But it was a good kind of crazy. They kept me on my toes, but they were the sweetest little things."

I'm having a hard time thinking of Knox as a sweet kid rather than the intense biker I know him as today.

"Things were great for a few years. I was home with my boys and my ex had a great job. It was everything I'd hoped for, the kind of home anyone would be lucky to grow up in. Until it wasn't." Tanya bites her lip and lets out a deep sigh. "He got laid off and started drinking. Heavily. I don't know, maybe he got fired for drinking. It all happened so fast. One day, he was going to work and coming home to play with his kids, and the next, he was drinking all day and only coming home if he needed money or he was mad and needed someone to rail on. I kicked him out so many times, and so many times, he promised to quit, to be a better dad and a better husband. Finally, I got him out of the house for what I thought was going to be the last time. It wasn't."

I look up at her tear-filled eyes and remove one arm from under the tightly tucked covers, placing my hand on her arm.

"He came back wanting money. I was a single mom waitressing at a little diner, trying to make ends meet for my boys and keep a roof over our heads. It wasn't easy, and I scrimped and saved every last penny. When he came in, he started tearing the place apart, thinking I was hiding money or that he had any right to the money I was earning on my own. He punched me in the face when I told him to leave. Knox came out and jumped on him. That boy was so damn protective, even at eight years old. My ex threw him off and Knox hit his head on the coffee table, splitting it open. Linc started screaming, grabbed a pan, and smacked his dad over the head. It dazed him for a few seconds, and me and the boys ran into the back bedroom and locked ourselves in my bathroom. I heard my ex get up and then heard truck tires screeching out of our driveway. We left that night with a couple suitcases and just drove. I had no idea where I was going, but I was getting the hell out of Nebraska."

"What brought you to Shine," I ask, completely engrossed in her story.

"Nothing, really. I thought we'd just be passing through, but there was something about the river and the clean air that made me want to stay. It was a small town, and everyone had a smile on their face, ya know? Like they were happy. It had been a long time since I'd felt that, and I hoped it would rub off on me and my kids. But I needed a job. I walked into the Black Roses bike shop and Janine was at the front counter. I asked if they needed a receptionist, figuring the hours would be good for me and the boys. They weren't open on the weekends or late at night, so I knew I'd be able to be home with the boys more than if I waitressed or bartended. And it was close to the school and the little duplex I'd found for us." Tanya starts laughing at whatever memory is playing in her head. "Janine was going on about the guys using her office as a giant trash bin. I told her I was new in town and had two boys of my own, so I was used to always having to clean up after them. She hired me on the spot."

"Wow, I didn't know all that," I say, thinking that's the end and she lived happily ever after.

"I'm afraid that wasn't the end of my ex, though. He found out where I was from my sister. He somehow convinced her that he'd changed and wanted his family back. He showed up one day when the kids were at school, and I was home grabbing something or other for the shop. He beat me to bloody hell and had me tied up, waiting for the boys to get back. Said he was taking us back to Nebraska. When the kids came home and walked in on my ex hitting me, Knox picked up a bat propped next to the door and swung as hard as he could. Nailed my ex right in the temple and knocked him out cold. I'd never been so glad they didn't listen to me when I'd yell at them to put their stuff away as I was in that moment. Linc called Trick. He and Gramps and a couple other brothers were there in mere minutes. They grabbed my ex and threw him in the back of a van." She looks me in the eye. "I never heard from him again. Trick helped to get me cleaned up, and my boys never saw another bruise on my face."

Tears spring to my eyes as she finishes her story. But something else too. I'm so fucking glad she had the club to turn to. If they hadn't been there...I don't even want to think about it.

"My point is, honey, the world isn't safe for women. Men like my ex, or that piece of shit they have chained up in the basement, they prey on women. They feel power from abusing and hurting women. That's why I made damn sure to raise my boys to be the men they are. No one gets away with hurting the people they love. People may scoff at their methods and put them in prison for what they believe to be the right thing, but you know what? I'd take a hundred of them over the men who walk around this earth as wolves in sheep's clothes because, make no mistake, that's exactly what my ex and men like Carlo Cataldi and his lot are."

"You seem to know a lot about what's going on?" Isn't that like against some biker code or something?

"Oh honey, Trick doesn't keep secrets from me. He lays it all at my feet, knowing that I'll love him no matter what because I know who he is. I know his heart, and I know my boys' hearts—all three of them." I remember Ozzy saying years ago that Tanya practically raised him alongside Knox and Linc. Janine made Tanya and her boys part of the family before she and Trick were even a couple.

I'm exhausted, and not only physically. It's that soul-deep exhaustion that makes me want to shut my eyes and not open them again until my world has righted itself.

"Will you stay with me until Ozzy gets back?"

"Of course." She smiles down at me. "I wasn't planning on going anywhere, sweetheart."

My eyelids fall closed, allowing the comfort of Tanya's presence to soak into me.

I'm roused from an uneasy sleep after what feels like only minutes later. Tanya is gone and Ozzy is climbing into bed next to me.

"Hey," I croak out as he settles.

"Hey, pretty girl."

He opens his arms, and without saying a word, I cuddle into his side as he wraps his strong arms around me. I don't know how to merge the part of Ozzy I know he had to be in the basement with the man who holds me so protectively yet gently in his arms. And for tonight, I don't need to.

CHAPTER TWENTY-THREE
FREYA

A week passes, and every day is the same. I wake up and try to put on the face of someone who hasn't been completely shaken to their core. I'd like to say it's been business as usual after getting home from the warehouse, but that would be a lie. The most I can muster on any given day is walking into the kitchen for coffee and letting one of the bunnies fix me a plate for breakfast, which ends up going uneaten in our bedroom.

Ozzy is worried as hell for me. I see it in his eyes every time he looks at me. Usually, he's all smiles and sweet words. But there have been several times when his mask slips and he looks downright scared for me and this spiral I've found myself in. The girls have tried to stop by and talk to me, letting me know they're here for me. Charlie especially, since she had a similar situation with the Cataldi organization only a few months ago. Nothing helps, though, and it's fucking exhausting trying to pretend. Every night, Ozzy crawls in bed with me and holds me while I sleep. He never tries to initiate any sort of physical intimacy between us, for which I'm grateful. It's not because I'm afraid to have him touch me or to touch him. Connecting with Ozzy that way has made me feel more alive than anything else in my life ever has. That's the problem. Feeling alive and being present is exhausting when it's taking everything in me to simply exist at this point.

Then there's the guilt. I'm not the woman I was a week ago when I was riding high on my conviction of Francesco Cataldi. It's a sad day when you realize the people you work with, the people you thought shared the same principles and ethics as you, turn out to be under the influence of the very criminals you're trying to put away. Everything about my career and the people I work with is called into question. I can't help but wonder who Cataldi was paying off to look the other way. How many times has someone else "lost" evidence? I worked myself to the bone for a farce, believing in a system full of liars. I'm questioning everything about what I thought was my impeccable judge of character, including when it comes to the man who has been doing everything in his power to make me feel safe. I feel like absolute shit about it, but the doubts won't leave my fucking head. Every last thing in my life feels like it's been turned inside out and upside down.

The clubhouse has gone from being my safe haven to being somewhere I don't feel like I have the right to stay. If there's one thing Ozzy deserves from everyone here it's complete faith in his ability to take care of his club and family. And he did take care of me in that warehouse, hell, even before then. Ozzy is still trying to take care of me, but how do I reconcile being the woman who fought for justice with the woman who's perfectly okay with Ozzy ending someone's life for me? How do I stay here when all my doubts and distrust seem to spill over onto everything in front of me, including Ozzy?

I'm in the kitchen when I hear shouting and a horn honking from outside the gate.

I rush to the main room of the clubhouse and see all the brothers running to the door with their guns drawn. I hurry to follow, and the scene outside nearly stops my heart.

"Put your guns down. That's my dad," I yell at the group of men.

Jude turns to me and scowls. "He has one hell of a way of saying hello." He holsters his weapon, and I step forward. Ozzy charges up behind me and wraps an arm around my middle.

"Did you call him?" he asks, just as confused as me at seeing my father.

I shake my head. "No."

Ozzy yells to the prospect to let him through the gate. Shooting the man a dirty look, my dad drives through, stopping feet from where Ozzy and I are standing. The other bikers go back inside, but I feel them watching from the clubhouse.

"Dad, what are you doing here?" I ask as he steps out of the car.

"I got a phone call, Freya. You were attacked. Again. And didn't tell your mother or me."

Shit. It sounds bad when he says it.

"I'm sorry. I didn't want to worry you with it."

My dad's head rears back as though I'd just slapped him. "Worry us? You're our daughter, Freya. You should be home recovering with us. Not with the men who nearly got you killed."

The truth is, I want to be with my parents. I want my mom to stroke my hair and tell me it's okay. I want the comfort of my old room and to feel the safety of being somewhere no one has ever hurt me. But I don't know how to tell Ozzy that. I don't know how to tell him I want my dad. He hates Ozzy and the last time they were in the same room, I chose Ozzy over him. But that was before the warehouse. Before realizing the evil I thought I was ridding the world of was lying in wait for the opportunity to rip me from my carefully constructed house of cards.

I don't know how to tell Ozzy that I can't breathe here with insecurity and fear and this never-ending loop of doubt circling through my head. It's too much being around him and not trusting every single decision I've made up to this point. Not just with him but with everything I thought to be true my entire adult life. I'm suffocating under all this doubt, but I can't make it stop.

"Get in the car," my dad commands.

"You can't tell her what to do, Mr. Campbell. She's an—"

"She's my daughter!" my dad yells. "She needs her mother and to be away from you and the danger you seem to constantly bring to her life. When are you going to get it through your fucking head that you aren't good for her? Trouble follows you and your club, and for the second time in her life, she's been swept up in it."

"You aren't going to come in here and talk to me—"

"I'll go," I say quietly, then clear my throat, repeating my words, even though I don't need to. You could hear a pin drop in the dead silence that's surrounding Ozzy, me, and my dad.

I turn to the man standing behind me, his arm still wrapped around me.

"I want to go with my dad. I can't take the fighting right now. Please, don't make this into one. I just want to go home."

Ozzy stares at me with anguish in his eyes. "I wasn't keeping you here against your will, pretty girl. You can leave whenever you want. This isn't a prison."

"I know, Ozzy. I just...I want to go home where I feel safe." And where I can breathe without worrying that I'm causing him or anyone else more worry.

"You don't feel safe with me."

It's not a question, but I can tell he doesn't understand why I don't. And I don't have it in me to explain. The anguish in his eyes cuts me to my core. I wish more than anything I could make sense of the unending turmoil I've felt this last week. I'm questioning *everything* right now. My world was toppled in a day, and I'm still in freefall. Ozzy and I dove in so fast. It's not fair to lay all of this at his feet when I can't make sense of anything myself.

"Please don't make this hard. I can't deal with it being hard," I say, tears gathering on my lids as I hold his tortured gaze.

Ozzy leans in and kisses my forehead. "Whatever you need, pretty girl. I'll give you whatever you need."

I nod once and turn on my heels, walking toward my dad.

"Let's go," I say, heading to the passenger door and climbing into my dad's sedan. I can't see my dad's face, but I see Ozzy's through the driver's door window, and by the looks of it, he and my father are having some sort of silent standoff.

"Dad. Please."

He finally opens the car door and sits behind the wheel before turning around and heading back out of the gate he just stormed through.

"You're making the right decision. You need to be home with your mother and me. Not in Shine."

I nod and lean my head against the cool window.

I don't answer because right now, I have no idea where I need to be.

CHAPTER TWENTY-FOUR
OZZY

The hardest thing I've ever done in my life is watching Freya drive away with her dad. I wanted to yell and scream that her place was here, beside me. But I know her well enough to know it wouldn't have done either of us any good. This last week she's been withering away, and there hasn't been a damn thing I could do about it. She's been working something out in her head, and the best thing I thought I could do was give her a little time and space to work through it. I'm beginning to think that may not have been the right approach. The divide between us kept growing, and I didn't do a damn thing to stop it.

When the taillights of her dad's sedan have disappeared down the highway, I turn and stomp back into the clubhouse. Walking over to the bar, I rest my hands on the edge. There're discarded coffee cups in front of me, probably from the brothers who stormed outside when they heard the commotion at the gate. I was in my office trying to work, but my thoughts kept going back to the scared, closed-off girl I'd been sleeping next to for the last week.

Blinding rage clouds my vision, and I swipe my arm across the bar top, sending the cups flying and shattering on the hard floor. Next, I let out a roar of anger and pick up a stool, sending that flying to the other side of the room. I do it again and again until the barstools are strewn all over the clubhouse. My chest expands and contracts with heaving breaths as I stand stock-still in the middle of the destruction and squeeze my eyes shut.

Fuck, she's gone again.

"Ozzy," Knox calls from behind me. "You need to get it together, man. Tearing apart the clubhouse isn't going to solve anything."

A dark chuckle breaks from me as I slowly turn to my vice president. "I wouldn't know. Never tried."

There has never been a situation I've faced and not been able to keep a level head. The only person to have ever been able to evoke this level of rage and hollowness in my chest just drove off, leaving me to my own devices.

If tearing every inch of this clubhouse apart and burning it to the fucking ground would bring Freya back, I'd do it in a heartbeat.

"Listen to me, brother. Your woman hasn't been the same since you got back from Boston. Something shook her to her core. Being here hasn't helped her. We've all seen it. Maybe being with her parents—"

I cut Knox off with a glare. "She's giving up on me. On us. And I couldn't do fuck all to stop it. Just like last time."

"Maybe it's for the best." Knox crosses his arms over his chest and stares me dead in the eye.

"Watch your fucking mouth, Knox. This is not the time to piss me off."

"Look at what you're doing, Oz. You're destroying our home and fighting with me. Maybe her going back to her life is the right move for everyone. We need a levelheaded president. When they attacked you, they attacked the club. Cataldi got away, and no one knows where he's hiding or what he's planning. The last thing this club needs is our president losing his shit over a woman."

"You always hated her. Since high school, you've acted like she was some stuck-up princess who meant nothing. She was everything to me," I yell.

"And look where you're at now," he yells back. "She never planned on staying in Shine when she graduated high school. Did you expect her to stay now? What happened to her was scary as fuck, I'm not saying it wasn't. But she was always going to go back to her life. You know, the one where it's her job to put criminals away. Criminals like us or the Irish. You can't honestly think if a case against the Irish ever came across her desk, she would just pass it off just because they helped her out once."

"Fuck you, Knox. You don't know what the hell you're talking about."

"Like hell I don't. You being with her would have brought down this club. Everything Gramps and Trick worked for would have been destroyed if there was a federal prosecutor in your bed."

It's not as though I hadn't thought about that. I'm sure Freya had too, but goddammit, we needed a minute to figure it out. Having her run away means we won't get that chance. Maybe Knox is right, but that doesn't mean I wouldn't have tried something— anything—to keep her and my club.

I push past Knox and step behind the bar, grabbing a bottle of whiskey. I'm not going to waste the high-end bottles the Irish sent over months ago. No, today calls for the gut-rot shit that's only good for one thing—getting blackout drunk.

"You gonna get wasted and hope that solves all your problems?" Knox barks at me.

"No, I'm going to get wasted and forget my problems. That okay with you, *Dad*?"

Knox scoffs and heads toward the door. "Whatever, man. It's your funeral."

He walks outside, slamming the door behind him. A few of the brothers I didn't pay any attention to while Knox was spouting off are now standing around and staring at the wreckage.

"Anyone else have shit to say?" I call out, opening my arms wide with the bottle grasped tightly in my fist.

"Nah, mate, do what you gotta do," Jude says, looking around the room. "We'll clean this up."

Jude wasn't here the last time Freya left me, and he isn't one to judge anyone for destructive outbursts or anything else for that matter. He's the one who'll have your back in any storm, even if it's one of your own making.

I walk out the back door into the frigid air and inhale deeply. Fuck it. Unscrewing the cap, I take a long swig of the cheap whiskey. It may be before ten in the morning, but I can't be bothered to give a shit. Knox can go fuck himself with his half-baked theories. Even if every time he opened his mouth, he was expressing every fear I had deep down but was too afraid to voice. That's what pisses me off most of all. He was throwing shit I didn't want to think about in my face.

And fuck Freya's dad. How dare he come to my home, to my clubhouse, and say that shit to me. It was almost as though I was reliving the day I went to their old house all over again. I was frozen and couldn't defend myself. I think part of me was afraid of what would come out of my mouth. That man hates me and my family. There will never be anything that will change his mind, and I'm not going to waste my energy trying.

I choke down another gulp of the alcohol, the whiskey beginning to take effect. It's not burning as bad as before.

I'm done. This day can go fuck itself.

If I thought yesterday was shit, I obviously didn't count on the anger still being here today. Only now, it's coupled with a hangover from hell. Groaning, I turn over in bed and notice a glass of water and a couple of aspirin sitting next to it with a note.

Here you go, asshole.

Knox

A chuckle, quickly followed by another groan, escapes me. It feels like I got hit by a fucking Mack truck.

Sitting up, I scrub my hands over my face and take a swig of the water. I wait a few moments, then when that stays down without any problems, I swallow the aspirin. This day is off to a great start.

I stagger to the bathroom and stare at myself in the mirror after turning the water on. Jesus, I even look like roadkill. The bags under my eyes, coupled with the dark circles, make me look as though I haven't slept in a week. Come to think of it, it's probably been that long since I have. Worrying about Freya and what was going on in her head made any sort of meaningful rest nearly impossible.

When I step into the shower, the hot water does little to relieve my headache or the tense feeling in my muscles. I need coffee and a greasy breakfast before I start this day.

After drying off and getting dressed, I head to the kitchen. Someone made breakfast sandwiches, so I grab a couple and a giant cup of coffee. Sitting down at the empty bar, I've just dug into my plate when Knox comes from his room.

"Hey, dickhead," he says, clapping me on the back.

"Hey. Thanks for setting me up this morning. I don't really remember much from last night. Hope I wasn't too much of a raging psycho." The scene from yesterday runs through my head. It was the last thing I recall before the whiskey did its job, and I blacked the fuck out.

Knox shakes his head and takes the seat next to mine.

"No more than usual." He shoots me a lopsided grin and grabs the other sandwich on my plate, shoving half of it into his mouth.

"There's more in the kitchen, fucker."

Knox shrugs, completely nonplussed by my comment.

"This shit between you and Freya," he begins, and my shoulders stiffen. "I'm not going to pretend like I don't have my reservations." I give him a side-eyed glance, but he takes his chances and continues speaking. "But I'll lay off. If you two can figure out a way to put your differences aside, I won't say shit."

His little speech makes me wonder what I said to him last night because I sure as shit don't remember.

"Thanks. Not sure if it matters, though. She seems to have made her decision already." The rage I felt when she left yesterday has *almost* turned back into that hollow ache I was used to dealing with for fifteen years.

Knox shakes his head. "Nah, man. She's confused and scared as shit right now, but I saw the pain in her eyes when she got in her dad's car. You guys aren't eighteen anymore. You can call and talk to her, or at the very least send her some texts—while you're sober." He shoots me a warning look. I noticed this morning my phone had been turned off. Doesn't take a genius to guess I tried to text her last night in my drunken haze, and Knox most likely saved me from that embarrassment. "Point is, you two aren't kids anymore. She felt abandoned by you all those years ago. If you don't reach out to her, she'll probably think the same thing is happening again."

"I never abandoned her. Her dad purposely kept her from me," I grumble.

"Oh, I know. I heard all about it last night."

Well, shit, I must have been one chatty son of a bitch.

It's not like Knox and I disagree on much. The only exception to that has been Freya, back in high school and now. I must have said something last night to make it click for him how much I love her and why simply letting her go isn't an option. Whatever it was, I'm glad he's done giving me grief about her.

"Thanks for understanding," I tell my best friend.

He gives me a half smile, which is about all anyone gets out of him, and gets up from his seat after giving me another hard slap on the back. I let out a groan of discomfort, and the asshole chuckles when he walks away.

And just like that, all is right between us.

Three days pass in a blur. The whiskey has stayed firmly locked in my desk drawer. No need for a repeat.

I took Knox's advice and have been texting Freya. Not to ask her to come back, just touching base and letting her know I'm thinking of her. To my surprise, she answers every time. It shouldn't be a shock to hear back from her. She's an adult with her own phone and her own mind. Knox was right; I was acting as though this was like the last time she left. We aren't kids anymore, but I was treating the situation the same. Her brief responses don't give me a lot of hope, but I'm holding on to the hope that at least it's something. She hasn't come out and told me to leave her alone or whatever we were starting is over, but she also isn't telling me she's coming back. I haven't asked either, though. Part of me is afraid of her answer.

There's no more putting off the work I need to do at the cabin. To my knowledge, no one has been up there since the fire, so I have no idea what shape the building or property is in. Instead of taking the truck like I probably should, I decide a long bike ride is in order. I put some trash bags in my saddlebags and start my bike, letting the thunderous roar drown out the thoughts swirling in my brain. Everything I sift through will have to stay until I bring the truck up, but it can wait; clearing my head with a ride cannot.

Pulling up to where the cabin once stood, I'm frozen solid while my bike still runs as I stare at the wreckage. The entire structure is burned to the ground. I don't know what I was expecting, but the reality of what I'm seeing is a punch to my fucking chest. There's no way Freya and I would have survived the fire. The place was old and looked like it went up in flames like a tinderbox. I park my bike next to a thicket of trees that were blackened by the smoke but are otherwise still standing strong. We're fucking lucky the fire didn't spread to the dense forest around here. Maybe a couple of Carlo's men stayed behind, or maybe Mother Nature was looking out for herself that day because the carnage could have been so much worse.

A couple hours pass as I sift through the rubble of the cabin before I hear a truck pull into the drive. It doesn't startle me though. I'd know the sound of that motor anywhere. I should, considering it was the first one I worked on as a kid.

My dad steps out of his old pickup and takes in the scene in front of him.

"I haven't been out here since you told me about the fire," he says, walking over to where I stand next to several trash bags. "You didn't bring your truck?"

"No, I needed the ride."

My dad nods, knowing what it's like to need your bike and the open road when shit gets heavy.

"Anything left?" he asks.

Chuckling, I walk over to a very small pile next to several bags filled to the brim with unsalvageable trash. I pick up the VHS tape and throw it to my dad, who catches it easily.

As soon as he sees what it is, a loud laugh booms from him. "Of course one of Gramps's old movies made it."

We don't have cable or satellite out here. Years ago, Gramps brought out an old VCR and a bunch of old Westerns. The man was obsessed with the Wild West.

"I think that one's his favorite, too," I say, pointing at the dirty VHS in my dad's hand.

He smiles and shakes his head, throwing the tape in his truck.

"How you doing, Oz?"

If that isn't the million-dollar question. I blow out a long breath, looking up at the bright-blue sky. "Not great," I answer honestly.

"I have to tell you something. You're not going to like it, but know it was done out of concern for Freya and nothing else."

My eyes narrow on my father as suspicion swirls in my gut. What the hell?

"It's about how her dad found out where she was."

That question has been plaguing me since he showed up to the clubhouse.

"Freya was in a bad way, son. It was obvious she wasn't sleeping and barely eating. Tanya knew her mom from years ago and reached out. She was sick about it, couldn't decide if it was the right move or not, but she knew she had to do something. We didn't expect her dad to show up at the clubhouse like he did."

I scoff. "Seriously, Dad? After what happened after the shooting, you didn't think the man was slightly irrational when it came to the club and his daughter?"

Blinding rage takes over, and my booted foot goes flying at one of the trash bags, sending the contents sailing through the air.

"How could she do that? And how could you let her?"

My dad stands tall, his chest puffed out and ready for the fight that's about to happen. "Because we're parents, Ozzy. Both of us knew Freya hadn't told her parents what happened. If you were going through something like that, and we didn't know about it, how do you think that would make us feel? They had a right to know what happened to their daughter, and they had the right to the opportunity to help her despite how they felt about you two being together." My dad's tone is even and leaves no room for argument. "I stand behind my reason for letting Tanya call her mom. As if I could have stopped her in the first place. But I am sorry for what happened after the call. Her dad should never have shown up like he did. No one has the right to make you feel less than, and that's exactly what he did. Shit, I thought enough time had passed that he would've seen reason and put the blame for everything where it belonged, on the Italian's shoulders, but I was wrong. And for that, I'm sorry."

It makes sense. Tanya loves Freya. She wanted to do what she thought was right. And my dad has a point. I should have insisted Freya call her mom. Neither my dad nor Tanya knew about the fight with Freya's dad at her apartment. Maybe the entire situation could have been avoided if the news came from her and not Tanya.

Who am I kidding? Her dad would have reacted the same, no matter what.

"Have you talked to her?" my dad asks.

"A little. Her world was turned upside down again because of me."

"Wrong. Her world was turned upside down because of what that piece-of-shit Carlo did. It was turned upside down all those years ago because of those assholes who stormed into the clubhouse. If her dad needs to figure out a way to put the blame where it belongs, so do you. If you don't, you're going to make the same mistake you did in the hospital fifteen years ago. You want that to happen again?"

"Fuck no," I spit out.

"Then be the man I know you are and buck the hell up. It's not over yet, son."

CHAPTER TWENTY-FIVE
FREYA

I thought going home was going to somehow make me feel better, but so far, it hasn't. My mom has been doting on me, but things between my dad and I are strained, to say the least. He thought my choosing to come home meant he could say whatever he wanted about the Black Roses and Ozzy. Our family dinners have ended with me storming off from the table and my mom yelling at him. She's not necessarily on Ozzy's side, but she's trying to do what's best for me. Hearing how much my dad hates the club and everyone associated with it is not it.

Ozzy has been texting me every day, and every day, I want to tell him leaving was a mistake and beg for him to come get me. Unfortunately, I haven't worked up the courage. The look in his eyes when I left gutted me. He hasn't asked me to come back, but he asks how I am and if I'm eating and sleeping. Sometimes, he sends me a picture of the sunset. We didn't get to enjoy enough of those together.

Leaving the clubhouse didn't make any of my doubts suddenly disappear. I'm still saddened by the realization that there are people in the federal prosecutor's office who work to undermine the good I thought we were doing, but I've stopped questioning how I could've been blind to it. I went into practicing law with the need to exact justice for those hurt by the criminal underworld, including myself. Nothing Carlo told me that day in the warehouse takes away the fact that I got it. It may have taken a little time and some space, but I've come to realize Ozzy and I aren't so far apart in what makes us tick. He may use different methods, but the end result is the same as when I put the bad guys behind bars. Justice is served. I don't know about anyone else, but I sleep better knowing there are men out there like him and his brothers. It's comforting to know that when the law fails and the bad guys get away, there're men like the Black Roses who make sure they answer for their crimes.

"Hey, sweetie," my mom says, coming into my room this morning. "Did I wake you?"

"No, I just haven't gotten out of bed yet."

I've been lying awake for the last two hours with my phone in my hand. Usually, Ozzy sends me a good morning text by now. Every day, I wait for him to ask me to come back, but he hasn't. He's done exactly what I needed. That man knows me better than I know myself sometimes. He knew I needed time and he's stood by and allowed me the space to work through my own shit, my own doubts. And I left him standing in the middle of a gravel parking lot at his clubhouse. I did the opposite of what I promised him when I ran away. We were supposed to figure it out. He knew that being with me could cause problems for him, but he was willing to put our future before any of that. He would have fought tooth and nail to make it work, and I bailed.

"Freya, you know I love having you here, right?"

I let out a humorless chuckle. "Are you kicking me out already?"

She shakes her head. "No, honey. But I was wondering if you've given any thought to what you're going to do? I could call your therapist, the one you had after the shooting."

"I don't need therapy, Mom. But thank you for letting me stay." A plan of what I need to do is forming in my head and it has nothing to do with staying in this room or going to see a therapist.

"What do you need? Because honestly, your dad and I are at a loss."

That one makes me laugh outright. My dad hasn't seemed particularly concerned with where I go as long as it's not back to Shine and the club.

"When I was growing up, I wanted to be a lawyer like Dad. For as long as I can remember, that was my goal. But these last few years, it's felt, I don't know, hollow, I guess. Like I'm in a hamster wheel and it's the same thing day in and day out. I hardly have any social life and forget about a love life. Who wants to date a woman who works sixty to seventy hours a week just to put some criminal behind bars who's going to get out and do the same shit that put him in there again?" That last part is more my spin on things than anything else, but that's how I've been feeling. "I thought I would be making a difference. Turns out, I'm just a small obstacle in their life of crime. One they can roll right over."

"Who rolled over you? You won the biggest case of your career a week ago."

I didn't have the heart to tell my parents what Carlo said about using my office to get the convictions they wanted and other attorneys screwing up cases on purpose. My dad believes in the law, and I know how hard it was to take that disillusioning punch to the gut firsthand. No matter how angry I am with the man, I don't want to be the one to deliver that particular blow.

"But what good am I really doing? That's one organization. There are plenty more to contend with."

"Then you go after those, too," she replies with confidence beyond my grasp.

That has always been my thinking, too. The only problem is knowing what I know now. Seeing the things I've witnessed as a US attorney makes me...tired. And frustrated. It's a sham. My career, everything I thought was important, it's all smoke and mirrors. I want to get the hell off the carnival ride, but I'm afraid. Thirty-three years old, and I'm afraid of letting my parents down.

"What if I don't?" I ask my mom. "What if I decide I want to do something else? Live somewhere else?" The thought has been circulating through my mind for the last few days. I could take what I know to my superiors and hope they aren't in on whatever the Mafia had going with my office, or I could leave. Walk away and decide for myself what I want to do, not what anyone else thinks is right for me to do. There's a certain freedom in that realization that's just now settling deep within me. Making a difference doesn't mean taking the one path that was laid out years ago. I don't have to be shackled to someone else's ideas of what that looks like. Hell, I can make it up as I go and figure out a way that feels right for me.

My mom straightens her spine and looks at the wall above my head like she's gearing up to ask me something she's not quite sure she wants the answer to.

"Somewhere like Shine?" she finally asks, looking me in the eye.

I hold her gaze, not wanting to disappoint her but wanting to be honest with her and myself. "Yes," I reply in a whisper. I clear my throat to speak again. "Yes." This time, my voice is strong with the finality of my decision. "I'm going back to Shine."

My mom nods, biting her lip as she processes the information.

"I knew from the moment I saw you look at Ozzy on that damn football field when you were in high school that he meant more than a friend or a passing fancy." She shrugs. "I don't know, call it mother's intuition or something, but I had a feeling." She looks to her hand resting on my ankle then back to me. "It's hard, this whole parenting thing. Your dad and I always counted our lucky stars with you. You were an easy kid and not too bad as far as teenagers went, either." A soft smile graces her lips. "Then, one day, you grew up. You wanted things we didn't see for you—hope for you."

I open my mouth to protest, offended that she's saying out loud she hadn't wanted Ozzy for me. I'm so tired of everyone telling me how wrong he is when he's the only person who's ever felt right.

"Let me finish," she says before a word leaves my lips. "That's how it's supposed to be, Freya. We raised you to have your own mind, and we did it well. It was inevitable at some point your dreams weren't going to align with ours. I think that was the hardest part for your dad. You wanted to be just like him when you were little, then all of a sudden, there was this other person who he knew would have a strong influence over you. He never had to worry about that before Ozzy."

"Ozzy always supported me going away to college and becoming a lawyer."

"That may be true, but how long was that going to last? We knew Ozzy wasn't going to leave Shine, but we wanted you to dream bigger. So much so that we didn't realize Ozzy *was* your dream. You don't usually find that at eighteen."

Would I have stayed? If the shooting never happened, would I have decided to stay in Shine and take a different path? In all likelihood, had the shooting never happened and I'd left for college, Ozzy and I would have fizzled out. Or maybe not. But now I can make the choice to stay. It may not be easy for my dad to understand or get over, but it's my choice to live the life I want. There's nothing holding me back. I've lived the life my parents, hell, even myself, saw for me, and I wasn't happy. I was just too busy to think about it, but these last few days have given me the time. I don't want to be the one at the office before everyone and leave after everyone else has gone home to their families. I did what I set out to do. I put Francesco Cataldi away. And you know what? It wasn't the victory I thought it was going to be.

"I'm not sure what I want to do with the rest of my life, Mom, but I know where I want to do it. It's not Boston."

My mom smiles. "I didn't think it would be."

My mom leaves soon after our conversation and I hop in the shower because I'm a fucking mess. There's no way I can spend another day without Ozzy. No, I don't have it all figured out, but I'm certain of two things. One, I don't want to work in the US Attorney's Office anymore, but I still want to be a lawyer. What exactly that means for the direction of my career, I'm not sure. And two, I'm not living the rest of my life without Ozzy. Yes, his life is dangerous, but the club wasn't responsible for me getting attacked. My job was. A job I don't want anymore, the one that hasn't been fulfilling in a long time. I was just too stubborn to see it.

Getting out of the shower, I towel off and throw on some jeans and a warm sweater. Thankfully, my mom and I have been the same size since I was in high school, so I'm borrowing her clothes for the time being. I need to go back to my apartment and grab some stuff, but I haven't had the energy.

Shit, I don't have a car here. I'm positive my dad will have major issues with me taking his, especially if he knows I'm going back to Shine. Sure, I could lie and say I need to drive to my apartment, but that's absurd. I'm thirty-three years old and lying to my parents is ridiculous at this age and completely unnecessary. He's going to have to get over the fact that I've changed direction. Which brings me back to my being an adult. There's no reason to hide my relationship, and I'm not going to. No one may understand my reasons for throwing away the career I worked for, but I do. It's not just to be with Ozzy. It's to be happy. It's so I can figure out what my path to happiness looks like and that *does* include Ozzy. How could it not?

I throw on the boots I left the clubhouse in. As I'm heading down the stairs to tell my dad I'm leaving and where I'm going, I hear the rumble of an engine I would know anywhere. It's the same sound I listened to on the way to New York and back just days ago. The same truck driven by the boy I fell in love with fifteen years ago and the man I'm still desperately in love with today.

I throw the door open as Ozzy parks his truck and steps onto my parents' driveway. We stare at each other for several long moments. I see the boy who never got the chance to say what he needed to all those years ago when my father tore him from my life. I see the man who saved me wearing his heart on his sleeve. I see a future I didn't dare think about.

Before I know what's happening, my feet are carrying me to Ozzy. I stop in front of him and regard the fear and hope warring in his gaze.

"I need a ride," I blurt out.

He cocks his head, confusion in his expression. "To where?"

"Home," I reply.

His face falls, and he nods. "I'll take you to Boston."

Before he finishes his sentence, I'm shaking my head. "No, not Boston. Shine. Take me home. Wherever you are, that's where I need to be."

He's still for a breath before he takes a step in my direction and pulls me into his body. "Even better, pretty girl," he says, then smashes his mouth to mine.

Before we break apart, my dad comes charging out of the house with fury raging across his face.

"What the hell are you doing here?" he yells.

I turn in Ozzy's hold and face my father.

"He's here to take me home, Dad," I reply for Ozzy.

"You are home, Freya. Get back in the house."

Shaking my head, I stand in front of Ozzy, who holds his strong arm around me.

"No," I begin, looking back and seeing my mom in the doorway. "You don't have to approve of my relationship, Dad, but you're going to have to accept it. I'm sorry this isn't the life you saw for me, but this *is* my life. I'm not going to spend it unhappy."

"Don't be ridiculous. He's not the only man in the world."

"He's the only one for me. I'm not wasting time trying to find someone who meets your standards. That's not fair to me. Or to Ozzy. I love you, Dad, but I'm not living my life for you."

Turning my head, I look into the eyes of the man I've already spent too much time away from. "Let's go."

Ozzy nods and walks me to the passenger door, opening it for me and helping me in.

"You're going to regret this, Freya," my dad calls.

"No, Dad. I'll regret it if I don't."

When Ozzy backs the truck out of my parent's driveway, I watch my dad. He's unmoving as he stares at me, surely thinking I'm making the biggest mistake of my life. Nothing I say is going to change his mind, and for the first time since I can remember, I'm okay with that. There's no anger toward him. Maybe a touch of sadness because he refuses to see reason, but that's something we'll have to live with. And I plan on doing all the living I've lost out on these last several years.

"He'll get over it, pretty girl," Ozzy says, laying a comforting hand on my thigh.

I slide my palm over his and smile. "Maybe, but not anytime soon."

"You okay with that?"

"I have to be. I'm not giving up on us, and for my dad, that's the only thing he wants from me. I can't do that, Ozzy. I've spent the last fifteen years without you.

And for what? So I could live a life free of danger? That backfired in my face spectacularly."

"Your dad's right though. My life can be dangerous."

"So can mine. I think that fact's been proven." Carlo didn't go after me because of Ozzy. He went after me because I wouldn't play ball.

"Have you given thought to what you want to do? Do you plan on going back to the US Attorney's Office?"

"Would you care if I did?"

"If that's where your passion is, then we'll figure out a way to make it work. I'm not afraid of a challenge, pretty girl, just as long as I have you."

I smile, knowing he will do everything in his power to figure out a way for us to be together, no matter what.

"I don't think I want to go back," I tell him. "After what Carlo said, I don't think I can." Could I make a difference knowing any one of my colleagues could be working against me behind the scenes? I don't know. And to be honest, I don't want to find out.

We drive in silence most of the way. Simply being in the truck with Ozzy, his hand resting on my knee and occasionally drumming the beat to whatever song is on the radio with his fingers is enough for me. I feel a contentedness I've never known with anyone before or since. When I asked him to give me a ride home what I should have told him was *you are home*. I should have told him there's no way I can live a half-life knowing he's somewhere without me. I already did that for fifteen years.

As we head through Shine, instead of staying on Main Street, which will take us to the clubhouse, Ozzy makes a turn into a residential neighborhood.

"Where are we going?" I ask, looking at the tree-lined street.

"Home," Ozzy says with a wide smile. "You know I don't live at the clubhouse. When we got back from Boston, I decided to stay there because I thought maybe being surrounded by the brothers would make you feel, I don't know, more at ease or something." We pull into the driveway of a single-story white bungalow with black shutters. "But that's not where I ever planned on living with you. I bought this place years ago. It was a dump, but Dad and Gramps insisted it was a good investment. Originally, I was going to flip it, but something changed my mind." Ozzy parks and helps me out of the truck. "In the spring, Tanya usually plants a bunch of flowers and shit for me. The first time she did it, I saw this place as more than a house. I saw it as what it could be. A safe place to land. And now you're here with me."

I smile and realize that's what we are to each other—a safe place to land.

We walk up the stairs, and he unlocks the red wooden door before opening it for me. I'm blown away by the refurbished hardwood and molding throughout the space. The walls are a creamy white, giving the wide-open living room an even more spacious, clean feeling.

"Wow, I'm impressed," I say, looking around.

"What? Did you expect dirty motorcycle parts and posters of half-naked girls all over the place?"

"Well, I figured there was a reason you didn't want me to see your place," I joke.

"Our place, pretty girl." He holds out his hand, which I immediately clasp with my own. "Let me show you something." He takes me through his kitchen, which is just as bright and clean as the rest of the house, not even a single coffee cup in the sink and leads me through French double doors to the deck outside.

"This is one of my favorite places," he says, sitting on a plush-looking patio recliner. He pulls me down to his lap and I take in his spacious backyard. It stretches for what looks like nearly a full football field to a copse of oak trees.

"This is all yours?" It sure beats the hell out of my place with no yard to speak of.

"*Ours*, sweetheart."

I smile and dip my chin. "It's going to take me a minute to get used to saying that."

Ozzy kisses me and rests his forehead against mine. "That's okay. We have plenty of time." His hand travels under my sweater as he dips his pinkie past the waistband of my jeans. "In the meantime, why don't I show you our bedroom?"

"Lead the way."

EPILOGUE
OZZY

Three Months Later

"I got in the shower alone so we wouldn't be late," Freya moans.

I look up from her delicious pussy and admire the blush that's covering her entire body. Could be from the hot water, could be from the orgasm she just came down from after I got to my knees and ate her out while she was attempting to wash her hair.

"You complaining, pretty girl?" I stand to my full height, my rock-hard cock jutting out between us. Her hand goes to my length, and she begins pumping slowly as I dive in for a wet kiss. Freya moans into my mouth when my fingers reach her tight nipples, and I tug hard.

"I'm going to be late for my meeting at the shelter, and you have Finn coming to the clubhouse today," she reminds me.

"I promise to make it fast," I offer, nuzzling into her neck.

"Sounds like a good time for me," she says with a laugh.

Looking down at her with a raised brow, I pinch her nipple even harder, and she yelps. "Turn around and stick out your ass. If you're a good girl, I might let you come again. Keep running your mouth, and I'm going to take you to the edge, then pull out and finish in my hand. Or maybe your mouth," I say, running my thumb over her bottom lip. "Mmm, I think I like that idea, actually."

Freya smiles wickedly, sucking my thumb into her mouth, then biting down on the digit with narrowed eyes.

"Fucking naughty girl," I tsk.

I remove my hand and smack her ass, the sound reverberating loudly off her wet flesh. "You're wasting time."

She turns and does what I tell her, leaning forward and resting her hands on the glass of the shower. Her back arches, and damn if I don't want to get on my knees again and worship her from behind. My cock, on the other hand, has other ideas, getting impossibly harder at the sight.

Positioning myself at her entrance, I push into her tight heat, eliciting a moan from both of us. Fuck, this never gets old. Being in my woman's tight cunt is nirvana, and I can't get enough, hence following her into the shower this morning.

"Goddamn, you feel so good," I moan, pumping in and out, hitting the spot deep inside her that makes her scream every time. "Play with your nipples, baby," I instruct as my hand comes around to her sensitive clit, and I begin rubbing in fast circles. If there's one thing that gets Freya there faster than anything else, it's intense nipple stimulation. She fucking loves it, and I love watching her come apart, so it works for both of us.

I rest my hand above hers on the glass and lean over her naked back, bringing my lips to her ear. "I fucking love being inside you, Freya. You take my dick so well." Her walls tighten and the moans that leave her mouth spur me on. "I want to come on your tongue while you're on your knees with your mouth open. Will you do that for me, pretty girl?"

When her pussy flutters around my cock, I know she's about to tip over the edge. "You like that, don't you? Being on your knees and taking my cum in your mouth."

She lets out a sharp cry as she strangles my cock, her second orgasm wrenching incoherent screams from her throat.

I pull out and grab her hips, turning her around and pulling her down to her knees.

"Open your mouth, baby."

She grabs my thighs as she opens wide and sticks her tongue out, welcoming the jets that spurt from me as I pump my cock viciously in my fist. My hand slows as

Freya leans in and licks the head of my dick, cleaning me off.

"Holy shit. You're going to get me hard again if you keep that up."

Freya looks at me through watery lashes and shoots me a devious smile that says that's precisely her intention.

Shaking my head, I chuckle and lift her back to her feet. "You were the one complaining about the time."

She shrugs and brings her lips to mine. "I think one more round won't hurt."

I laugh, then hear my phone ring from the other side of the shower. I peek my head out to see whose name is on the caller ID and take notice of the time.

"We really do have to get going, sweetheart."

Freya lets an adorable pout spread across her lips, and I lean down to kiss it.

"Come on. I made coffee before I got in here."

That perks her up, and she rinses her body one more time before stepping out of the shower.

It's been three months since she moved into our house. The day after she got here, we called a realtor in Boston and put her apartment on the market. At the time, she hadn't decided exactly what she wanted to do for a job, but she knew it wasn't going to be in Boston. She had an offer on her apartment the next day and about a month after that, the keys were in the hands of the new owners. Her neighbor, Mrs. Flemming, decided to take her daughter up on the offer to move in with her when she found out Freya was leaving. We get little cards from the woman about once a month, and every one ends with her reminding us to send her a wedding invitation. I haven't asked yet. Freya insists there's no rush, but the ring sitting in my nightstand drawer says fifteen years is a long enough wait. Tonight, that's going to change.

When I bought the ring, I called her dad. I wasn't under the illusion he was going to give his blessing, but that didn't change the fact that I needed to come to him as a man and tell him my intention. It went about as expected, with him telling me I'll never be good enough for his daughter. He may come around, or he may not, but we're not waiting to start our lives until he finally accepts his daughter's decision.

About a week before the sale of her apartment was final, Freya went with Jude and Lucy to the women's shelter to check out their self-defense class. She came home that afternoon fired up and ready to go back to work. If people were scared of her reputation as a bulldog before, they need to watch out now. She's an absolute terror for the men the women at the shelter ran from. She found her calling in fighting for the women who were in similar situations to Tanya's and went full steam ahead with her family law practice. It's not so different from what the club does to men who abuse women. She just does it in a courtroom and without the bloodshed. Though the men she fights against probably feel like they've been bled dry by the time she's finished with them.

I'm in the kitchen when she comes out in what I like to call her lawyer uniform. Those tight skirts still turn me the fuck on.

When she walks up to me to give me a light peck on the lips, I grab her by the back of her neck and deepen the kiss, tangling my tongue with hers. The blush that covers her cheeks when I pull away makes me chuckle.

"See you tonight, pretty girl," I say with a wink, grabbing my truck keys before heading to the door.

I'm sitting at my desk when there's a knock at my door, and Knox pokes his head in. "Finn's here."

"Bring him back."

Shuffling my papers into a neat pile to work on later, I open my desk drawer and pull out the bottle of whiskey I keep in there and two glasses.

Finn walks into my office and I stand, shaking his hand over my desk.

"Good to see you, Ozzy."

"You too. Drink?" I ask, pointing to the bottle.

"Please."

I pour us a couple fingers each and hand him a glass.

"So, what's this visit about, Finn?" It isn't like the head of the Monaghan family to request a sit-down with me.

"I wanted to talk to you about two things. First, my contacts in Nevada have heard some rumblings from the Bone Breakers. About how they don't believe that you don't know what happened to their men who came out several months ago to discuss doing business out west. They're still moving product, but it seems they found a different supplier. I heard Carlo was making some trips out there before he went underground."

The fucking Bone Breakers. Those assholes are right to not believe me. We made sure three of their men ended up six feet under after trying to take Lucy back to her psycho father and the cult compound she grew up on. I figured it would eventually come back to bite me in the ass. We had a strong suspicion they were working with the Italians, and Finn all but confirmed it.

"Now, I'm not going to ask what happened. That's between your clubs." I nod at the show of respect, and he continues. "But since they were out here on my behest, I thought I would let you know it sounds like there's trouble brewing on that front."

Finn wanted us to vet them and see if they would be a club we would be interested in working with for him.

They weren't.

"Thank you for letting me know," is all I say in response.

"The second is Carlo Cataldi."

That bastard's name still sends rage through my blood, but I tamp it down as Finn continues.

"There's been no sign of him. His capos have no idea where he slithered away to, but my man doesn't think he's down for the count. It's only a matter of time before he resurfaces. Right now, his organization is still floundering with him in the wind. It doesn't hurt our cause that he was the one making deals with the skin traders. Thankfully, his capos don't have his connections, but that could and probably will change."

"Not that I don't appreciate the visit, but you could have told me this over the phone. Why the face to face?"

"Because I'm a man of honor, Ozzy. I told you we would handle the Italians and we failed you. You and I have always had a good working relationship, and I let you down. The Cataldi situation took us by surprise. I don't like surprises, especially when they get my friends kidnapped and nearly killed."

I smile at the word *friends*—interested to see where he's going with this.

"I wanted to tell you personally, man to man, that we're more determined than ever to handle the Italian situation. It won't touch you or your club again."

I nod and hold out my hand to shake his.

"Thank you, Finn. I appreciate the heads-up. If you need us, you know where to find us."

"Appreciate that, Ozzy," he replies, firmly grasping my outstretched hand. "We'll be taking it from here."

The End

Thank you so much for reading Ozzy and Freya's story! I wanted to leave a little note to tell you what's next. The next book in this world is going to be Finn's and more of the Monaghan family. When he told Ozzy he's going to take care of Cataldi, he means it! But there's still those damn Bone Breakers to deal with. I have a feeling Knox will have a few things to say about how that's handled...

If you enjoyed Ozzy and Freya, I would be forever grateful if you left a review. You can do that by visiting Ozzy's book page where you purchased. Reviews are so incredibly helpful for us authors, and a great way to spread the word about our stories.

Do you want to know what it was like for a few of my guys growing up in Shine? Join my newsletter by going to my website www.katerandallauthor.com or scan the QR code to get the free prequel, **Rose Colored Glasses,** when you subscribe. It's an angsty first-love novella featuring Ozzy and Freya. See where they got their start!

Stalk me on my socials!
TikTok
Facebook
Instagram

Goodreads

BookBub

Or you can scan the QR code below for a link to all my socials and to sign up for my newsletter and get your free copy of **Rose Colored Glasses!**

Also By Kate

The Ones Series
The Good One
The Fragile One
The Other One

The Black Roses MC
Linc
Jude
Ozzy
And more coming...

ACKNOWLEDGEMENTS

Holy cow! Thank you so much for continuing on this adventure with me. Having you take the time to read my books means everything to me. Life is busy, so thank you for spending time with my words.

Thank you Kiki, Megan, Colleen and Anna with Next Step PR. Y'all have been my cheerleaders from the beginning and keep me on top of all the other authory things that goes beyond writing. You ladies are the BEST!

Molls, my sister from another mister, you keep me sane and remind me words are magic and this is what I'm meant to do. If it wasn't for you, I would never have taken the plunge into writing and publishing. You mean the world to me, sis.

And always, thank you to my husband. You keep me fed and keep our ship from sinking when I'm chained to my desk because I have another ridiculously tight deadline. Then when I emerge from my cave, you celebrate with me and cheer me on for the next one. I love you, babe.

ABOUT KATE

Kate is a lover of all things books. It doesn't matter what genre, as long as there's a HEA, she's in. She started reading romance in high school and would hide novels in textbooks to read during class. Becoming an author was always a dream she had and finally decided to put pen to paper (or finger to keyboard) and write what she loves. She grew up in the beautiful upper peninsula of Michigan then became a West Coast girl where she lives with her amazing husband and hilarious son. She would love to hear from readers so check out all her socials and sign up for her newsletter so she can keep you up to date on her books and whatever other ramblings come to mind.

Made in the USA
Columbia, SC
08 March 2024

32281472R10214